# PRAISE FOR AMELIA DIANE COOMBS

"Compulsively readable, *Drop Dead Sisters* is perfect for readers who love shows like *Bad Sisters* and *Dead to Me*. A mystery about three estranged sisters who accidentally kill someone? Yes, please."

—Mindy Kaling

"*Drop Dead Sisters* is a delightfully twisted romp through the woods with an all-too-real cast of quirky and endearing characters that leap off the page. While the mystery of what happened to Guy Moran's missing body keeps the pages turning at a quick clip, the Finches infuse the story with humor and warmth, along with the bizarre frustrations that seem to always accompany large family gatherings. Amelia Diane Coombs beautifully captures just how messy and complicated family, and especially sisters, can be, while simultaneously weaving a captivating caper that kept me on my toes from beginning to end!"

—Lauren Thoman, author of *I'll Stop the World* and *You Shouldn't Be Here*

"Not only is this mystery packed full of hilarious hijinks and incredible, entertaining twists, it's also a heartwarming exploration of the unique and often complex relationships that can only form between sisters. I loved it!"

—Natalie Sue, author of *I Hope This Finds You Well*

# DROP
# DEAD
# SISTERS

## ALSO BY AMELIA DIANE COOMBS

*All Alone with You*

*Exactly Where You Need to Be*

*Between You, Me, and the Honeybees*

*Keep My Heart in San Francisco*

# DROP DEAD SISTERS

**AMELIA DIANE COOMBS**

MINDY'S BOOK STUDIO

Published by Mindy's Book Studio, New York

www.apub.com

Amazon, the Amazon logo, and Mindy's Book Studio are trademarks of Amazon.com, Inc., or its affiliates.

ISBN-13: 9781662525551 (hardcover)
ISBN-13: 9781662522758 (paperback)
ISBN-13: 9781662522741 (digital)

Cover design and illustration by Jarrod Taylor

Printed in the United States of America
First edition

*For the Coombs, Smith, and Balfour families, and all
our summers at Donner Lake*

# A NOTE FROM MINDY KALING

There's a reason stories about family have captured our attention through time. Nothing is more relatable and juicy than a complicated family. These dynamics are unique but somehow universal, each more tangled than the next, and most revealing what feels like an inescapable truth: that blood is thicker than water. Family.

Although at the beginning of *Drop Dead Sisters*, our protagonist, Remi Finch, isn't quite convinced. Remi has spent years avoiding her sisters, Maeve and Eliana, and now she's stuck in the woods on a camping trip with her whole family. But when Remi has an encounter that turns deadly, Maeve and Eliana do everything they can to protect their sister.

The sisters set off on a murder mystery that has them hiding evidence from the authorities, their family, and maybe even a hot park ranger. These ladies totally have it under control (not really). But, hey, at least they're finally bonding?

Compulsively readable, *Drop Dead Sisters* is perfect for readers who love shows like *Bad Sisters* and *Dead to Me*. A mystery about three estranged sisters who accidentally kill someone? Yes, please. Hope you enjoy it as much as I did.

# CHAPTER ONE

*July 3 / Early Evening*

If you have an older sister, there's a good chance that she's almost killed you at least once since childhood. Maybe not intentionally—or hey, maybe it was intentional—but between pretending you're a life-size doll and generally neglecting you during Friday-night babysitting, it happened. Trust me, it happened, but you survived. Which, more or less, was the motto of my childhood. Shit happened and you didn't die. Best of luck with your trauma and therapy bills.

My first memory of Eliana and Maeve accidentally almost killing me was from when I was five. Maeve was ten. Eliana was thirteen. We were playing hide-and-seek on our grandparents' farm in Humboldt County, and before the game began, my sisters "whispered" about how the best hiding spot was outside the farm, past the back gate. So, off I went when it was my turn to hide. And *straight* into the pot farm next door. The security guard found me before my sisters did, pointed his shotgun at the stack of fertilizer I'd been crouching behind, and barked for me to get out. I peed my pants.

Mom and Dad grounded my sisters for a week.

Seems lenient, in hindsight.

Then there was the time they insisted I cook dinner when they were babysitting, and I almost burned down our kitchen—with me in it. Once, Eliana locked me in her car during the summer; horrifying, considering she's now the mother of two. Another time, Maeve decided to test if my pediatrician was right and I was *actually* allergic to avocados; I had to go to the emergency room. Those are the highlights. I'm sure there are dozens of other accidental almost-murders that my childhood memory has repressed.

I only see my sisters for holidays, graduations, and the rare Finch family medical emergency. This is on purpose—not because we hate one another, because hate is an actual emotion you would need to have toward another person. No, we're indifferent to one another, which I sometimes think is worse. Doesn't help that Eliana and Maeve are a mere three years apart, and I have five- and eight-year age gaps with them. I'm perpetually the youngest, something no one ever lets me forget.

My car hits a pothole as I merge off the freeway and curve along a pine-shadowed road, following the forest-green road signs for Fallen Lake State Park. *Camping*. Why did my parents have to pick camping to celebrate their fortieth wedding anniversary? As an introverted workaholic with an intolerance for family bonding, I've never been camping with my family. Never had the desire—or death wish—to strand myself in the wilderness with the entire Finch family, both sisters included. Until this weekend.

I shouldn't be surprised about the locale, though. My parents are hippies. Weed-smoking, Birkenstock-wearing free spirits who sold my childhood home the minute my dad retired, used the money to buy an RV, and took off across the United States and parts of Canada. Their honeymoon was a twenty-day backpacking trip in Yosemite, so maybe I should be thankful we're just camping. *Just camping* sounds like an oxymoron inside my head, but I drove five hours and cashed in three days' worth of precious vacation time. Might as well try to enjoy it.

My therapist thinks my less-than-traditional childhood is how I ended up in the blandest soul-eating job on earth: community manager for Warp, a popular online video game company. *I'm* the one who reads all those angry emails your nephew sends at one in the morning when his *Rift of the Realms* account gets locked for profanity.

I've made great life choices.

Life choices that have been coming back to haunt me lately. Yesterday, I received a job offer from my old college roommate Tasha. Unsurprisingly, I didn't go to college to learn the art of managing an incel's anger issues. I studied graphic design, and Tasha—who fund-raised over $4 million to launch Soft Cat Interactive in Seattle—handed me a shiny new job offer on a plate.

Most people would celebrate. Chug champagne with one hand while emailing their letter of resignation with the other. But all I did was panic-reply to Tasha that I'd be out of town camping until the following week and I'd get back to her later. Then I spent three straight hours googling how risky start-ups are and reading articles about how moving is considered a "life stressor."

Thanks, but no thanks. I have enough life stressors as it is.

I appreciate Tasha's offer, but I don't see myself packing up and leaving San Jose. Voluntarily moving closer to Eliana, who lives in Seattle, was never on my adulthood bingo card. Maeve and I live six hours away from one another, and it's a nice buffer, but I enjoy keeping a state line, minimum, between Eliana and me. As deeply unenthused as I am about a long weekend of camping with my family, it should be a welcome distraction from the career anxiety (does it count as a career if I've been at the same dead-end job for over five years?) and the constant low-level hum of what my therapist jokingly calls my *millennial ennui*, which has only gotten exponentially worse the closer I creep to my thirtieth birthday.

Fallen Lake finally comes into view outside the passenger window: dark waters lapping up against docks and rock sand beaches, with a backdrop of peaked mountains with torched trees from last year's fires. I've never been before, but my parents love Fallen Lake. Mom spent her childhood summers here, and my parents often stay in the camp-ground when they make their way down along the West Coast to visit our scattered family. From Seattle to visit Eliana to Los Angeles to visit Maeve, with me sandwiched somewhere in between, in the armpit of Northern California: San Jose.

I drive through the downtown to reach the campground. The small tourist town is made up of Mexican restaurants, run-down motels with flickering vacancy signs, a sporting goods store, the occasional frilly bed-and-breakfast, an upscale art gallery, and a Dairy Queen. Mom describes Fallen Lake as charming, but I don't see the appeal.

I flick on my blinker and slow, turning in to Fallen Lake State Park. The entrance is a glorified dirt parking lot surrounded by crooked pine trees. A row of six cabins sits on the far side of the parking lot—lodging for the rangers, if I had to guess—and a few haphazardly placed parking cones steer me toward a cabin-style check-in kiosk. An open shed is on the other side, stacked full of firewood for sale, and a sign beside it lectures visitors about campfire safety, which just makes me think about s'mores.

Okay, this trip might have one upside, because I do enjoy a good s'more.

I park beside the kiosk and roll down my window, then lean into the back seat to check on Buffy, my Cavalier King Charles spaniel, who whines in anticipation. Someone is not a fan of long car rides, and I can't say I blame her. "Almost there, girl," I tell her, and scratch her floppy ears.

As I wait for the ranger, I inhale the pine-fresh air that's supposedly good for my mental health, but I'm not any calmer on the exhale. Probably because something like three hundred people a year die in state parks. What can I say? I'm an almost-thirty-year-old white woman who lives alone. I listen to a lot of true crime podcasts.

"Checking in?" The ranger ducks to peer into my open window. He's tall, early thirties, dressed in a green khaki uniform, dark hair curling around his earlobes, sunglasses pushed on top of his head.

"Yeah, last name Finch. Campsite 34. I think."

"You think?" The ranger smiles, and if I weren't oozing dread from my pores over seeing my entire family, I might appreciate that smile more. It's a good smile, dimples and all.

"The perils of having your disorganized parents book your camping trip," I say. "My mom said she'd send the reservation confirmation but never did."

"Hey, no worries," the ranger says with a chuckle. "Can confirm you're in Campsite 34. I checked in your parents earlier."

"Mmm," I say with a nod. "My condolences."

This earns me yet another smile, and s'mores might not be the only good thing about this trip. If I'd known park rangers were this hot, maybe I would've gone camping years ago.

"Your sites are in the Buckeye campground," Mr. Hot Park Ranger is saying now, and he passes me a highlighted camp map through my window, along with a slip of paper with a piece of painter's tape dangling off the edge. "Just follow the highlighted route. And here's your parking permit; place this in the driver's side of your windshield."

I stick the piece of paper to my windshield, then glance at the map. Yikes. This campground is big. Rather than contemplate my mortality and odds of getting chainsaw murdered in a state park, I smile at the ranger. "Thanks."

Mr. Hot Park Ranger taps the roof of my car twice before saying "Happy camping" and moving on to the next car in line.

I follow the highlighted route on my map to the cluster of campsites my family rented, and seven minutes later, I'm pulling into the paved parking spot at Campsite #34. I pop open the car and duck out, every bone and muscle groaning as if I'm sixty, not twenty-nine. But I only stopped once, at the In-N-Out in Davis, and my entire lower body fell asleep an hour ago.

"Hey, good girl," I coo at Buffy as I open the back door and unclip her harness from the safety seat. I lower her onto the ground, then attach her leash to my belt loop. Buffy stretches out her back legs, then looks up at me with her expectant puppy face, tail thumping.

5

Hot Californian sun sizzles against my pale indoor-person skin.

Damn it. I forgot sunscreen.

I brought ten cans of prescription dog food but forgot sunscreen.

"Remi!" Mom's campsite is beside mine, and she's seated beneath a giant sunshade lofted over a wooden picnic table. Her blonde hair is roped back in a braid, streaked with grays, and she's wearing cargo shorts and a T-shirt from the San Diego Zoo with a giant cartoon ostrich on it. She waves her arms above her head like I'm on the other side of a Target parking lot, not thirty feet away. Yes, I was embarrassed to be seen with her in high school.

Buffy strains at her leash, eyeballing all the squirrels and birds and random humans, as we walk over to my parents' site.

My parents booked five sites in a row for the long weekend, near a bathroom that's tucked among the trees. I sag with relief when I spot that squat brick building. No chance that I'd pee in a ditch. I do have a line, and ditch peeing is it. But, as Buffy drags my reluctant body toward Mom, I mentally count the number of people attending this weekend and frown. Unless the numbers have changed, we're two campsites short. Meaning an unlucky few will be grouping up.

Ten bucks and a case of prescription dog food that those unlucky few are me, Eliana, and Maeve. The last time I was in the same room— or general space, indoor or outdoor, breathing the same air—with the both of them was at my college graduation. Seven years ago. Eliana has a family. Maeve travels a lot for work. And I'm . . . *me*.

If our lives were a video game, we each adventured off on our own side quests nearly a decade ago and never returned to the main storyline.

Great. This is going to be *great*.

Mom hops up from the picnic bench and rushes over to me before I can reach their sunshade, enveloping me in a bear hug.

"Oh, baby." Mom smooshes her lips to my cheek and sways me back and forth like a rag doll, or one of those wacky blow-up tube men set up outside used car dealerships.

"Hey, Mom." I extricate myself from her hold and readjust my glasses, my smile mostly genuine. Even if I'd prefer reading death threats from fourteen-year-olds (yes, this happens) instead of camping, I need to pretend like I want to be here. Because I love my parents, even if they're weird and embarrassing. Against all odds, they've stuck together for forty years, and though I'm far from a romantic, we should celebrate that.

Or, at the very least, acknowledge it with a grocery store sheet cake and some balloons.

"How was the drive?" Mom kneels down to scrub Buffy on the head, the dog's tail thumping ecstatically.

"Long. Traffic was gross." I moved to San Jose after college. Before my parents sold the house and became transient seniors, we lived outside Eureka, California. San Jose was enough distance between me and my hometown to feel independent, but not too far away to make visiting inconvenient.

Mom beams; then she hooks her arm through mine and leads me to their campsite. Their trusty RV—which they named Atlas, like they're a teenage boy with his first car—takes up the entire parking bay, and the solar panels mounted on the roof glint beneath the sun. The RV is ancient, and my parents tried to make it as eco-friendly as possible, remodeling it with a waste-grease fueling system. The door creaks open, and Dad clomps down the stairs, wearing an outfit nearly identical to Mom's. His shirt has a meerkat on it.

I wave to Dad, then say, "But all in all, not too terrible. A little boring. No offense to Buffy."

I listened to a four-part podcast series on flesh-eating bacteria. Riveting. And I'm not being sarcastic. The podcast kept my brain occupied enough to forget about Tasha's job offer *and* this trip for five hours. Was that the smartest thing to listen to before going camping on a lake? Probably not, but I'm not known for well-informed decision-making.

Dad reaches us and pulls me in for a hug—and into a cloud of citronella, all-natural bug spray that he must've coated himself with. "You need to hit the road more often, Rem. Does wonders for the mind." At this, he taps the side of his balding head.

"I'll do my best," I say with an awkward laugh. Because my parents like to act as if I don't have a full-time job and we live in a society where one week of vacation a year is a privilege. See: free spirit hippie parents who don't understand student loan debt and the importance of a decent credit score.

Dad tousles my hair, mussing my dirty-blonde waves, then heads to the ice chests inside the open bear-proof bin. "We're grilling up some portobello mushroom burgers for dinner," he calls over his shoulder, and I refrain from making a joke about my parents doing shrooms.

Because they did once, when I was in high school. On my prom night.

Mom nods toward a few camping chairs encircling the campfire, and I follow. "Hey, um," I say, and glance over to my campsite, "is anyone else staying at my site? I'm trying to figure out where to put my tent."

"We could only get five sites," Mom says, like that's an explanation. "It'll be nice, won't it? Catching up with your sisters?"

My mostly genuine smile falters. "Did you run this plan by Eliana and Maeve?"

"It's my anniversary weekend, and I want you three girls to get along. Just think, Rem, of how wonderful it'll be! You three can stay up and roast s'mores, fill each other in on your lives, talk about your dreams—"

I snort at her kumbaya fantasy, and Mom's face falls. "Sorry, but did you confuse us for your *other* three daughters who all get along?"

"Breaks my heart," Mom says with a sway of her head, "that you're not closer to your sisters. One day, your dad and I won't be here anymore, and your sisters will be all you have."

Oh, cool, she's going the emotional "someday I'll be dead" manipulation route. That's a low blow, even for our mom. "Seriously—"

"Try for me," she interrupts and grabs my hands, holding them within hers. "Your sisters haven't always made it easy for you, but you are all adults now. Times change, so change with them."

"You sound like the inside of a fortune cookie," I tell her, and Mom smiles, as if that was a compliment and not a dig at her crackpot wisdom. "But fine, sure, whatever, I'll try. Remember that this is a two—no, three-way street we're talking about. I'm not the issue."

Mom raises a pencil-thin brow, as if calling BS on my entire statement.

"Not . . . the only issue," I amend, and the brow lowers.

"Attagirl." Mom pats my cheek before reclining back in her chair; I'm disturbed how similar her tone of voice is to mine when I praise my dog for not eating out of the trash can.

No, the three of us have never gotten along, and despite my mom's delusions, I don't expect that to change this weekend. I never sat my sisters down when I was younger and asked why they didn't like me, but I can hazard a few guesses. I was an anxious kid, annoying at the best of times, a brat at the worst. Eliana and Maeve—while radically different in personality—had this closeness I could never, ever infiltrate, no matter how hard I tried. The fact that I tried, embarrassingly hard, was what annoyed them the most. I was a shadow, an echo, that they couldn't wait to escape when they left for college.

My sisters never understood me, which isn't a crime, but their general disinterest in ever trying to understand me as an adult bothers me more than I'd like to admit. I almost wish we'd had some big fight, something I could point to as the reason for why we fell apart, but the truth is that we were never together to begin with.

Also, no matter how much my parents deny it, they each have a favorite. All parents do. They might love their children equally, but there's always one kid they prefer spending time with. The one kid whose absence is missed during holidays and vacations, who gets the more personal gifts for their birthday, not to mention casual texts throughout the week.

Maeve's always been Dad's favorite. Like our dad, Maeve's idealistic, a dreamer. And our mom's always loved Eliana *slightly* more than the rest of us. Maybe it's because Eliana was the firstborn, or because she has the picture-perfect life, or the fact that she made our mom a grandmother. Who knows.

If I want to be fair, it's technically not their fault for being our parents' favorites—that's all on Mom and Dad for their poor choice in offspring—but sometimes I wonder if the fact that my sisters had our parents to themselves for years before I came along made it impossible for me to ever catch up.

A fancy minivan inches along the one-way road that encircles the campsites, as if reading each and every plastic tag attached to the posts by the car and RV stalls. No doubt looking for Campsite #34. I squint through the glare on my glasses and catch sight of my oldest sister in the driver's seat. She drove, even though it's a twelve-hour trek from Washington, but Eliana has always had an irrational fear of flying. If you ask me, I think she has an irrational fear of any situation where she can't be in complete control.

Mom spots the minivan a moment after me and perks up in her lounger.

"That must be Eliana. She made great time!" Mom smiles as she groans to her feet, and I swear her smile is wider, more joyful, than the one she wore when I arrived. I deflate, ever so slightly, since I barely had fifteen minutes with my parents before one of my sisters showed up.

I hang behind as my mom walks across her campsite and into mine, waiting as Eliana parks her minivan beside my sedan. I tear my gaze from her arrival and drop my head back, staring up at the sky as the sun slides like yolk to the west. *It's just a long weekend,* I remind myself, *barely seventy-two hours.*

I survived an entire childhood with Eliana and Maeve. Three days is nothing.

Like my mom said. We're all adults now.

Allegedly.

Eliana's a *mom* now. Surely, she's grown up and stopped being a judgmental shrew. And Maeve's always been in her own materialistic world, a borderline narcissist. And me? Who knows what they say about me. Probably something like how I'm the Finch sister who never met her potential and whose anxiety coping mechanisms are crying in the bathroom or collapsing in on herself like a dying star.

They wouldn't be wrong.

Between my extended family and various family friends, we don't really even need to interact with one another. Sure, we're sharing a campsite, but I'll pitch my tent as far away from them as possible. We'll trade polite smiles, make bland small talk, and sign off on Monday morning with a hearty *See you in another seven years. Or better yet, make it an even ten!*

With a sigh, I march across the dusty campsites toward the parked minivan, Buffy trotting beside me. Mom squeals as Eliana steps out into the bright sun and tosses her arms around my oldest sister. Eliana's tall with toned calf muscles peeking out of her cropped leggings, an oversize T-shirt knotted at her waist. Her long wavy golden hair is soft and fluffy, reaching the middle of her back, a braided headband holding her bangs from her blue eyes. The smile on her face freezes as she spots me over Mom's shoulder.

"Hi," I call out and awkwardly wave before shoving my hands into the back pockets of my jean shorts. My shoulders creep up to my ears, and I can practically hear my therapist gently reminding me not to wear them as earrings.

The last time I saw Eliana was two years ago, when our mom had shoulder surgery. That particular visit began with Eliana's judgmental comments over my hospital-gift-shop-sourced flowers and ended with her cornering me outside the bathroom and saying I was "stressing out" our convalescing mother because I complained about the hospital cafeteria food. I found a *Band-Aid* in my lasagna. There was no way I wasn't going to talk about that.

Eliana steps around Mom—the smile still locked into place, but that's probably due to the Botox, not affection—and walks over. "Hey," she says and leans in to hug me. But it's a ghost of a hug, her body barely touching mine.

"It's nice—" I begin to say, but Eliana's turning toward our mom, continuing their conversation as if I'm not standing three feet away. My cheeks burn with a mixture of annoyance and embarrassment, and I mutter "Guess I'll go put up my tent, then" before walking to the trunk of my sedan and popping the lid.

# CHAPTER TWO

*July 3 / Night*

A mosquito lands on my forearm as I sit beside the fire, the incessant buzz ceasing as it samples me like a human Capri-Sun. I smack my arm, wincing as bug guts smear across my skin. Then I shudder. Who voluntarily does this? Goes *camping*? I wasn't kidding when I said I'm an indoor person. My skin has that bland, almost sickly glow of someone who usually keeps the company of a laptop, a Costco-size bin of cheese puffs, and a coffee-stained hoodie.

When I find a spider in my apartment, I usually trap it beneath a jar and slowly suffocate it to death. Or wait until my best friend, Stephanie, visits, and I'll have her relocate the spider outside for me. Although, ever since Stephanie got married in April, spider rescue—and our friendship—has fallen low on her list of priorities.

Let's just say I've let a lot of spiders suffocate to death lately.

I use a crumpled Starbucks napkin from my pocket to wipe away the guts, then try to focus on the various conversations. We're all crowded around the firepit at Mom and Dad's campsite, flames licking the sky and the air sweet with smoke. Eliana is seated beside me, her body canted to one side as she leans in toward our mom.

There are eight of us in total. Other than my immediate family—Maeve has yet to arrive, in typical Maeve fashion—there's Aunt Lindy, my dad's sister. She's probably the most eccentric of the Finch family, and that's saying something. She rolled into the campground in a Tesla convertible and with absolutely no camping gear. Mom's best friend forever—and maid of honor—Salli arrived during the middle of dinner, carting with her what looked like half an REI floor display; maybe she'll share her boon with Lindy. And Grandma Helen and her younger lover, Bill, showed up as I was chopping firewood like an off-brand Paul Bunyan. I mean, good for Grandma, but awkward for everyone else.

For someone who lives alone, this is a lot of human interaction for one evening. Buffy is curled up on the dirt by my feet, dressed in the new acorn-patterned dog sweater I ordered online before the trip. And even though there's nothing inherently wrong about this gathering, I can't get comfortable. Can't breathe in that fresh air that's supposed to be good for my brain.

Maybe because I'm too busy playing a loop of the various state park murders that I've learned about. Or maybe it's because I stopped belonging with my family years ago, if I ever fit in with them in the first place. Early on, I realized I was different from my carefree parents—who have never expressed an ounce of anxiety between the two of them—and my unaffected older sisters. This would've been alienating enough if it weren't for the fact that neither of my parents believes in traditional medicine.

Instead, they send emails about how microdosing psychedelic mushrooms is the cure for what ails me and that the only therapy I need is a social media detox and the great outdoors. The entire sales pitch makes me want to scream into a pillow. As an adult who has had a *lot* of therapy (real therapy, with a therapist, not a tree), I've come to terms with the fact that my parents are harmless. This is how they show they care.

Sometimes, though, I wish they didn't care so much.

"Juliet! Remind me, who else is coming for the big day?" Aunt Lindy hollers at my mom from across the firepit and snaps me out of my spiral, waving her arm so the bell sleeve of her caftan flutters. "I want to make sure I have enough sambuca for my signature vow renewal cocktail on Sunday."

Eliana's mouth pinches, annoyed at the interruption, but Mom turns toward Aunt Lindy with a smile. "Damien and Andrew," my mom says, naming her brother and his husband. Then she adds, "Rem, they were so excited to hear you'd be coming!"

I perk up at the mention of my favorite uncles, who, by Finch standards, are pretty normal. Well, normal-ish. Not like there's a high bar for normal in this family. "Oh, awesome," I say. "I haven't seen them in years."

"Yeah, that's what happens when you bail on five Christmases in a row," Eliana mutters beneath her breath, and Dad lovingly whacks her on the knees. And *this* is why I don't open my mouth around my family. Eliana always has some barb, some criticism, tucked into her pocket, and she's nothing if not patient, waiting for the perfect time to strike and make me feel like crap.

Mom's smile falters, but she recovers quickly. "The cousins from Nevada," she tells Aunt Lindy, who counts the number of guests on her nicotine-stained fingers, her nails tipped in acrylic. She claims to have quit smoking decades ago, but that's a lie. Everyone goes along with it, though, like our own family folklore. "And the Morans were supposed to come but canceled last minute."

"Please tell me you didn't invite Guy." Eliana stabs a marshmallow onto her roasting stick, then licks the sugary guts off her fingers.

For once, I agree with a sentence that has come out of my sister's mouth. The Morans were my grandparents' neighbors in Humboldt County, a common fixture during my childhood summers, one month of which I spent at their farm with my sisters. Jim Moran was my dad's best friend growing up, and their son, Guy, was inescapable. Like that one cousin you hated but had to see every Thanksgiving.

Guy's four years older than me. A year younger than Maeve. Four years younger than Eliana. Perfectly slotted between our age gaps. On

15

paper, this would've been perfect, but Guy was an absolute dick. A real "boys will be boys" poster child.

"Well," Mom says, fluttering her hands around in front of her face, "not on purpose. I invited Jim and Barbara, of course. Why're you looking at me like that, Eliana? Jim was your dad's best man. As I was trying to say, when I invited them, they assumed Guy was *also* invited. But he's not coming, either, so you can cool your jets."

"That boy gives me the willies," Salli says from beside Aunt Lindy, her hands busy with a knitting project. The yarn dangles over the side of her camping chair, disappearing into the dirt.

Aunt Lindy snorts, still holding her hands out with the guest count. "The willies are an understatement. Do you remember when he broke into Rico's gun vault during my Christmas party?"

My uncle Rico passed away a decade ago during a hunting accident, and he was an avid gun collector. I think it goes without saying that my hippie parents were deeply unenthused that their brother-in-law loved firearms, and it sparked more fights between them than I care to remember. When I was in high school, Aunt Lindy and Uncle Rico threw a Christmas party, and Guy broke into Rico's gun vault to—and I kid you not—impress the girl he was dating at the time. Jim Moran had to literally beg my uncle not to call the cops.

"A menace," Grandma Helen says from across the firepit, and it makes me think of my own Guy Moran horror story.

When I was eleven and Guy was fifteen, he tried to drown me in the public pool. My dear old grandma told me that Guy probably liked me, as if this type of behavior was a compliment, something that should make me blush—not something we should've reported to the police as an early sign of sociopathic behavior. As an adult, nearly two decades later, I know that Guy wasn't flirting with me, or trying to kill me. Honestly, he was probably just a shitty kid trying to get attention, but I still remember the shame when I went to my grandma for help, how she brushed off my concerns.

After so many years, everyone's heard the story—I was a very dramatic child—and I don't bother bringing it up. There's not much I hate more in this world than being the center of attention during a family event. But I won't lie—it's nice knowing that I'm not the only one in my family who can't stand Guy Moran. Or the Morans in general. I have no idea why my dad has stayed friends with them over the years. Then again, my parents are the type of people who, once they choose you, they choose you for life. They're kind of like dogs in that way.

"Guy's had some hard times," Dad says as he bites into a s'more, "but Jim mentioned that he's been doing really well lately. Got a new job, even!"

"Good for him," Eliana says sarcastically, and I snort in agreement. But my sister doesn't look over at me, doesn't latch onto this rare flare of camaraderie. She turns to our mom again, pulling her back into a private conversation made for two.

I linger for a few more minutes, then stand and announce that I'm going to bed, and I walk Buffy back to my tent. I set her up in her crate, then carry my toiletry bag with me to the bathrooms, my phone's flashlight my only guidance. The bathrooms have a cement floor with a peaked, open-air roof that's great for ventilation but terrible for bugs. I lock the heavy door behind me and wrinkle my nose at the damp mystery stains on the floor and the moths bumping into the walls and lights.

I balance my bag on the toilet paper dispenser and then brush my teeth, trying to ignore the embarrassing fog of homesickness surrounding me. I was always that kid, the anxious one who hated sleepaway camp and turned down sleepover requests with such ferocity a rumor started that I still wet the bed. In middle school. But I'm an adult now. Even if my brain is its same panicked self, and it gets even more panicky and insecure when I'm with my family.

In San Jose, I'm Remi Finch. I have a life. Is that life borderline pathetic? Extremely. But it's *my* borderline pathetic life. I take my meds and go to therapy weekly, and I have a cute dog to make up for the lack of boyfriends lately. This last part is by choice, because after a few terrible dating app dates Stephanie convinced me to try, I decided to punt my phone into the sun and *never again.* Around my family, I'm the youngest. Anxious and inefficient and, somehow, still not an adult even though I'm turning thirty in September.

When I'm around my family, it's like I can't escape the worst parts of myself.

After I spit in the sink and wash my face with the disposable bio-degradable washcloth Mom gave me, I dry swallow my meds and duck into the darkness. And bump *straight* into Eliana, who must've been doing her version of a campground nighttime routine, a near-identical toiletry bag in one hand—did our mom buy them for us?—and her phone with its flashlight glaring into the other.

"Oh my god." Eliana clasps her hand to her chest, breath ragged. "You scared me, Remi."

"Sorry." I slide my own phone from my back pocket and tap on the flashlight. As I start back toward camp, leaves crunch behind me as my sister follows. My sister is taller than me, her legs longer and stronger from her years as a soccer player in high school, and we fall into step within seconds.

"So. Mom didn't think you'd make it," Eliana says, as if we were in the middle of a conversation that got interrupted. A phone call dropped due to poor reception.

"I'm here, aren't I? Their anniversary is a big deal." I eye my tent with longing, but it's still on the other side of the clearing. Trees and rocks block my escape route.

Eliana removes her headband, futzing with her bangs, and then wraps the band around her wrist like a bangle. "I'm sure Mom and Dad are glad you could find the time."

The words *might* seem nice on the surface, but those bitter under-tones leave a bad, yet familiar, taste in my mouth. I'm not a bad daughter. I visit our parents several times a year and call every other week. Sure, I've bailed on the bigger holidays and gatherings, but I still show up when it counts. The problem is that Eliana has never failed to rub it in that she's the golden child. The oldest, the overachiever, and the one who gave our parents grandkids—thank god, because my entire life is a kid-free zone—and has the picture-perfect life.

Speaking of . . .

"Why aren't Chad and the kids here?" Yes, my sister married some-one named Chad. Yes, I have a brother-in-law named *Chad*. And no, I don't know why he doesn't go by Charles.

Eliana's whole demeanor stiffens, sharpens. "Guess the Finch family gossip train doesn't have any stops in San Jose," she says flatly.

I glance beside me, nearly tripping over a rock in the pathway. "What?"

"I'm getting divorced." She says this without any emotion, a state-ment of fact. "We separated nine months ago. There's this huge . . . custody battle. Chad agreed to me primarily having the kids but walked it back a few weeks ago. Now he wants the kids half the time, which is comical because he can't keep a houseplant alive. My lawyer said leaving Clara and Connor with him over the holiday was 'in good faith' and might smooth a few things over."

I press my lips together, to hold back whatever inappropriate remark is bound to pop out of my mouth. Because I joke when I'm uncomfortable, and Eliana unloading something personal onto my shoulders makes me itchy. I wait and count to three. Then I say, "That's a bummer. I'm sorry."

Eliana snorts. "A bummer. Yeah, that's one way of putting it."

We've reached our campsite, my tent on the outskirts, whereas Eliana's fancy domed tent with two rooms inside is set up closer to the picnic table. My sister waves good night, then disappears into her tent.

I stand beneath the inky sky and hate—I absolutely *hate*—that I'm the tiniest bit sorry for my sister.

# CHAPTER THREE

*July 4 / Morning*

A body slams into mine so violently that I almost bounce off the air mattress and onto the dirt-and-pebble-strewn floor of my tent. I flail, pure panic taking over because—as a woman who lives alone in a city—I'm appropriately concerned about getting murdered in my sleep. But as I open my mouth to scream, I recognize the body on top of me. Or to be more specific, the wild caramel curls half smothering me to death.

"What the hell, Maeve?" I shove my sister off me and sit up, fighting to free myself from the sleeping bag tangled around my limbs.

Maeve repositions herself at the end of my air mattress. "Nice to see you too."

I grab my glasses from the floor and shove them on my face, the tent coming into crisper focus. "That wasn't funny when we were kids, and it's not funny now."

With an eye roll that belongs more on a teenager than my thirty-four-year-old sister, Maeve sticks her hand out of the open tent flap and grabs something. "Am I forgiven?" she asks and hands me an enamel mug of coffee. The script on the side says *The Mountains Are Calling*. Probably from Salli's REI haul.

I inhale the fresh coffee, shrug. "When'd you get in?"

"Late." Maeve sips her own coffee and motions toward Buffy's crate. I nod and she unlatches the door. Buffy hops onto the air mattress and sits between us, my sister smothering her with kisses. "I got stuck in traffic and missed my flight."

Maeve moved to Los Angeles fifteen years ago. One would think she would've adjusted her schedule to fit within LA's hellish traffic patterns, but she's as disorganized as she is stubborn. The last time I saw Maeve was for lunch last year, when she stopped by San Jose on her way into San Francisco for a work event. She runs a small social media empire called Maven Maeve, which is a lifestyle blog with a very aesthetically pleasing Instagram. She's a glorified influencer, and as someone who hates social media, I can make absolutely no sense of her life.

"I need to let her out." I gesture toward my dog, and Maeve scoots out of my tent. I leash Buffy and tug on a sweater, then check my phone. Nine fifteen. Today is the Fourth of July, and last night Mom droned on and on about some fireworks display down at the beach we're all supposed to attend.

I frown at Buffy. This will be our first Fourth together, and I brought some gabapentin and a ThunderShirt, but I have absolutely no idea if they'll be enough. I make a mental note to put them in my backpack for later. "Sorry in advance, girl."

Buffy wags her tail blissfully.

I slide out of my tent and zip it behind me, waiting as Buffy does her business behind a bush. As Buffy pees, I watch Eliana and Maeve seated at the picnic table fifteen feet away, catching up over cups of coffee. It's frustrating, how easily they get along. On paper, my two sisters couldn't be more different, but that's never been a problem. Part of me wants to walk over and join them, as if I can fit into their dynamic if I try hard enough.

Then I imagine how awkward that would be, the questions they'd ask. Or, more importantly, the answers I'd give. *Nope, no boyfriend, and haven't been on a date in a year. Yes, same job that's slowly sucking the soul from my body; I am a husk of a human being.* I won't mention Tasha's job offer—because I'm not taking it—and then awkward silence will ensue.

The worst kind of small talk is with family, the people you *should* be able to connect with. Yeah, no thanks. I haven't had nearly enough coffee yet to suffer that much.

Rather than insert myself like the third wheel I've been since birth, I tug Buffy over to Mom's camp, following the scent of Tofurky bacon and blueberry pancakes. The campground is quiet and still, other than the early rustlings of our family—and the few others who were unfortunate enough to book campsites across the street from the Finches, who stayed up long after I fell asleep, playing a rousing game of Pictionary—as coffee is percolated on tiny, propane-fueled stoves and people trudge to the bathrooms.

"Morning, baby." Mom's standing at the edge of the picnic table in front of a propane grill, Tofurky bacon sizzling. A lone wasp circles, darting back and forth, as Dad tracks its movement with today's rolled-up *Sac Bee* in one hand, his eyes slitted. My dad's a pacifist. Usually.

"Good morning." I slide onto the picnic bench, the morning sun warming my back as I sip my coffee. The weather in the mountains is more volatile than back in San Jose. Hot days and freezing nights, and as cold as I got last night in my tent, sweat is already gathering along the band of my sports bra.

While I caffeinate, Mom makes breakfast, rattling off today's long list of activities, which gives me a headache. Lunch in downtown Fallen Lake at noon. Kayaking for those interested at one thirty; there's a rental shack at the beach in the campground. Cornhole, card games, and horseshoes from three until dinner, which is a proper "'Murican" meal of hot dogs and potato chips—if you look beyond the fact that the hot dogs are plant based. Then we're heading to the public beach, which is on the complete opposite end of the lake, for the fireworks.

"Salli organized everything," Mom says.

Like any good best friend, Salli has strengths that complement my mother's weaknesses. She's the organized calm to Mom's disorganized storm. When I was a kid, Mom always forgot to sign my field trip permission slips, boycotted the power company due to their lack of eco-policies (which resulted in our power being turned off for three days), and would randomly pull me out of class to go on day trips to the beach.

Salli would let me sleep over at her house—Mom's eco-warrior crusade didn't kick off until my sisters were out of the house, which I'm not bitter about at all—during the power outages, and she would pick me up from school when my parents were busy with work or that one time they were detained at the local jail after a protest. Salli never had kids of her own, but she loved our mom enough to help out when needed. She never shamed me for not wanting kids. Even my super-liberal, pro-choice mom guilted me when I told her.

Unlike Eliana, who wasted no time popping out babies after she married Chad, or Maeve, who eagerly devolves into baby talk at the sight of a toddler, I've never wanted kids. When I was younger, though, I never really thought I had a choice. Everyone *assumed* I would have kids due to the whole ovaries-and-uterus thing, and it wasn't until high school that I began to realize that not having children was an option. No big reason—yeah, the planet's on fire, and we're probably all doomed—but for me, I don't *want* them. It wouldn't be fair to the kid, and it wouldn't be fair to me. Besides, I'd much rather live in regret of not having a kid than regret bringing one into the world.

Dogs and houseplants are much more my speed. And if that ever changes and my eggs are all shriveled up, there's always adoption. I'm not so obsessed with who I am that I feel the need to replicate myself. No one in their right mind should want my anxiety- and allergy-ridden DNA, not to mention my poor eyesight.

Mom chatters, and I make listening noises, keeping an eye on Buffy as she gets a little too brave around some ground squirrels.

"Why didn't you tell me Eliana was getting divorced?" I ask during a rare lull in the conversation.

Mom slides a plate of Tofurkey bacon and pancakes in front of me, then sits down. "Because I didn't want you to gloat."

I shove the Tofurkey bacon, which is a poor and flavorless imitation of the real thing, into my mouth. "Why do you think I'd *gloat*?"

"You aren't Chad's biggest fan," Mom points out.

"Who is?" I joke, and she gives me a meaningful look.

Guiltily, I shove more of the pathetic excuse for bacon into my mouth. But my mom's not wrong. Not that I'd gloat. Okay, maybe a *tiny* bit, because Eliana's life has always been perfect. Effortless. Up until now, I don't think she's ever failed at something, and as a humble mortal who fails on a daily basis, my schadenfreude is warranted. Not saying that divorce is a failure, but it's the end of something. Something I'm sure Eliana—at some point—wanted to last forever.

The schadenfreude might make me a bad person, but I've been jealous of Eliana over the years. Not because of Chad, because, well, *Chad*. But I've never had good luck with relationships. Eliana is driven and precise and knows what—or who—she wants. Maeve always has a new boyfriend or girlfriend to show off on her social media. The last guy I dated was a dude who used to work at Warp. He ended up cheating on me with one of our interns. Not only was it humiliating, but it also caused a *massive* HR scandal that blew up on social media. After that and the disastrous dating app situation, I threw in the proverbial towel.

Dad thwacks his newspaper against the table, flattening the wasp, and says, "Honey, your sister could use your compassion right about now." He uses the newspaper to sweep the carcass onto the ground; the wasp guts smear across the *Sac Bee* headline, something sensational about a teenager killed in a hit-and-run last night.

Here's the thing. I actually have compassion for Eliana. Loads of it. Buckets of compassion over here. But Eliana hates when people feel sorry for her. She also has no idea how to fail. Unlike my sister, I'm intimately familiar with failure, but if I ever tried to talk to her about it, she'd tell me I had no idea what I was talking about. Because Eliana has to be right, constantly. It's exhausting. And after a literal *lifetime* of indifference from my oldest sister, I'm not sure why I should bother.

"The divorce wasn't my news to tell," Mom says. "Maybe you should call your sister more if you want to know what's going on in her life."

"Eliana doesn't call me either," I point out, and cringe at the childish tone in my voice. Barely twelve hours around my family, and I'm regressing into something I don't like. I refuse to take back the comment, though, because it's true. My sister doesn't call me, and I'm not even sure I'd pick up if she did.

Actually, that's a lie. I would pick up, because Eliana calling me is such a rare occasion, I'd assume one of our parents was in the hospital.

I slide the *Sac Bee* across the table, gingerly peel off the front page with its smooshed wasp guts, and flip for the crossword.

Mom nibbles on a piece of her sad, pathetic excuse for bacon. "You girls, I swear . . . so stubborn. I don't know where you get it from."

Across the table, Dad raises his bushy brows—which are only rivaled by his even bushier mustache—and smiles knowingly. Because we get it from our stubborn-as-a-mule mom. He hands me a pencil from the knickknack holder attached to the propane lantern stand that's clamped to the table.

"What's new with you, Rem?" Dad changes the subject, and I'm equal parts grateful and intimidated by the shift in conversation.

I tap the pencil against the crossword. Tasha's job offer looms over me like a complex cloud. Because my parents would tell me to take the offer. Leave my soul-sucking job behind in San Jose and go commune in the Pacific Northwest, close enough to my sister to have weekly dinners together.

"Um, nothing really," I say, and fight the urge to tell my parents, to ask them for their advice. Because I've tried, desperately, to be an adult. Self-sufficient and successful, despite the anxiety that's weighed me down since its first flares in my early childhood. "I actually just heard—"

"Dad," Maeve calls from our campsite as she flounces toward us, "are you finally ready for that cribbage rematch?"

My dad turns toward Maeve, his mustache dancing as he grins. "I've been waiting since Christmas for a chance to defend myself," he says, and opens his arms as my sister slides onto the bench beside him.

Eliana calls our mom to our campsite, and Mom wanders over with a cup of freshly percolated coffee. And I feel myself retreating. Back into my role of the youngest, the quietest, the one who matters the tiniest bit less than everyone else.

If I've learned one skill from working as a community manager, it's the art of pretending to listen to someone while you're really trying to remember the title of a movie starring Nicolas Cage you watched when you were fourteen. Seriously, it's an underrated skill, and one that I've mastered. And that's all I do as the Fourth of July slowly inches along. I attend lunch with my entire family, us Finches taking up the giant banquet table at the Mexican restaurant downtown. When addressed, I make appropriate small talk, then zone out and stare at a blob of guacamole on Aunt Lindy's inappropriately low-cut shirt.

I forgo kayaking because if there's anything I hate more than exercise, it's exercising with my family on a body of water. I'm also too horrified by that flesh-eating bacteria podcast to dip my pinkie toe into Fallen Lake, let alone my entire body. Instead, I hang out on the shore in my awkward one-piece bathing suit and prescription sunglasses while Maeve frolics around in a thong bikini. No joke, a woman *covered* her husband's eyes as my manic pixie dream girl of a sister walked past them on her way to the bathroom. I wonder how I'm related to these people sometimes. The only person who seems to be having a worse time than me is Eliana, which admittedly makes me feel better. Constantly on her phone, that line between her brows—the one that surfaces when she's upset, despite Botox injections—grooving deeper and deeper.

Now, it's fireworks time. Also known as the bane of existence for those with sensory disorders, dogs of all shapes and sizes, and veterans.

As a kid, I loved fireworks, but as an adult, the cons outweigh the patriotic pros, especially with Buffy in tow. To make matters worse, the bag I packed with the ThunderShirt and gabapentin was accidentally left behind at camp. When I realized my blunder, I tried to leave the festivities to grab them, but my mom insisted that Buffy would be fine, that I was *overreacting*. But the fireworks haven't started yet, and Buffy's whining, as if sensing the impending doom.

We're set up near the volleyball nets, a hodgepodge of lawn chairs and blankets staked out across the sand. Fallen Lake stretches out before us beneath the almost-night sky, a few lights from the police boats glinting on the water. Dad explained, even though no one asked—as all dads love to do—that boats are forbidden during the show since the fireworks are shot off over the water.

The first firework pops. Then another.

And Buffy commences the full-on meltdown I feared was coming. She barks, cowering against my legs and somehow pulling on her leash at the same time. Someone's blasting "Goodbye Earl" by the Chicks so loud that barely anyone turns toward the noise. Mom is seated beside me and frowns, lifting her brows in concern, which pisses me off way more than it should. Dad doesn't notice; the fireworks reflect in his glasses as his face lights up with delight over the show.

I try to calm Buffy, but she's freaking out.

Hey. Maybe this is my out.

"I'm gonna go," I yell toward my family.

There's a flurry of offering to help and suggestions on how to calm Buffy, but in the end, I shake my head, scoop up the dog into my arms, and do what I should've done thirty minutes ago: leave.

As I walk, I coo in Buffy's ear, telling her she's okay. Buffy's my first pet, and I only adopted her in January. We had a few goldfish and hamsters when I was a kid, but nothing furry and companionable. Mostly because Eliana and Maeve could never agree on a cat or dog to adopt before I was born, so instead of compromising, our parents decided to give them a little sister. Seems fair. Anyway, I know dogs hate fireworks, but this is my first time witnessing their complete lack of chill on the country's most patriotic of holidays.

The drive back around the lake takes twenty minutes, the speed limit comically low, not to mention all the drunken tourists and teenagers darting across the road to reach the lake and public docks. Like bandy-legged deer in red-white-and-blue-spangled board shorts and bikini tops, crossing with abandon. I drive slower than Grandma Helen, horrified by the thought of accidental vehicular homicide.

By the time I reach the check-in at the campsite, I'm exhausted, and there aren't any lights on inside the kiosk. There's no hot park ranger there to check my tag, and I don't stop at the stop sign; I just roll on through. It's dark, with only a few campfires and lanterns speckled out across the various sites. As I drive, I murmur comforting words back to Buffy as she whines with every pop-pop-pop. The road snaking throughout the campground is one way and windy, confusing during the daytime and ten times worse in the dark.

Once I'm parked at Campsite #34, I lean into the back and stroke Buffy's head, relieved that she's calming. Then I toggle on my phone's flashlight and proceed to relocate my traumatized dog. I unzip my tent and crawl inside, nudging Buffy by the butt into her crate. Then I wrangle the ThunderShirt over her squirmy body and cover the crate with a heavy woolen blanket my mom left on my air mattress, probably because I mentioned how cold I was last night. I sneak a few treats— giving her a hearty dose of gabapentin in a pill pocket to help her calm down—and nuzzle her, then lock the front.

I stretch out onto my back and stare at the domed ceiling of my tent. My air mattress lost some air overnight—which makes me think of my neighbor, who bought one of those giant blow-up Santas that always ends up deflated on their lawn every morning—and it's wobbly like a waterbed, but I'm too wired to track down wherever my mom keeps the air pump. The anxiety over Tasha's job offer and Eliana's divorce and Maeve's Maeve-ness ping-pongs around inside my brain like radio static.

When I'm around my family, and my sisters in particular, it's hard to release my choke hold on the past. I wasn't a happy kid. I didn't have the stellar grades like Eliana. I wasn't charismatic like Maeve. My anxiety went untreated, and my family acted like all I needed was to exercise or meditate, and I'd be all better. Fixed. As if I was *broken*.

My eighth-grade English teacher had a parent-teacher meeting with Mom and Dad before graduation, where she gently told them I should *really* see a therapist. Apparently, all the angsty poetry I'd written that year and the fact that I had almost no friends was a "red flag" to Mrs. Hong. Poor woman didn't know what she tipped into motion when she shared her concerns with my parents, though. My parents thanked her, then enrolled me in this New Agey summer day camp where I was supposed to heal my anxiety with trust falls and guided meditation. I broke my arm horseback riding and spent the first eight weeks of my freshman year of high school in a stinky hot-pink cast. And I still had anxiety.

Also, I'm now afraid of horses, which is fun.

Being here, surrounded by Finches, is a constant reminder not only of all the ways I'm different but all the ways in which I'm *wrong*.

A thump echoes throughout the campsite, and my heart skips. I refocus on my surroundings. Not a firework. Closer, deeper, than the fireworks on the other end of the lake. The woman-who-lives-alone rears her paranoid head inside me, but there are other people at the campground. Maybe not at these adjacent sites, but we're not alone. *I'm* not alone. Even though most people left during the fireworks.

"Hello?" a voice calls out, and I sit up. Hold my breath. "Anyone here?"

The voice is familiar, but in an echoey way. Distant, brushing up against the edges of my memory, and my heart rate picks up with something that feels like fear. *Paranoid,* I tell myself, *you're being a paranoid weirdo*.

I kneel forward and unzip my tent. Readjust my glasses and squint into the darkness. "Guy?"

In the center of my campsite stands Guy Moran. I recognize him immediately, even though it's been years since I've seen him in person. I follow him on social media, as much as I begrudge it.

Guy turns toward my tent, a smile breaking out across his face, only visible due to the lantern he's carrying in one hand. "Remi?" His dark-blond hair is coiffed, swept to one side, and he's in jeans, a long-sleeved thermal top, and a heavy camel hair jacket on top. A messenger bag hangs from one shoulder. The heady smell of a bougie cologne stings my nostrils. Santal 33. During my dating apps stint, there was a fifty-fifty chance in San Jose that whatever douchebag you ended up with wore Santal 33. I'm not a fan.

I scoot out of my tent and zip it behind me. "Yeah, hey," I say, standing up and crossing my arms.

Guy's gaze travels across my body, and something tightens in my gut. Even though Guy wasn't trying to *actually* drown me that summer, it comes rushing back. His hand on my head, pushing me down. My fingernails grasping and scraping the side of the pool, legs kicking.

"Where is everyone?" Guy sets the lantern on the picnic table Eliana decked out with a cherry-patterned table cover, topped with random camping accoutrements she borrowed from Salli—a stove, a propane lantern, enamel mugs flipped upside down to dry on a rag. He sits on the bench, his legs falling open to each side, taking up all the space he can.

I stick near my tent. Weirdly, I want to lie. To tell him everyone's just . . . in their respective tents or the bathrooms or off fetching firewood. Anything other than the fact that every other member of the Finch party is over twenty minutes away from here and I'm alone with Guy Moran. But I'm being paranoid, defensive. Guy was the worst as kids, but I've barely interacted with him in a decade. Sure, he seems like a douche online, but so do 85 percent of men. He's harmless.

"They're watching the fireworks at the beach." My answer comes after a long pause, and Guy's brows pinch together. He knows something's wrong. He knows I'm uncomfortable.

The suspicion fades so fast I wonder if I imagined it. Guy smiles, flashing obscenely white teeth in my direction. "Damn, I hoped I hadn't missed the show," he says with a sigh that sounds forced, all hot air.

I hesitate, because if he'd wanted to see the fireworks, why didn't he go straight to the lake? It's not like they're setting off fireworks in a state park. Discomfort scratches at me, and I say, "My mom said you couldn't make it."

"No, yeah, my plans changed last minute. Thought I'd come up and surprise everyone." Then he winks.

The whole exchange is like a bite of something too sweet—something that's *almost* good, for a half second, but it's too much and false. Overwhelming, raising your heart rate and turning your stomach, rotting you from the inside out.

I bob my head, arms still crossed over my chest. "Sure. I'm sure they'll be back soon. Everyone will be . . . so happy to see you." I add this last bit sarcastically, but Guy doesn't pick up on my tone. He doesn't strike me as the type of person who could fathom someone disliking him, let alone an entire family.

"Wanna keep me company until they get back—"

"Oh," I interrupt with a shake of my head, "no, I'm actually not feeling very well."

He drops his head back with a groan. "Oh, come on, Rem-cycle. Lighten up. I brought some libations for tomorrow. Got a few I can spare."

I bristle. "Rem-cycle" was the nickname Maeve gave me when I was thirteen and she was eighteen. She thought it was *hilarious*. Clever wordplay, sure, but no one likes being called boring. Over half my life later, and I still hate it. I'm not going to be swayed as a near-thirty-year-old woman, but the thing is, I am being ridiculous. I'm on edge, due to the fireworks and being alone in a new, different place.

"Sure. Fine." I walk over, slide onto the bench opposite him. He grins and holds up one finger, then scoops the lantern off the table and walks off into the darkness.

I wait, sitting on my sweaty hands. Not like I need to prove to Guy Moran that I'm different now. But maybe . . . maybe I do want that, the tiniest bit. Someone to treat me differently. Like an adult. Like someone they *want* to spend time around, rather than just tolerate.

# CHAPTER FOUR

*July 4 / Night*

Guy finished off three limited-release beers he brought with him; his new job is working as an alcohol distributor for a brewery in Sacramento. I barely sipped mine, since alcohol and Prozac aren't friends, and the last thing I want is to get blackout drunk around someone like Guy Moran.

The fireworks have begun to fade, even though a few unofficial ones pop and crackle in the distance. Other than that and the rush of the traffic up in the mountains, it's quiet. Guy and I chatted a little, mostly about work and our families. With anyone else, it could've been nice, but my company leaves everything to be desired.

Once Guy runs out of beers, I gather the bottles and dump them in the nearby recycling. Even though I only sipped at my beer, then dumped it in a bush when Guy wasn't looking, I'm exhausted, all of yesterday's travel and the depleting anxiety that comes from being around my family catching up with me all at once.

Guy stands when I return, lingering beside the table.

"Thanks for the beer," I say tightly, hoping he'll finally leave my campsite and set up wherever he's staying. Probably at Salli's or Aunt Lindy's campsite, maybe a local hotel. I haven't asked. I don't care.

"Anytime, Rem." He rakes his fingers through his hair and glances around the quiet—even quieter than earlier—campsite.

When he doesn't move, I say, "I'm gonna get some sleep." I haven't washed my face or brushed my teeth, but I'm okay with plaque and clogged pores if it means curling up in my sleeping bag right now. Plus, Guy's been eyeing me a little too closely all night. I might be paranoid, but I'm also not naive.

I step past him, toward my tent, and *there it is*—Guy's hands slip around my waist.

"Hey," he murmurs, and holds me in place.

A tall woman I am not, barely five feet. Not thin, but not muscular either. Guy is taller, wider than me, and he easily stops me, holds me. His fingertips press into my skin, hot through my sweater, burning through the layers beneath, a tank top and long-sleeved shirt. The taste of that beer floods my mouth, tinged with acid, and I jerk back. Guy's grip tightens. I'm staring straight at his chest, unwilling to look him in the eye; I don't want to see what's there, what I missed earlier.

"Let me go." I say this calmly and politely, reaching to pull his hands off. And one hand does, lifting from my waist—but only to catch my wrist, pinning my arm to my body. The taste of beer is stronger now, and my heart rate is a physical force. "Guy. Stop."

Guy twists me, pulls me closer. His mouth against my ear as he says, "Remi, come on. I told you, you need to lighten up."

I shove against him. Claw at his other hand, but he does the same thing—grasping my wrist and bruising my skin as he pins it against my side. Awkward and constrained. And his mouth is on my neck, the breath hot and yeasty. Trailing up, sucking on my skin. Covering my mouth, his tongue forcing my lips apart.

*No, no, no.* That's all I hear in my head, over and over again, as he shuffles me closer to the tent. I shove and wriggle, trying to use my lack of height as an advantage; I'm smaller, faster. When I manage to slip one hand free, he just grabs it again. Tighter, his skin chafing against mine from the friction. The scents of Santal 33 and cigarettes and his lemony detergent burn at my nostrils. Then . . . Guy's loosening his hold on me to unzip the tent, and I break free. My glasses fall from my face, disappearing into the dirt and darkness.

"Damn, you're feisty," he says with a laugh. Catches me by the waist. I didn't even make it past the firepit. His hands are *everywhere* now, and I don't know which direction is up or down. My vision is blinking in and out, my hearing rushing.

Every move I make, he counters it.

I've never felt smaller than I do in this moment.

All I want is to disappear, to block out what's happening, to run away inside my mind. And I drift, pull back. The fight in me fading because *I can't stop him.*

"Get off of her," a voice almost screams, and suddenly Guy's hands are no longer everywhere. The last flame of fight inside me reignites, and I shove out wildly, my palms connecting with his chest, and scramble backward. Far enough back to see Maeve's curly hair as she drags Guy away from me.

*Maeve. Maeve?*

"We're just having some fun," Guy says, and holds up his hands.

"She's crying, you asshole." Eliana says this, and I blink in confusion. *Where did Eliana come from?*

My breath is ragged in my chest, rattling, and I'm shaking. Crying. When did I start crying? Guy turns toward me, eyes widened in innocence. He steps toward me, and Eliana snarls, "Get away from my sister, Guy. I'm serious. Back off."

"Remi," he says, but this time it's strained. Worried. "Tell them we were messing around. Having a little fun."

Eliana and Maeve turn toward me, and I don't even have to say anything for them to know. But a whimper, a pathetic noise they'd usually mock me for, escapes my lips. And something shifts, hardens, in Eliana's eyes. She turns toward Guy. "Leave, Guy. Or I'm calling the cops." Then she pulls out her phone.

The cajoling *Who me?* look on Guy's face drops like a curtain, and he lunges at Eliana, reaching for her phone. I run forward. Not even thinking, just doing. I need to stop him now because I couldn't stop him before. I collide with Guy, and Maeve does the same. He grunts, swearing and pushing, his elbow slamming into my rib cage with so much force that bile spills into my mouth and I gag. Buckle forward and scramble backward, all in one unsteady motion.

My foot catches on a rock, and I lose my balance, falling hard, my elbow scraping against the ash-stained firepit beside me. Guy trips too—on a rock, our tangled feet, I don't know—and stumbles. For a moment, I panic. He's going to fall *on* me, pin me down, and I kick the heels of my boots into the dirt, scooting away as he falls.

But Guy falls weird, not straight back like I did.

The side of his head cracks against the rim of the firepit, and he crumples to my feet.

The campsite is quiet.

My haggard breath, the faint wheeze of my asthma. Maeve's hiccuping inhalations. Eliana's sharp intake, like a gasp.

Guy doesn't make a sound. Not a cry of pain, a choking lungful of air, a yell of anger.

*Nothing.*

I dig my heels into the dirt, pushing back and farther away from Guy.

"Um." My voice is strangled, too loud in the night. "Is he—is he okay?"

Maeve blinks down at Guy, her breathing still staccato and offbeat.

Eliana pokes Guy with the toe of her Keds. "Guy," she hisses. "Get up. This isn't funny."

Guy groans—a low, loud wail—curling onto his side as he clutches his head. I'm relieved in a sickening way. Almost comically. Because of course Guy's not dead! That'd be ridiculous.

I search the ground for my glasses. The cat-eye frames are coated in dirt but not broken. I manage to push myself to my feet, my vision blurring with a bout of dizziness as I right myself. After wiping off the lenses, I put them on and back away from Guy's writhing body—giving him a wide berth—my elbow throbbing painfully with each panicked heartbeat.

Guy pulls his hand back from his head, and the lantern light shines against the blood slicking his fingers and palm. Stumbling to his feet, he says, "You're dead. All three of you are dead. When my dad hears about this—"

"Oh, shut up," Eliana interrupts. "And sit down before you pass out and hit your head again. We need to call an ambulance."

"And the cops," Maeve adds from beside me, and she wraps an uncharacteristically protective arm around my shoulders. "You *assaulted* Remi."

The reality of the situation unravels around me. What am I supposed to tell the cops? The word *assault* ushers bile into my throat, that lingering taste of expensive beer and plant-based hot dogs coating my tongue and teeth. I squeeze my eyes shut for a moment and sag against Maeve, fully aware of how that can't happen.

Guy assaulting me would not only ruin this weekend but ruin my parents' anniversary and my *entire* family's relationship with the Morans. Sure, we all hate Guy—who doesn't?—but Guy's father was our dad's best man. We're practically family. My stomach churns with nausea at the consequences of Guy's behavior.

"I didn't—I'm fine," he spits, and backs away from us like a caged animal. Blood trickles down the side of Guy's face, drips off his sharp jawline. "You don't need to call the cops."

"Sit down," Eliana's calm, cold voice commands.

Guy swipes at his face, smearing blood across his cheek. "Fuck that." He grabs his bag off the bench and stumbles backward, disappearing into the shadows between the trees.

"What," Eliana says flatly, "a stubborn asshole. But if he wants to run off into the woods with a concussion and a head wound, fine!"

"Good riddance." Maeve rubs her hand up and down my arm, then turns to me. "You okay, Rem?"

No, I am not okay. On a good day, I'm rarely okay, and today is *not* a good day. My mind is skittering and wired, flashing through the events of the evening. The smell of Guy's spit on my neck. The blood that dripped from his jawbone onto the collar of his nice camel hair jacket.

"I'm fine," I lie after a moment and force an awkward smile. Anything to throw the attention off me, to get me out of here. I want to burrow into my sleeping bag and forget that this night ever happened. But I still ask, "Does Guy need medical attention or anything? We shouldn't let him run off if he has a concussion."

Eliana sighs heavily. "Guy isn't the person we should be worried about."

I shrug both shoulders. "I'm just saying, that was a lot of blood."

"Head wounds bleed easily," Maeve says casually, and I lift my brows in concern. "What? I dated an EMT last year." Maeve pulls the sleeves of her puffy sweater down around her hands and adds, "Guy's trash—always has been, even when we were kids—but Remi's right. We should find him. And call the cops. We're not letting him get away with this, are we?"

Maeve's not wrong. Guy's not a good person, or even an okay one. But that doesn't mean he should bleed out in the woods. I'm not sure if I could live with that on my conscience. The fact that Guy Moran's head wound is something I care about after he tried to shove his hand into my pants makes me want to vomit. But I'm conditioned to care, even about the worst kind of men.

Eliana hesitates, which surprises me. She's always been the more responsible one out of the three of us, always on her high horse. But then she nods. "Okay, let's go find that douchebag." Her cell phone is still clutched in her hand, and she taps on her flashlight, illuminating the trees.

What I want is to stay behind, to curl up into a ball and sleep this horrific night off. But I also don't want to be alone right now. Even if my only option for company is my sisters, I'm taking it. So, I follow Eliana and Maeve, my arms still wrapped around myself, both for warmth and for comfort.

I force myself to focus on my surroundings, on the now, so I don't think about what happened. What *almost* happened if my sisters hadn't shown up. I'm not sure how to thank them, and I wrestle the words around in my head as we set out in the general direction Guy ran off toward. I can't even remember the last time I expressed an ounce of gratitude toward my sisters. Which probably says a lot more about me than them, now that I think about it.

I've opened my mouth—forming the words *Thank you* on my tongue, testing them out silently—when a thunk echoes ahead of us in the darkness, and I smack face first into Eliana's back as she skids to a stop. I peer over her shoulder as she sweeps the beam of her flashlight between the trees, and I squint through my dirt-smudged glasses. The light cuts across a flash of khaki. A sprawl of legs. Then I understand what I'm seeing: the unmoving form of Guy Moran, face down in the dirt.

"Seriously?" Eliana mutters, and—even though every bone in my body is telling me to run in the opposite direction—we rush forward. "He must've passed out. I told him it was a bad idea to run off with a concussion. C'mon, help me get him up."

"Ugh, let him sleep it off out here." Maeve crosses her arms over her chest. "And if he so happens to freeze to death, then that's just nature taking its course."

"*Maeve*," Eliana says admonishingly.

"I was joking," she says dramatically, then whispers to me, "No, I wasn't."

Eliana turns off her phone's flashlight, then grabs Guy's arms and motions for us to each take a leg. Gingerly, I grip Guy's ankle and we hoist him off the ground. Even though it was my idea to go after Guy in the first place, I can't believe I'm doing this. Guy attacked me, and here I am, ferrying him to safety so he doesn't get eaten by a bear or die of hypothermia or whatever.

I readjust my hold on his boot as we shuffle back into our campsite. My gaze darts to all the darkest corners of our campsite. Everyone else must've returned from the fireworks around when Eliana and Maeve did, but no one's propane lanterns are lit. Atlas's lights are out. Everyone else went straight to bed. "What're we going to do with him?"

Eliana wipes her forehead with her shoulder. "Um," she says as she glances around the darkened campsite. "Your tent?"

"Dude, really?" I groan. "Where am I going to sleep?"

Eliana begins to shuffle-walk Guy over to my tent, which is still unzipped, the fabric door panel flapping in the breeze. "You can bunk with one of us."

"Fine." Grunting, I lift Guy and hoist him over the threshold into my tent. We flop him onto my air mattress and into *my* sleeping bag. I left the dome light on earlier, before Guy arrived, and as the three of us crouch in my tent, catching our breath, I get a better look at the man in my bed.

Eliana flings the rest of the sleeping bag over him, then reaches to turn off the dome light, but I grab her wrist, stop her.

"Uh, why are his eyes open?" My stomach churns, slow and aching, with dread. "Is he *awake*?" Because Guy Moran is staring blankly at the dome of my tent, a trickle of blood dripping off his jaw and onto my sleeping bag. Wood splinters and blood mat his dark-blond hair.

Eliana uses her index and middle fingers to press against his neck. Holds her palm over his nose. "Guy's not awake," she whispers. "He's dead."

# CHAPTER FIVE

*July 4 / Night*

I lurch back and nearly topple out of my tent. My gaze darts from my sister to the . . . body in my sleeping bag. "Dead?" I hiss. "He was fine ten minutes ago!"

Maeve pinches her cheeks, her weird go-to childhood panic move.

"I mean, was he?" Eliana whispers. "He was bleeding everywhere, Rem. But he doesn't have a pulse. You can check him yourself if you want."

"Nope, I believe you!" I hold up my hands, and my mouth fills with stomach bile. I'm lightheaded. I hear it again—the thwack of his skull against iron—and shudder.

"Oh my god, was he dead when we carried—" And yep, now I vomit. The thought of carrying a dead body is what sends me over the edge, and I lean out of my tent in time to puke up the sips of bougie beer, the plant-based hot dogs from dinner. Wiping my hand across my mouth, I sit upright and glance between my sisters, who are pale, sweat on their upper lips.

"Did we," Maeve says, her cheeks blossoming red beneath the pinch of her fingertips, "kill him?"

Eliana crosses her arms and tucks her hands into her sweatshirt sleeves. "He fell," she says sternly, and I'm not sure if she's trying to convince me or herself. "Right?"

"Uh-huh," I say, not even sure if I believe the words I'm saying. My blood rushes in my ears, my stomach twists and turns, and my hearing goes muffled, distant. Guy's dead. We don't know how or why, but I'd bet my entire bank account that him smacking his head on a firepit earlier had something to do with it. "We need to call 911."

"Remi, we can't call the cops," Eliana says in the lecturing tone of hers that makes me feel bad for her kids.

"What? Why?" I bug my eyes out at my sister, the responsible, law-abiding one.

"Guy's dead, inside your sleeping bag, in your tent," Eliana points out. "This looks bad. You understand that, don't you?"

I've been avoiding the body on the air mattress, but my gaze is drawn to it now, like I'm rubbernecking at a bad accident on the 101. The lump of his body beneath the nylon fabric, the dark splotches of his blood, moist and damp. The wood splinters in his hair, the congealed mat of blood and hair on his forehead.

*We didn't kill him.* That's what I keep telling myself, over and over again, a frenetic loop. Because Guy was fine. He was standing and talking and had enough cognizance to run off when we mentioned the cops. How'd Guy go from fine, albeit concussed, to *dead*? "It was a freak accident. The longer we wait, the worse it's going to be. You were fine with calling the cops earlier."

"Yeah, well, that's before this douchebag turned up dead," Eliana hisses. "The custody case with Chad's been messy, and I can't be wrapped up in something like this, freak accident or not."

I squint at my sister in disbelief. "You don't want to call the cops because of your custody case?"

"Can we continue this conversation outside of the tent?" Maeve asks, her voice pitched with panic. "I know he's dead, but I swear he's staring at me!"

Buffy whines in her crate. Shit. I almost left my dog inside a tent with a corpse. I am a horrible dog owner, on top of being a horrible human being. I grab the crate, murmuring calming words to Buffy as I exit the tent.

My sisters climb out, and Eliana zips the tent shut before turning to me, her arms still crossed tightly over her chest. The campsite is dark, and just the light from Guy's forgotten lantern on our table illuminates the area. But desperation radiates off my sister. Rarely have I ever seen Eliana scared, but she is. She's terrified.

"Remi, please?" Eliana's voice cracks a little. "You realize that this looks really bad for you too. He's in your tent—"

"Yes, I'm not an idiot," I snap. "But if we were responsible, shouldn't we call the cops? Like, *now*? It was an accident."

"Last we saw him, he was alive," Eliana says fervently. "We don't know if we were responsible. We were even trying to do the right thing, going after him when he was injured."

"That's true," Maeve says, and nods along. "We are not the bad guys. Why don't we call the cops in the morning? Say we returned from the fireworks and found him passed out in Remi's tent. We saw the beers, assumed he'd been drinking . . . accidents happen all the time."

"Yeah, that's not a bad idea," Eliana says, and this train is fully off the rails now. Because while I'm sure—okay, *pretty* sure—we didn't kill Guy, not calling the cops seems like the opposite of what we're supposed to do. This, right here, is how we end up on a Netflix true crime documentary. "We have no idea what happened to Guy after he ran off. Maybe he fell, hit his head again. Or maybe someone else . . ."

My resolve is cracking. But then again, I've never been good under pressure. It's, like, the *one* thing I'm known for. Poor decision-making and cracking under pressure: that's me. "Wait. You think someone else killed him?"

Eliana's mouth twists, a facial tic for whenever she's thinking too hard, analyzing a situation to death. "You both heard that noise before we found him too? I didn't imagine that?"

"I heard it," Maeve says, and now that they both mention it, I remember a thunk, a splintering noise that echoed in the trees before we stumbled across Guy.

Is someone else out there?

"Me too." I wrap my free arm around myself now. As my sisters stare expectantly at me, I cave to the peer pressure like an awkward teenager. "Okay, fine, we can call the cops in the morning."

Eliana's shoulders slacken with relief, and we walk over to her tent. "Thank you. And c'mon, we'll stay in my tent. The last thing we should do is split up right now."

Maeve sighs. "Yeah, okay. I'll go get my stuff."

I kick off my hiking boots and climb into Eliana's tent, which is somehow immaculate. No dirt on the tarp floor. No suitcase with its guts spilling out beside the giant air mattress.

"I didn't know they made air mattresses that big," I comment awkwardly as I busy myself with tucking Buffy's carrier into the corner, because I have absolutely no idea what to say to my sister.

"It's a California king." Eliana peels off her dirty clothes, and I avert my eyes as she puts on her pajamas. All of this is upsettingly . . . normal. Except, it's not. Guy attacked me and now he's dead, and I'm pretty sure we didn't kill him, but I'm also not sure that we *didn't* kill him, and I have no recollection of the last time Eliana, Maeve, and I slept in the same room. Seriously. Not a single vague or fuzzy memory.

Maybe a vacation? When I was in elementary school? Usually, our parents would book two rooms—one for Eliana and Maeve, and one for the two of them with me on a rollaway bed or fold-out couch. I had my own bedroom back home. There have always been walls, if not miles and state lines, between us. Until now.

I look down at my dirt-smeared jeans and sweater. All my clean clothes are back in my tent. With Guy.

"Here." Eliana grabs sweatpants and a long-sleeved top from her suitcase and tosses them to me.

"Thanks." I peel off my clothes, not entirely sure what to do with them. I'll never look at my favorite pullover the same way again. Not without envisioning Guy's hands on the fabric against my waist, his mouth forcing its way onto mine. I shudder. Balling them up, I stuff the clothes in the corner behind Buffy's crate.

Eliana crawls onto her air mattress, which has two sleeping bags spread on top of it, zipped together to create one giant mega sleeping bag, topped with a few blankets. I slide in beside her and stare up at the domed ceiling. Eliana's silent beside me, still and unmoving.

Then she asks, "Are you okay?"

"Depends wholly on your definition of 'okay,'" I say and close my eyes. "But thank you. Don't know what would've happened if you and Maeve hadn't shown up."

"You're welcome," Eliana says after a beat. "It's weird. I always knew Guy was shitty—on a gut level, you know—but I had no idea just how shitty he could be. When I saw you, I didn't even think, I *reacted*."

"Almost like you care about me or something."

"Would that be so shocking?"

I grunt in response, too ashamed to answer. Because I've never really seen or felt my sister's care before. My entire life, all I heard from Eliana was that I overreacted, that I was too sensitive, that I needed to get out of her way. Maeve forgot my last four birthdays, never returns my phone calls, and once tried to make out with my college boyfriend. It's depressing that this might be the first time that I can remember when my sisters have *chosen* me. When they've put themselves in harm's way to help me, rather than look the other way because it's more convenient.

A rustle outside the tent pulls me from my mental spiral.

A shuffle. Twigs crunching.

Oh god. What if Eliana's right and there's someone *else* out there who killed Guy? And is going to kill us? The zipper begins to tug, and I sit up, wildly looking around the tent for any kind of weapon. My gaze lands on Eliana's curling iron, on top of her suitcase, and I snatch it, holding it like a baseball bat.

"Hey." Maeve pops her head in before crawling inside. She's carrying a pillow in one hand, her phone in the other.

I drop the curling iron but keep it within grabbing distance. "Dude. Announce yourself first."

Maeve tosses her extra pillow on the air mattress. "What? Who'd you think it was?"

"I don't know," I answer quickly. Do I really think someone else killed Guy? Or do I just want there to be a killer? Someone to absolve me of the guilt that's left me with a permanent stomachache. Sure, what happened tonight was an accident. And we tried to help Guy, we really did. But none of this would've happened if it weren't for me.

If I hadn't gotten out of my tent.

If I hadn't said yes to the beer.

If I hadn't shoved him when he tried to grab Eliana's phone.

*No,* I tell myself, and curl my hands into fists, my fingernails digging into the soft flesh of my palms. *No, this isn't your fault. You're not responsible for what Guy did.*

As much as I know that—and desperately want to believe it—I sometimes still feel like that eleven-year-old kid, running to my grandma at the Arcata Community Center pool. Water in my lungs, panicked, and being told I was overreacting, that Guy *liked* me. I spent an entire childhood being told I overreacted, when in fact, my reactions were fine. Normal, even. You know what's not normal? A teenager trying to drown an eleven-year-old girl. A man trying to force himself onto a woman.

My heart rate slows, slightly, as I remind myself of this, and I open my eyes. Maeve is now curled up on her side, and a silk eye mask is pushed up into her curls, a sight that is so quintessentially Maeve I almost laugh. Eliana's still sprawled out on her back, staring blankly at the dome of her tent.

"So, what's going on with Chad, Eli? Why're you so against calling the cops?" I ask, my voice faint and hushed. The childhood nickname slips out, and surprise shadows my sister's expression.

Eliana inhales slowly—her stomach rising with the deep breath beneath the sleeping bag—and exhales before saying "I lied when I told you Chad wanted partial custody of the kids. He wants full custody, which the lawyers have told him is impossible unless I can be proven as an unfit mother. That's been his little side project over the last month," she says, her tone acerbic. "Not because he actually wants the kids, but to mess with me. And being wrapped up in Guy's death—or murder or whatever we want to call it—won't look good. Chad would have a field day with it. I mean, I got a parking ticket last week, and I swear, the man acted like he'd won the lottery."

"Seriously?" I ask in disbelief, both over Chad *and* the parking ticket; my sister has been an anal-retentive driver for as long as I can remember. As for Chad, I've never liked him, but trying to win custody of your kids purely out of spite is diabolical. As much of a douchebag as I've deeply believed Chad to be all these years, I didn't know he had that level of hatred in him.

"Chad wants to hurt me as much as I've hurt him," Eliana says, and there's still so much she's not telling me—not telling us, as Maeve has now rolled onto her other side to listen to our older sister. "Best case, Chad uses this against me and wins full custody. Worst case, Chad gets full custody because I'm in prison. Even if it was an accident—it *was* an accident—I can't."

Maeve readjusts on her pillow and pets Eliana's hair. "I've always hated Chad," she says idly.

"Not helpful, Maeve," Eliana sighs. Then she adds, "I'm exhausted. Let's try and sleep. Tomorrow's going to suck."

Maeve snugs her silk sleeping mask over her eyes, yawns. "Good night."

I murmur my good nights but don't shut my eyes. Every shadow outside the tent makes my heart hammer; every noise makes my stomach dip. Rather than dwell on tomorrow, my mind focuses on Guy's wound. How it was a scrape—a bad scrape—when he hit his head on the firepit. And the wood splinters and blood, so much blood, that now mat his hair.

Guy could've tripped on a rock or run into a tree. The noise we heard could've been him falling. Or maybe it was none of those things. But the thought that lingers, haunting me as I drift into a fitful sleep, is that if we're not responsible for Guy's death—and it wasn't an accident in the dark—then someone else is.

Someone else killed him.

I dream of Guy.

Not in the dirt, by the firepit, with a head wound. Or burritoed in my sleeping bag, wound weeping.

But as a fifteen-year-old boy with his hand on my head. Pushing me beneath the turquoise-blue water of the pool at the Arcata Community Center, my legs kicking out, my fingernails scraping against the tile, my breath shortening into gasps as I inhaled water. For those few moments, I honestly thought I was going to die. Dead at eleven. Never been kissed. Never even had my period. All gangly and quiet, living in the shadow of my sisters.

As Guy tried to drown me, all I could think about was how *this was it*. I was going to die before anything real ever happened to me. Before I could be myself instead of the youngest Finch sister. I don't know why I was so obsessed with that thought as I choked on water, my asthma flaring and tightening my lungs, filling them with cotton. For so much of my childhood, I was intent on being something other than what I'd been since birth: Anxious, happy to hide in the shadows, the easy target. The one who never, ever fought back. A human doormat.

I don't know when that stopped. When I became so *fine* with my mediocrity. Because that's what I am: mediocre.

Maeve is social media famous.

Eliana's a successful CPA and a mother of two.

And I've never escaped my sisters' shadow. If anything, I've sunk deeper into it.

When Guy let go of my head and I broke through the surface, gasping for air, he laughed. Floated onto his back and splashed me, a lazy flick of his hand across the water. "Lighten up," he'd said with a wink.

Just like he said when I turned down the beer. Before he convinced me otherwise.

I remember scrambling out of the pool and running to my grandma. Explaining to her what had happened. How—for the briefest moment—fear flickered across her face. But it was gone as quickly as it had appeared. She brushed it off.

*Boys will be boys.*

# CHAPTER SIX

***July 5 / Early Morning***

Eliana, Maeve, and I file out of the tent around six thirty.

I barely slept, which, given my dreams last night, was probably a good thing. After Eliana aggressively shook us awake, we went over the plan. We'll "stumble" across Guy's body, under the guise that we found him passed out—drunk, maybe; the more details the better—in my tent the night before. But only this morning, he's dead. One of us will call 911. Hopefully, it'll look like an accident, blow over. After all, people die in state parks all the time, and Guy had alcohol in his system.

While I'm queasy at the fallout—Guy's body being found on my parents' actual anniversary is a major vibe killer—I'm ashamed over how relieved I am that I won't have to report the assault. My entire life, I've been the dramatic kid, and not in a fun, theater-camp way like Maeve. My knee-jerk instinct as an adult is to not voice my discomfort, to not tell anyone. To not cause waves, after a childhood of rocking the calm seas that my parents tried to cultivate.

The dead body in the tent will cause enough drama as it is.

I squint at the bright morning sun and pull the too-long sleeves of my borrowed shirt over my hands as Buffy sniffs some nearby bushes and pops a squat; the morning breeze ruffles her ears. Camp has barely begun to stir around us, and my hypervigilance kicks into high gear as I scan each neighboring campsite. The tension in my shoulders softens when I realize the only person awake is Salli—her white pixie cut smooshed on one side, eyeglasses hanging around her neck on their bauble chain—and she blows us a sleepy kiss as she walks toward the bathrooms.

If Salli finds it odd that the three of us bunked together and are spending time together of our own free will, it doesn't show. Under normal circumstances, I'd be worried that she might tell our mom that the three of us are getting along. The horror. But I have bigger problems. Like Guy Moran's corpse warming up in my tent like it's inside an Easy-Bake Oven.

"Are we doing this now?" I ask in a groggy whisper, wiping crust from the corners of my eyes as we walk over to my tent.

Maeve turtles into her puffy coat. "Yeah, do we want more witnesses around to . . . witness us finding him?"

Eliana twists her mouth to one side. "No? I don't know, it doesn't matter. Let's get it over with." When neither of us moves toward the tent, she sighs. "Fine. I'll do it." She unzips the tent, lowering herself to her knees, and pokes her head inside. I wait for a theatrical gasp, something to signal that we should call 911 and get this extremely morbid show on the road, but my oldest sister is silent.

Then Eliana shuffles out but leaves the tent flap unzipped, then stands up. "Guy's gone."

I stare at my sister. "Well, yeah. He's . . . *you know*," I say and lift my brows meaningfully because I am not uttering the phrase *Guy is dead* in broad daylight with Salli twenty feet away from us. The woman might wear hearing aids, but I'm not convinced she can't turn them up to eavesdrop on conversations when she's bored.

"No," Eliana whispers, flustered as her cheeks pinken, "he's *gone*. The tent is empty."

An awkward laugh burbles out of my lips. "Stop. This isn't funny."

"Does it look like I'm joking?" Eliana's words come out as a hiss, and she crosses her arms over her chest.

I shove past my sister and fling back the tent flap.

The air mattress where we dumped Guy last night is empty, strewn at an odd angle across my small tent. No body, no sleeping bag. Absolutely no sign of Guy Moran. I stare, as if this is some illusion I need to clear by concentrating hard enough, but the tent is empty.

"We—we put him in here, didn't we?" I ask Eliana as I push to my feet, racking my brain. It was so dark last night; I was exhausted and probably in shock. My memories and thoughts are jumbled together. What did we do with him? Leave him outside? But then I remember Buffy whining, how I almost left her overnight with a dead body.

"No, Remi, we put him in a different tent," Eliana mutters sarcastically, and I resist the sisterly urge to punch her in the boob.

"Stop fighting," Maeve says beneath her breath. "There has to be a reasonable explanation for this."

"Other than zombies?" I deadpan.

"Hello, chickadees!" A chirpy voice grates at my ears, and I look around wildly, my gaze landing on my grandma approaching our campsite.

Grandma Helen is eighty-six, more active than I am, and, despite her younger lover, is extremely traditional and believes a woman's place is in the kitchen. She's an enigma, my grandma. This morning, she's dressed in khaki slacks and a warm sweater, her knobby and frail hands wrapped around a mug of coffee.

"Remi's hungover," Maeve says, way too loudly.

I shoot her a withering look. But I'm sure I look hungover. Pale, nauseated, dying slowly on the inside.

"Oh dear." Grandma Helen stops beside my tent and gives me a pitying smile. "Bill's feeling a little ill himself. Did you have some of Lindy's punch too?"

I force a smile, realizing my grandma has no memory of me leaving the festivities early. That's convenient. "Yeah. I should've known better."

"What're you three looking for?" Grandma Helen asks curiously, her hawkish eyes darting around our campsite. How long has she been watching us? The thought makes the back of my neck prick with sweat. The dried splatter of my vomit darkens a patch of dirt beside my tent.

"My ring," Maeve says without missing a beat, holding up one of her chunky antique rings before slipping it back onto a slender finger. "Fell off last night."

"Ah." Grandma Helen nods and smiles serenely. Then she turns toward Eliana and asks her something about her kids, and Maeve drags me over to the picnic bench by the sleeve of my borrowed shirt.

We lower ourselves onto the bench seat, and my undercaffeinated brain tries to puzzle out the mess we're in. Guy *was* dead last night. Not like I checked him for a pulse, but Eliana did. And Eliana's never wrong. I swallow back the bile in my throat as I remember the head wound, the way his eyes stared sightlessly at the dome of the tent. Guy was dead, no question about it. And, unless my life has taken a supernatural turn, is probably not a zombie. Which means someone moved Guy's body. But who would move him? What would be the point of moving him?

Unless . . . unless whoever finished him off last night took him from my tent.

"Oh my god, stop," Maeve snaps, and wrenches my hand from my mouth. "That's so disgusting, Remi."

I blink and stare at my hand in hers; I've been chewing my nails as I spiraled. Small specks of blood smear across my short, unpainted nails. Dirt and something else, dry and darker—Guy's blood, maybe— smudges beneath them. I really should take a shower. "Sorry," I whisper and tug my hand free. "I'm just trying to figure out what the hell is going on. I'm freaking out."

Why did I agree to this family vacation? Why am I not back home, in San Jose, reading death threats written by sixteen-year-olds whose characters were nerfed in a recent patch update? Why did I ever think a Finch Family Function would be a good idea?

"Good. I'd be more worried if you were calm right about now," Maeve says, and leans down to pet Buffy, who's perched on her butt in front of us like the most unintimidating guard dog of all time.

Lowering her voice so only I can hear, Maeve says, "Someone had to have moved him."

I resist the urge to gnaw at my fingernails again, and I sit on my hands, watching Eliana make easy small talk with our grandma three feet from where Guy hit his head. Our grandma is a talker, especially when she hasn't spent much time with us lately, but Eliana manages to end their conversation quickly, and our grandma wanders off toward her campsite. "Yeah, but who?"

Maeve lifts her narrow shoulders to her ears. Then she sighs. "Why can't we ever have one normal family vacation?"

"Maeve, this isn't like when you got food poisoning at Disneyland."

"Well, duh, this is way worse, but I'm not wrong. Our family vacations are cursed," she says darkly.

If I weren't dying inside, I might point out Maeve's hypocrisy. If anyone in this family has had cursed family vacations, it's me. There's a reason why I loathe Finch Family Functions to my core. Because, historically speaking, they never end well for me. Not like I break down or get into a fight with someone, but the Finches are rowdy extroverts, and I am . . . the exact opposite of that. Something always goes wrong—and it's always my fault—and usually ends in my stress tears after Eliana snaps at me too many times.

For example, take my high school graduation trip to Maui. Eliana and Maeve were also invited—it became less of my graduation trip and more of a family vacation, but whatever—and they hyped up this big surprise for the first half of the trip. And like the dummy I am, I bought into their hype. Their surprise was a half-day zip-lining course, which would've been fun if I weren't afraid of heights. Eliana thought the experience would "help me get over my fears" and that I was being dramatic. I had a panic attack, and Eliana yelled at me for me being both thankless *and* selfish; then Maeve took off with a cute local and stranded us without our rental car.

Eliana marches over to the picnic table, arms crossed over her chest. "Are you two thinking what I'm thinking?"

Maeve yawns loudly and readjusts the collar of her puffy jacket around her neck. "That we need coffee."

"No—I mean, *yes*, we need coffee, but we need to figure out who moved Guy's body," she whispers, sliding onto the bench seat beside me. "The more I think about last night, the more convinced I am that something else happened to Guy after he ran off. His wound looked worse, and, until this morning, I thought it was an accident. Like he tripped. But someone went through the effort of moving him, which means they didn't want him found. Because they killed him."

I drag my hands through my hair. The thought I had last night returns: Do I desperately want someone else involved so I won't feel guilty? Last night is a chaotic blur, like I'm actually hungover, trying to pick apart my hazed memories. But Eliana's making sense, as reluctant as I am to admit it. Why move the body if there was nothing to hide? And that head wound definitely looked worse than the gash from the firepit.

A morning breeze ripples through camp, and my tent flap flutters, revealing the empty air mattress.

"We need to look for the body," I say suddenly. "Whoever moved him also took the sleeping bag." I spent four hours researching sleeping bags before this trip and picked a fancy one that zipped all the way around since I always get cold when I sleep.

Now that I think about it, it has the hallmarks of a great body bag.

"All of our DNA is on him from last night." Eliana massages her immovable forehead. "Oh, this is bad."

My elbow throbs from where I smacked it against the firepit, and I cup my palm over the inflamed skin. "Yeah, we really didn't think this through. We should've called the cops last night, told them we found him that way—"

"Shut up." Eliana braces her hands on her knees now. "Who would've thought that *the body would've gone missing*?" She says this last part through clenched teeth. "I wanted to think everything through, get some distance from what happened. To make the most rational decision that wouldn't come back to bite us in the ass."

"We're not blaming you, Eliana," Maeve says and rubs her back, but I snort.

"I mean, we technically didn't call the cops last night because of Eliana." I don't mean to sound like an asshole, but I've always had a knack for saying the wrong thing around my sisters. "What? That's just . . . factual. I would've called the cops."

Eliana's gaze lands on mine, challenging me. "You so sure about that? Remi, you hate conflict and figures of authority more than anyone I know. It's *pathological*."

I open my mouth, about to argue my case, but Eliana has me doubting myself. Would I have called the cops? The thought of telling them what happened, explaining the assault—and the accident—makes me want to vomit my guts out. The anxiety over explaining what Guy did, as well as the possibility of the police thinking I killed him . . .

"That's what I thought," Eliana says after I flounder in the silence. "Anyway, we need to stop panicking and figure out a plan. Are you two game with trying to find the body? We can also ask around. Guy wasn't exactly everyone's favorite person."

Maeve's mouth drops open. "You think someone in our family killed him?"

Eliana throws her hands up. "I don't know what I think, okay? My main focus is finding Guy's body before anyone else and making sure we're not tied to whatever happened to him. Are we all on the same page? Yes or no?"

Maeve unwinds herself from our sister and stuffs her hands into the kangaroo pouch of her puffy, fuzzy sweater; it makes her look like a poodle. "Sure. Contrary to what people say, not all press is good press, and I can't afford a scandal right now."

Eliana not-so-subtly rolls her eyes. Most of Maeve's income relies on sponsorships, and while influencers can be dropped because of scandals, Maeve has the least amount to lose with this situation. Not surprising, because Maeve is the kind of person who defies logic. She has amazing luck—seriously, once she won ten grand at a casino—and a completely unflappable mental state. She also follows the pleasure principal, avoiding *anything* that might cause her discomfort.

"Mom said everyone's going to Lake Tahoe," I say, "so we should have camp to ourselves for a few hours if we hang behind. We can search the area and come up with a game plan. Then we can try talking with everyone this afternoon before the party?"

Maeve frowns, tapping her chin with her flawless acrylic-tipped fingernail. "You don't think Mom and Dad might find it a little weird that we start questioning all the guests about if they killed Guy at their fortieth anniversary party?"

"We'll be subtle," I insist. "Casual. Just try to get some information. I don't think anyone in our family did it, but it's possible someone overheard or saw something without knowing it. Grandma Helen said Bill was drinking Aunt Lindy's punch last night, and I doubt he was the only one. Memories could be a little foggy."

"Sounds good to me," Eliana says. Then she surveys the crime scene—I mean, campsite. "Is there anything Guy left out here? Phone? Keys? Do we know where he parked?"

Each campsite has enough parking for two cars. Anyone else has to park at the entrance or in an overflow lot. Last night, I never heard Guy's car pull into camp, only him walking on foot. He must've come from one of the overflow lots. I explain this to Eliana and Maeve; then we do a visual sweep around the campsite. The beer bottles—which I swear I left on our picnic table—are gone. Only Guy's lantern remains. "Just this. No idea on the car, but he walked that way to get the beers."

Eliana and Maeve look to where I point, and we wordlessly acknowledge that Guy must've been running off toward his car last night, since it's roughly the same direction as where we found his body.

"We can look for the car after everyone leaves. No one knew Guy had a change in plans? That he was coming?" Eliana asks as I get up and grab the lantern off our table. It's a generic Coleman, battery operated.

"I don't think so. He made it sound very . . . impromptu," I say and hold out the lantern. "What do we do with this?"

"Toss it," Eliana says, and I frown at her wastefulness. But it's not waste if it's potentially incriminating detritus, I guess.

With Buffy in tow, I walk the trash over to the gigantic dumpster by the bathrooms. I hoist up the heavy lid and fling the lantern inside. It clatters as it disappears into the darkness, and I lower the lid back into place. As I walk back to our campsite, I try to get my head on straight. Inhale that pine-fresh air and think of the irony that my mental health has only gotten exponentially *worse* since entering this campground.

The great outdoors is overrated.

Back at our campsite, Eliana's doing a lap like a German shepherd, searching for anything we might've overlooked.

"You're really good at this," I tell her, and it's a genuine compliment, even if my default tone is snarky. I have the verbal equivalent of a resting bitch face.

"Seriously," Maeve says from the picnic bench. "If Chad ever disappears . . ."

Eliana shoots us both a dirty look. "Oh, shut up. Sorry for not wanting to go to jail or losing my kids because Guy's a massive, rapey tool."

I hold up my hands. "What? I'm serious. I'm freaking out, and I'm glad someone's thinking straight."

"I'm freaking out too," Eliana says, and stands before us, hands on her hips. "But, unlike you, I know how to perform under pressure."

Sisters. They're the worst. Even when they're helping you avoid jail for an accidental murder.

As I feared, everyone partook in Aunt Lindy's punch last night and is hungover to varying degrees. If it weren't for Guy's missing body, I might enjoy the humorous state of my hungover parents. They rarely drink, preferring more "natural" ways to inebriate themselves. Mom's braid is half undone; the ghost of her makeup rims her eyes. Dad's shirt is on backward, and he seems to be constantly, vaguely nauseous as they settle in at their picnic table later that morning.

After we all wish them a happy anniversary, Eliana offers to make breakfast, and Maeve percolates coffee over the firepit. Our parents are utterly delighted at us doting on them—and the fact that we're not at each other's throats is icing on the proverbial cake—and the charade keeps my mind off everything that's gone wrong since I left the beach last night. Sure, my fingernails are bitten down to the quick, and the dark splotch on my hiking boots *might* be Guy Moran's blood, but I haven't thrown up again or broken down in the bathroom yet, both of which I consider small victories.

Am I a bad person? I'm way more focused on Guy having assaulted me and how his missing body—covered in my DNA and sleeping bag—implicates me than the fact that the man died. Or was murdered?

Wait, should *I* be more worried about being murdered?

My head throbs, and I grab my coffee, which Maeve topped off, and take a scalding-hot sip. The burning sensation doesn't even hurt, and I'm pretty sure I'm in shock. Not only is Guy dead but Eliana, Maeve, and I have gotten along decently all morning. But we're probably *all* in shock. Bonding over an extremely traumatic experience that'll probably hit us tomorrow. Or when we're back in our respective homes. Or randomly, while we're grabbing a coffee and scone at the local café three weeks from now.

Until then, I'm content to ride this delusional high. I mean, what other choice do I really have?

"Look at you three," Mom says, delighted despite her hangover, as she curls her fingers around the mug of coffee Maeve served her. She relocates into a camp chair in the sun, a lounger that leans back, and beams at us. "All getting along. This is so nice."

Eliana glances up from the small camp stove she's using to make french toast; her fluffy blonde hair is knotted into a bun on the top of her head. Maeve presses her lips together as she taps out the percolator basket into the dirt. I bite the inside of my cheek. Yeah. We're definitely in shock.

"The best gift we could've asked for," Dad says, tugging at the neckline of his T-shirt, no doubt realizing it's on backward as the tag scratches his Adam's apple.

I'm pretty sure our parents wouldn't be nearly as thrilled if they knew the reason *why* we are getting along.

I serve my parents each a plate of french toast and say, "When are you all going to Tahoe? We're thinking of hanging around here."

Mom and Dad exchange another gleeful expression, and I almost feel bad for them.

"Whenever everyone's ready," Mom says, and balances her plate on her lap. "Hopefully before it gets too warm, though. Salli and I want to play mini-golf, and her prescription—you know, the one for that fungal growth?—makes her sensitive to sunlight."

I wish I didn't know what my mom was talking about, but Salli's never understood personal boundaries. One time in middle school, Salli picked me up when I was sick since my parents were working, and I had to tag along to her gynecologist's appointment. She used the anatomically correct model of the female reproductive system in the waiting room to point out the locations of all her cysts.

"What're your plans?" Dad asks, munching on his breakfast.

A near-hysterical laugh threatens to break free from me, but I choke down some coffee instead.

"We're going on a hike," Eliana says with a casual shrug. So casual I'm a tiny bit concerned with how fine she's acting right now. "Nothing too exciting."

Maeve sits beside me at the picnic table, across from our dad. As if she can tell I'm the loose thread, the one about to snap and fray. Rather than squeeze my hand in comfort, she elbows me in the ribs. A silent *Keep it together.*

"Yeah." I nod, way too eagerly. "Hiking."

Dad stares at me for a beat—his indoor kid, the one with zero athletic skills or hand-eye coordination. Then he smiles widely, his Sam Elliott mustache curling around his lips. "That's wonderful, Rem. Anxiety is congestion of the soul, and spending time outdoors might be the medicine you need right now."

The medicine I actually need is Prozac. But you try convincing my hippie parents that any of their Big Pharma conspiracy theories are, in fact, complete bullshit. I refrain from pointing out that I'm outside *right now*, and three seconds away from a panic attack. But Eliana joins us at the table and raises her brows. Another warning. Because, for whatever reason, my sisters are handling this Guy situation way better than I am.

Maybe it's because I feel guiltier than either of them. Or maybe it's because of my "congested soul" or whatever. Or because of what almost happened before they showed up. I'm not sure if I should be more upset or thankful that I have two people making sure I don't turn myself in to the Fallen Lake Police Department just so my brain will finally shut up.

So, I shove a piece of french toast into my mouth, laugh way too loudly at Dad's cheesy dad jokes ("How much does a hipster weigh? An Instagram!" Maeve hated it. I loved it.), and ignore the missing body.

# CHAPTER SEVEN

## *July 5 / Late Morning*

Eliana, Maeve, and I wave as the convoy of cars loops around the campsite and drives off toward the front entrance. The taillights of Aunt Lindy's Tesla disappear around the bend, and I drop my hand, sag against a nearby tree.

Over the last two hours, a baby ulcer has begun to burn through the layers of my stomach—that or a hernia from lifting Guy's dead body last night. The stress, being constantly on edge, all of it makes me wonder if I'm murder- or crime-intolerant. My entire body is rejecting this.

"Thank god," Eliana says as she turns from the road. "I thought they were never going to leave."

"Seriously." Maeve readjusts her outfit—she changed into a clingy sundress after breakfast, which seems like a poor choice when we need to search a campground for a dead body. But hey, who am I to judge? I've already changed my shirt *three* times due to the nervous sweats, and I look like a troll doll in the free *Rift of the Realms* shirt I got from work compared to my effervescent sister.

"What first?" I grip my water bottle with both hands and take a long sip. Even though everyone from our campsites is gone, I'm on high alert. Probably because we're not alone—there are still people nearby at other campsites, minding their own business and having nice, normal camping trips that don't involve dead dudes—and I'm finding it much harder to talk about Guy Moran during the daytime than I did at midnight, running off adrenaline.

"Okay," Eliana says, her hands akimbo on her waist. She's traded her casual sweats and messy bun for a tight, no-nonsense ponytail, high-waisted jeans, and an old T-shirt from her soccer-star days knotted above her belly button. "Maeve and I will fan out and search the surrounding campgrounds. Remi, are you willing to search the nearby trails?"

As a general rule in life, I don't hike. But maybe I've never had the proper motivation. "Yeah, sure." Then I hear it—the thunk in the woods, an echo in my memory from last night. "Hey, uh, is splitting up right now a good idea? What if there is someone else out there?"

Eliana's face falters, ever so briefly; then she says, "I have pepper spray in my car?"

"Works for me," Maeve says, as if she has no survival instincts. At all.

"Remi, everyone will only be gone until after lunch," Eliana says as my expression remains stubborn and skeptical. "We don't have much time."

I waver. Because this is ridiculous—if my life were a horror movie, I'd be yelling that you do not split up—but it's eleven. We only have two hours. Tahoe is a short drive from Fallen Lake, and lunch followed by a round of mini-golf won't take my family long. Not when they have a campsite they need to decorate before tonight's vow renewal party.

"Fine," I say, and silently bemoan the fact that I skipped out on the self-defense classes Warp offered a few years ago.

Eliana returns from her minivan with three key chain–size bottles of pepper spray and doles them out. "While we're looking for the body, let's see if we can find any clues."

The corner of my mouth twitches, and I rotate the pepper spray, check the expiration date. "Clues?"

"Guy's backpack or his phone. A trail of blood. Drag marks. *Whatever.* Something to help us find him," Eliana says. "Keep track of where you search, in case we need to go back out tonight. If someplace looks like it'd be a good place to stash a body, check it out. Thoroughly."

I tuck my water bottle into the side pouch of my small backpack and clip Buffy's leash to the belt loop on my shorts. "What are we supposed to do if we . . . find him? Do we call 911?"

"Yep, after getting your sleeping bag back." Eliana takes out her phone and starts tapping at the screen. "Plus wiping down anything that might have our DNA on it."

I take a half step forward, peering at her screen. "Are you seriously making a to-do list?"

Eliana lifts her gaze from her phone to meet mine. "What? I don't want to forget anything. Priority one is finding Guy and the sleeping bag, then his car or his belongings. It'd be great if we found out who moved him but, I don't know about you two, I can live with the mystery of whoever killed Guy Moran if it means we get out of this scot-free."

"*If* someone killed Guy Moran," I point out. Then add as an afterthought: "Just make sure to delete that sociopathic list off your phone and the cloud later."

"The more I think about it," Eliana says, "the more convinced I am someone killed him. Also, there's nothing sociopathic about being *thorough*, Remi."

"Not sure if the cop who finds that list on your phone will agree."

Eliana smiles thinly at me, tucks her phone into her back pocket. "Meet back here at twelve thirty."

"Good luck!" Maeve shouts cheerfully as we spread out.

I reach into my bag for the campground map that hot park ranger gave me when I checked in. There are four clusters of campgrounds, each named after a different tree. Our campsites are in the Buckeye campground, which has several trails within walking distance. The Jellystone Trail is closest and has an asterisk beside it, denoting that it's the most popular, most kid-friendly trail in the park. If our body dumper was smart, they'd choose a more remote trail, so I pick the Lakeview Canyon Trail and head for it on foot.

Buffy trots alongside me, a stick in her mouth, absolutely loving the change in scenery as we leave camp behind. Not for the first time in my life, I'm thankful dogs exist. Because a woman wandering alone could, possibly, catch someone's attention. A woman walking her dog, however, is perfectly ordinary.

"Don't get used to this," I tell her. "We are *not* hikers."

Despite the questionability of splitting up, I won't lie; it's a relief to be alone. To have time and space away from my sisters, who I have spent more time with over the last twelve hours than I have the last seven years.

Pine cones snap beneath my weight like bones, and I scan my surroundings. Trees and more trees, the occasional ground squirrel or bird. When I began therapy, I remember my therapist saying that anxiety isn't inherently *bad*. In fact, I can thank anxiety for keeping my ancestors alive. That hypervigilance is what saved them from being eaten by tigers or whatever. But today, we don't live in a constant state of danger; we don't need to constantly tap into our fight or flight. Not like our ancestors did, at least. Because as last night proved, the simple act of being a woman in this world can put you in jeopardy.

Comical how all the anxiety in the world did absolutely nothing to help me survive last night. If anything, my anxiety made me freeze the moment I realized I wasn't a physical match for Guy.

Buffy sniffs around, straining against her leash, and as we reach the trailhead, I wonder if she has any latent bloodhound instincts in her that might come in handy, but all she does is get distracted by an exceptionally chunky ground squirrel. The late-morning sun warms my shoulders and the back of my neck, reminding me that I really need to pick up sunscreen sooner rather than later. But a sunburn or even skin cancer seems like small potatoes when Guy's body is missing.

The Lakeview Canyon Trail, according to the map, is "beginner friendly." I hope that's accurate. As I start my hike, I try to think like a killer, like someone who would need to dispose of a 180-pound man in his thirties. If you're going to hide a body anywhere, a state park isn't a bad option, I guess.

Fallen Lake State Park has over one hundred campsites, spread across miles of state-protected forest. While not complete wilderness—there are roads, trails blocked off from public access, and park rangers who zoom around on UTVs and trucks—the woods are prime body-dumping real estate.

The trail is flat, the dirt path worn into grooves from bike-tire treads. I clutch my pepper spray in one hand, my phone in the other. The sun's only gotten warmer, more unrelenting, as the day creeps toward noon, and sweat trickles down my spine. It makes me think of the blood on Guy's head, the way it sluiced down his jaw.

I shake the morbid thought from my head and focus on my surroundings. On my task. As much as I want Guy's body found, I'm not sure if I want to be the one who actually finds him. But I keep my eyes peeled for his camel hair coat, for the flash of denim blue between the trees, or the heels of his hiking boots beneath the bushes that line the trail.

I turn a corner and pause, frowning at the gigantic pile of scat in the center of the trail. Bear droppings, a quick google confirms, and a whole new fear lodges itself into my heart. *Awesome.* But I need to look on the bright side. A bear might find Guy and solve our problems for me. No body, no crime. I mean, bears . . . eat people. I think. Honestly, I don't think I've ever spent any time in the woods since that summer before high school, when I broke my arm at camp.

I'm so far out of my comfort zone, it'd be funny if it weren't tragic.

My calves burn, an unnecessary reminder about how I spend most of my days in a desk chair staring at a computer, and fifteen minutes into my hike, I have to slow down. Pause to sip my water and consult the campground map. Ahead, the Lakeview Canyon Trail will fork, and I decide to take the path to the left, which leads farther away from any of the nearby campsites; the other loops closer to the campground entrance.

I tuck my water bottle away, take a deep breath that inflames my usually dormant asthma, and soldier on. The trail to the left of the fork is overgrown, unkempt compared to the rest of my hike, and weeds itch at my ankles. Buffy is up to her shoulders in foxtails but is having the time of her life.

A branch cracks behind me, and everything inside my body stills. The Lakeview Canyon Trail is remote—that's why I chose it—with thick woods on either side, and I grip the pepper spray tighter. Prepare myself to turn around. To defend myself.

"Excuse me, miss?"

I whirl around, my finger hovering on the pepper spray release— only to find a park ranger headed toward me.

If someone were to attack me, they probably wouldn't call me *miss* and announce themselves first. But I don't release my death grip on the pepper spray, even though my palms are slippery with sweat. Buffy wags her tail, not sensing the danger as the man approaches. The ranger stops his advance, leaving a good ten feet between us, and through the haze of my panic, I recognize him from the day I checked in—Mr. Hot Park Ranger.

"Can I help you?" Despite the pepper spray in my hand and prob- ably feral look in my eye, I try to act like any other woman walking her dog. Not like someone trying to find the missing body of the guy she maybe-accidentally killed the night before.

"Sorry if I startled you," the ranger says, and his eyes linger on the pepper spray in my hand, "but this trail is closed due to safety concerns. I'm guessing you didn't see the sign?"

I blink. Sign? What sign? I mean, I was more focused on the map, not the actual trailheads. "No, I didn't. Sorry," I say, my words tripping over one another on their way out of my mouth. My cheeks flush. "I have had the worst twenty-four hours of my life—which is really say- ing something—and I guess I wasn't paying attention to where I was walking. So sorry. Won't happen again."

Inwardly, I groan. I shouldn't talk to strangers, especially those in authority positions. I'm a nervous talker, and mark my words, it *will* be my downfall.

The ranger smiles, and even in my flustered state, I'm reminded how nice of a smile it is. He's not upset; I am not in trouble—beyond the whole missing body thing—and I will my heart rate to slow. "Not a problem, miss. If I can have you head back to the main trail . . ."

"Oh! Right, yeah, of course." I whistle to get Buffy's attention—she's nose deep in a squirrel hovel off the side of the path—and retrace our steps.

As I pass the ranger, he says, "You're with that huge group, aren't you?"

I glance at him. Did he see something last night? Or this morning? Is this all a ruse? The ranger stares at me for a moment, his expression morphing not into suspicion but embarrassment.

"Sorry." He laughs, and it's kind of adorable. "I'm good with faces; *not* a creep, I promise. I checked you in the other day. We've never gotten noise complaints over a game of Pictionary before. Your family was the talk of the rangers' kiosk yesterday."

Yes, my family got the park rangers called on them due to that rousing game of Pictionary during our first night; Dad told me and Maeve all about it yesterday. The offending clue? *Landfill.* We're a competitive bunch, us Finches, and that's not always a good thing.

I study Mr. Hot Park Ranger's face. He's sincere. I think. Or very, very good at hiding his ulterior motives. Besides, rangers aren't cops. They're like . . . glorified Boy Scouts. Mall cops, but for forests. So, I laugh. Try to ease the tension in my face, shoulders. "They can be pretty rowdy, yeah."

"I'm Leo." The ranger taps a pin on his button-down: *L. Zebrowski.*

"Remi." I tuck the pepper spray into my back pocket. "And this is Buffy."

Leo smiles again, and my stomach flutters, which is extremely not helpful right now. "Is she the chosen one?"

I crack a genuine grin, not the *Hey, I maybe killed a dude last night and his body is missing, but I'm fine, everything is totally fine; don't mind the fire burning down my world around me* smile I've been practicing all morning in my phone's camera. "I'd like to think so. She's a badass when she's not cowering due to fireworks. But no one's perfect."

Leo laughs, even though my joke isn't funny. And it hits me that he's, quite possibly, flirting with me. The eye contact. The smiling. I could be wrong. I should *want* to be wrong, given the messy circumstances. But I genuinely can't remember the last time someone I felt any level of attraction to flirted with me. I lower my guard even further and take in Leo. Dark, slightly curly hair—long enough to curl around his earlobes but not messy. Grayish-brown eyes. A strong jaw, sharp cheekbones.

Everything about him reminds me of the fact that I haven't had sex in a year.

Last night, that almost changed.

The thought is dull and searing. I'm normally not an angry person—anxious, yes, but rarely angry—and I'm overwhelmed with the urge to break something. Not like I wasn't aware how close Guy came to assaulting me last night, but I hadn't thought of it that way. That my unintentional dry spell almost ended because some dude refused to hear the word *no*.

Slowly, I suck in a low, deep breath and try to calm myself down.

"Not to alarm you," Leo says as he falls into step beside me, his words drawing me out of my rage-tinted mental spiral, "but it's probably best you stick to the more crowded trails."

"That's an inherently alarming statement," I say, trying to joke, but an uneasiness is cloaking my shoulders, the back of my neck. "Why?"

"Our license plate recording system flagged a wanted vehicle entering the park last night," Leo explains, sliding his sunglasses from his head and hooking them through the front of his shirt. "But don't worry, you're not in any danger. Only a precaution while we work with local law enforcement to track down the fugitive and their vehicle."

My mouth is uncomfortably dry. "What kind of fugitive?"

Leo smiles and it's lopsided. "That's above my pay grade, sorry. I'm actually with AmeriCorps—I'm only here until the end of the season—so they don't tell me much. I'd say be aware of your surroundings, but you did almost pepper spray me in the face."

"Well, to my credit, you crept up on me. In the woods."

"I didn't creep," Leo insists. "Besides, I'm just doing my job. You're the one wandering where you shouldn't be."

I smile, but I'm distracted by this new piece of information. Theoretically, let's say that Guy *was* whacked in the head last night. That the sound we heard was someone finishing him off. Am I supposed to believe it's a coincidence that Guy was killed the very night a fugitive entered the park?

But I focus, very hard, on acting like a normal human being around Leo. Even if he's basically a mall cop, but for trees, I don't want to set off any alarm bells in that pretty head of his. Not like my sisters and I did anything wrong. I *think*.

"That's weird about the fugitive," I blurt out after a moment of silence, and shake my head in disappointment at myself. Subtle.

"I wish I could say it was the first time. Criminals sometimes take to the woods, often state or national parks, to avoid law enforcement. Not sure why."

"Probably seems off the grid. Safe." I try to convince my nervous system that I'm not in mortal peril. If anything, walking beside Leo is the safest I've been since I arrived in the park. But the fact that a fugitive is loose in the woods and very, very likely is the same person who killed Guy makes my body buzz, like I've downed a triple shot of espresso. My pepper spray feels meek and useless. "Did you know something like three hundred people go missing in state parks every year?"

Yeah, I should not be allowed to talk to figures of authority; I've lost my filter.

Leo glances sideways at me, his gray eyes widened. "I . . . did not. That's probably going to haunt me for the rest of my career. Thanks for that."

"You're welcome." *Stop talking about weird, inappropriate shit,* I tell myself, and am relieved as we reach the main trail.

Leo pauses to pick up an empty plastic water bottle from the side of the trail, and a genuine stab of affection for Mr. Hot Park Ranger warms my chest. He isn't just hot—he's a good guy. Someone who works for a nonprofit and saves the trees and picks up trail litter and probably recycles his toilet paper rolls. Until this weekend, I could confidently say that I'm an okay person, neither good nor bad, but sort of . . . hovering in the middle of the morality scale.

After last night and this morning, I'm worried I'm tipping the scales toward *bad*. Not like serial killer status or Chris Pratt levels of bad (he gave up his incontinent fifteen-year-old cat for adoption because she was too much trouble, which is the purest form of evil in my book). Maybe I didn't kill Guy Moran, but he's dead because of circumstances *involving* me, and someone like Leo Zebrowski would turn me over to the police in the hottest of seconds.

"You don't need to babysit me," I tell Leo as he returns with the trash in hand. "I can walk back on my own. I swear I won't wander off on any other closed trails."

"I'm headed that way," Leo says, and my face flushes from my assumption that he'd go out of his way to walk me to safety. "Not to say that you and Buffy haven't been good company."

The flush in my cheeks is much more pleasant this time, and I stare down at my hiking shoes because I am so, so not good at flirting and it's written all over my face. Buffy keeps pace with me, and for the first time, I get a look at her stick. The one she's carried around with her for the last hour, ever since we left on our hike.

The end poking out of her mouth is bright red with blood.

# CHAPTER EIGHT

*July 5 / Late Morning*

"Remi?" Leo stops once he realizes I'm frozen in place, turning back to me with a frown. "Hey, are you okay?"

I force my gaze from the bloody stick in my dog's mouth and smile way too aggressively. "Yeah. Sorry. Just, um, realized something."

All I want to do is rip that stick from Buffy's mouth. But that would require (1) me touching a probable murder weapon and (2) drawing Leo's attention to the aforementioned probable murder weapon. Neither of those things are happening right now. They can't happen right now.

Leo's gray eyes crinkle around the corners, but not in a smile. He's legitimately weirded out by my behavior, and I can't say I blame him. So, I force myself to keep walking and add, "Sorry, I'm—" I make a chaotic motion with my hand. "Family vacations really mess with my head."

The expression drops and he laughs again. The tender sound warms my chest. "I went to a family reunion earlier this summer, and I still haven't recovered."

The hiking trail feeds into the main road, and we walk alongside the asphalt, keeping out of the sparse traffic's way. The Buckeye campsites are now within sight, and I check the time. My sisters should be back from their own search party. What're the odds they found something more compelling than the murder weapon?

"So, uh, what do you do when you're not suffering through family vacations?" Leo asks when I don't reply.

For one bizarre second, I consider lying. Even though Leo knows my name, he doesn't need to know everything about me. But I find myself telling the truth. "I'm the community manager at Warp Games in San Jose. Basically, I read all the hate emails and complaints on our Discord, log them, flag the ominous ones, monitor our social media accounts. Rinse and repeat for forty hours a week."

"Seriously? People send you hate mail?"

"Not *me*, personally," I say, which is true if I ignore the incident from a few years ago when some "passionate" fans took things too far. "But the company, yeah. You get used to it, after a while. The all-caps yelling and misused profanities because, roughly, eighty percent of the complaints are from fourteen-year-old boys."

Leo laughs, tips his head back. "I'm sorry, but that sounds awful."

"Yeah, it's not great." As surreptitiously as possible, I sneak a glance at Buffy, my anxious mind gnawing at the unknown. Where did Buffy even find the stick? Back at camp? I rack my brain, unable to remember where exactly she picked it up. And it's most definitely because of the murder weapon, my nerves, and the fact that I like Leo's face and I don't know how to be a normal person around figures of authority, but I add, "My old college roommate actually offered me a job at the company she launched."

"That's really awesome," Leo says, and he sounds genuinely happy for me even though he doesn't know me. "Congrats."

"I'm probably going to turn it down," I tell him with a shrug. *Definitely* turning it down. Not probably. "I'm not really . . . I don't know. I'm not a huge fan of change. Besides, my job isn't that bad."

Even I don't believe the words that have just left my mouth.

We reach the cluster of Finch-infested campsites, Leo slowing on the road beside Campsite #34. Eliana and Maeve are seated across from one another at the picnic table, leaning in conspiratorially as they talk.

No doubt about Guy Moran and missing bodies and how our family vacations are cursed. They look up as Leo and I approach.

Leo turns toward me and smiles. "Change gets a bad rap. Maybe keep an open mind," he says, walking backward down the road. "Thanks for the company, Remi. Stay safe."

I wave, then all but sprint into our campsite.

Buffy, murder stick in her mouth, trots beside me.

Maeve leans back on the bench seat and lets loose a low wolf whistle. "If I knew park rangers were hot, I would've gone camping ages ago. Puts a whole new meaning on the great outdoors, don'tcha think?"

I'm embarrassed that I had literally the *exact* same thought as my sister when I met Leo on Friday. So embarrassed that I nearly forget about the bloody stick in Buffy's mouth. Then my dog parks herself beside the firepit and begins gnawing at the bloody end.

"No, Buffy!" I drop into a crouch beside her and unzip the baggie of treats hooked to my belt. Dangling a dehydrated chicken treat in front of her face, I say sternly, "Drop it."

Buffy growls protectively, tail thrashing side to side as if we're playing.

"Remi, what is going on?" Eliana pushes up from the table and walks over to me. "Hot or not, why were you with a ranger—oh my god, is that *blood*?"

"Yeah, I think Buffy found the murder weapon," I say, my voice pitched low even though the rest of our family hasn't returned from Tahoe yet. Somewhere nearby, a car door slams shut, and Buffy, as hypervigilant as her owner, turns toward the noise. But that's all I need to swipe the stick from her.

When she turns back to me and whines, I feed her the treat, and she forgets all about the chew toy murder weapon.

Gingerly, I hold on to the stick from the nonbloody end that's unfortunately also covered in dog spit. "Um. Okay. Do we need to preserve this for the cops or . . . ?"

"Given *your* fingerprints are now on it, Remi, I think not," Eliana says—sounding way more pissed at me than she has any right to be—and wraps a paper towel around the stick before pulling it from my disgusted grasp. She flings the stick into our empty firepit and glances around. "Matches! Where are the matches?"

Maeve dashes off to our parents' campsite in search of matches.

I wipe my hands off on my jeans, then perch on a rock and press them to my temples, my jaw, which are sore to the touch. Yeah, I've definitely been stress-grinding my teeth this vacation, and I forgot my mouth guard back in San Jose. How am I considered a functional adult?

"I shouldn't have grabbed it," I admit, dropping my hands to my lap. "Sorry."

"Yeah, well, you did," Eliana snaps, and I'm more irritated at myself than my sister. My desire to get the stick away from Buffy momentarily overrode my logical decision-making. I should've kicked the stick away from her or used a paper towel like Eliana.

Maeve returns with a trendy little box of matches, and as my sister burns the stick that undoubtedly clubbed Guy Moran in the head into ash, I fill them in on everything else I discovered on my walk.

"Why didn't you lead with 'fugitive in the park'?" Eliana stands over the fire, where she watches the wood burn with a kind of reverence that makes me worry my sister might be an arsonist.

"Sorry, I figured the *murder weapon*," I say, "was more important to deal with first."

"We didn't kill him!"

"Obviously!" I fling my hand toward the firepit, where the bloody stick crackles as it burns.

"Except we can't prove that. Because the evidence that would exonerate us and prove someone else hit him was contaminated by dog slobber and your fingerprints, so we had to destroy it," Eliana says. "Meaning we're still at risk of someone discovering the body—wrapped in your sleeping bag and covered in all our DNA."

I open my mouth to respond, but Eliana barrels on before I can.

Drop Dead Sisters

"And let's not forget that if someone else *did* kill Guy, maybe it was that fugitive the hot park ranger told you about," Eliana adds, "and then all of us—Mom, Dad, Grandma, everyone—could be in danger. I don't know about you two, but I don't want to die on this fucking camping trip."

"Because I'm dying to spend my final moments with you two," I mutter, but I think over what my sister just said. We didn't kill Guy. At least, not directly. Whoever wielded that bloody chunk of wood killed him, and at the very least, not having his death on my conscience makes me feel the tiniest bit better.

Maeve fluffs her fingers through her curls before dropping her arm to her side with an annoyed sigh. "Can you two stop fighting for five minutes? This is exhausting."

"What?" I say, affronted. "Sorry for not wanting to be criticized for every single choice that I make!"

Eliana turns back to the flames and taps the toe of her Keds into the dirt. "Sorry, okay?" She says this so quietly, I'm pretty sure I hallucinated the apology, but Maeve's baby blues widen in surprise. Eliana isn't known for her apologies; I can count how many I've received from her on one hand.

"Whatever." I sink deeper into my camping chair and stare up at the cloudless sky. A headache pounds against my brow, and other than the breakfast I picked at earlier today, I haven't had much in my system except coffee. "Did you two find anything?"

Eliana wanders over to the picnic table, grabs something off it. "Yeah," she says, and her voice is even, calm. Her rare "peacekeeping" tone. "Maeve found Guy's phone."

I perk up in my seat. "Really? How do you know it's his?"

"Well, for one . . . ," Eliana says and clicks the side button, lighting up the screen. The lock screen background is a close-up of a woman's cleavage. "There's also some blood on the back of the case."

Last night, I never saw Guy's phone. But the device in Eliana's hand looks like the most recent iPhone, in a leather case with a smear of

77

blood swiped across the back. Guy Moran always liked shiny toys, the newest and most expensive, even when we were kids. I want to point out the hypocrisy of Eliana holding the phone with her bare hands, but even I know there's a difference. We can easily wipe the fingerprints off a phone. Handling a murder weapon is a different ballpark of bad decision-making.

"I put it on airplane mode, in case someone tries to track it," Maeve says from the outdoor pantry—a small set of wooden shelves that's installed at every campground. They're old and crooked, the doors missing, a relic from before increased bear safety measures, like the massive metal bear-proof bins. "Hey, do we have any food? The only thing in here is bug spray, Eli."

"Mom took the coolers with her in the car," Eliana says. "Pretty sure I told her we were getting lunch after our hike, so she probably didn't think she was stranding us without food."

Maeve wanders over from the pantry, arms crossed over her chest. A sunburn peels at the tanned skin on her shoulders, and her left arm is spotted with bug bites. "I vote we get lunch," she says. "Everyone will be back in a half hour, anyway. If we haven't found Guy nearby, I doubt we will. Besides, I really don't want to be wandering alone on the trails if a fugitive is on the loose." She shudders, and the strap of her flimsy dress slips down her shoulder.

"I gave you pepper spray," Eliana says, almost defensively.

My stomach growls, fierce and petulant, and both my sisters glance over at me in alarm. "What? Unlike you two, I was too nervous to eat breakfast earlier. Let's find something to eat and see if we can get into Guy's phone. That's better than nothing?"

Eliana and Maeve agree, and I peel myself off the chair. Buffy is sprawled in the shade beneath the table, her leash attached to a stake in the dirt. Completely and blissfully unaware that she trotted around a state park with a murder weapon in her mouth. I'm not sure how one goes about disinfecting a dog's mouth, but I make a mental note to look it up later.

"Can you two watch Buffy for me while I use the bathroom?" I ask my sisters, and they wave me off.

Washing my hands for five solid minutes after I pee isn't the refreshing shower that I'm craving, but it feels good to scrub Guy Moran's blood out from beneath my fingernails. I have to focus on these small, simple victories. If I don't, I'm fairly confident I'll have a breakdown. My last twenty-four hours has been more turbulent than my sisters', but I have no idea how they're handling this so well.

Don't get me wrong, I'm glad to have my sisters' help, but it's complicated. I don't pretend to be the most capable almost-thirty-year-old woman on the planet, but whenever I'm around my family, it's hard to shake the incompetency I've tried to outrun since childhood. I was always the weird, anxious kid—and my family *pushed* me. As if nudging me hard enough might break me out of my shell rather than send me tunneling in the opposite direction, like a hermit crab.

They say anxiety's genetic, but you'd never think that looking at the Finches.

I turn off the tap, grab a wad of paper towels, and dry my hands. My gaze lifts to the warbled, fingerprint-marred mirror above the sink. My sisters loved to joke that our parents found me on the side of the road as a baby. Because being adopted wasn't cruel enough—I had to be a ditch baby. In addition to our massive personality differences, I also don't look like my sisters. We might all be various shades of blonde, but Eliana and Maeve are tall and have blue eyes with ski-slope noses like our mom. I'm short, and I have green eyes and features I can't find in either of our parents. My dad wears glasses, the only genetic link I've been able to connect.

I'm not a ditch baby—I have, unfortunately, seen my tub-birth home video—and know that I belong to this chaotic family just as much as my sisters. Maybe I don't make unhinged to-do lists on my phone like Eliana or emotionally disassociate from the situation like Maeve, but I *have* to keep it together this weekend. Once I get home, then I can have my breakdown.

The thought makes me feel better. It's nice to have things to look forward to.

The Hilltop Café that overlooks downtown Fallen Lake has outdoor seating and allows dogs, which were our two criteria for lunch, and I order a cheeseburger. After three days of almost exclusively eating my parents' vegan cuisine, I'm ravenous when my food is slid in front of me by our waitress. The early-morning nerves that chased away my appetite during breakfast have nothing on the gnawing sensation in my stomach. The first bite of the cheeseburger does something to my brain, and the anxiety I felt in the bathroom earlier ebbs as I stuff myself with meat and carbs and dairy.

The phone sits in the center of the table—our morbid centerpiece—and we have an unspoken agreement that we all need to get some food in our systems before we try breaking into the phone. Buffy's stretched out by my feet, and the outdoor patio is nearly empty except for an elderly couple in the corner.

Maeve pops a sweet potato fry smothered with aioli into her mouth. "Did you realize," she says, bouncing her foot, and the jelly sandal thwacks tunelessly, "that this trip is the first time we've all been together since Remi's graduation?"

"Yes," Eliana and I say in unison, not looking up from our respective meals.

"We should do this more often," Maeve continues. At my horrified expression, she adds, "Spend time together, not, *you know*. It's kind of nice, all of us hanging out together, like when we were kids."

I snort at my sister's revisionist history. "We never hung out, Maeve. You and Eliana hung out. You both hated me."

Her blue eyes go big. "I didn't hate you! You were—"

"Annoying," Eliana interjects as she bites into her third shrimp taco. "You were so annoying."

"I was a kid. We were all annoying."

"Speak for yourself," Maeve says smugly, and coifs her curls.

"Come on," I say with a laugh, "do you really think this weekend will change things between us? I'm grateful you both stepped in with Guy—seriously, I really am—but whatever happens this weekend . . . we're all going to go back to our lives. And, if you haven't noticed lately, we *aren't* in each other's lives. That's not an accident."

Maeve's smug smile fades, but she knows I'm right. Every year, I send Maeve a birthday gift and text. If I don't badger her to follow up, her text message response rate is something like 30 percent. She's forgotten my birthday for the last four years—for all I know, she thinks I'm still twenty-six—and was an hour late to that lunch last year when she stopped in San Jose on her way to San Francisco. It's not hatred or cruelty. This is what indifference looks like. If I'm there and it's convenient, she pays attention to me. But my sister has no object permanence. The moment I'm out of sight, it's as if she forgets I exist.

Maeve clears her throat and sits up straighter, fiddling with the straps of her sundress. "Whatever, Remi. What I'm trying to say is that we can all make more of an effort, me included. I'm pretty sure if we can survive this weekend without murdering one another, then we can survive anything." She wrinkles her nose, then adds, "Poor choice of words, but you know what I mean."

I finish off my burger, the meat heavy and comforting in my stomach. "How about this? I'll make an effort when Eliana does."

"Screw you," Eliana says, and pops a lone shrimp that fell from her taco into her mouth. "I'm going through a divorce."

"For the last seven years?" I ask sarcastically, because it's not like she tried when she was younger either.

A few years ago, Eliana wanted to put together this hour-long montage video for Dad's birthday. Over three decades of birthday parties and Christmas mornings and family vacations, and she tasked Maeve and me with reviewing possible footage. As a professional doormat who doesn't know how to say no, I agreed to help despite being swamped with work, and I spent an entire weekend watching home videos.

The most surprising thing? Eliana seemed like she liked me when I was younger. Maeve was, in typical Maeve fashion, distracted by anything shiny or remotely edible—and considering I was neither, she lost interest quickly—but they were both sweet to me. Eliana encouraged me to walk and played games with me and smooched kisses on my cheek. Maeve dressed me up and stole Mom's lipstick, smearing my lips bright red. The shift occurred in high school, when Eliana's interest in me dimmed into disdain and Maeve's short attention span somehow became even shorter, her little sister the least of her worries.

Rewatching all those home videos—one after the other, for an entire weekend—made me ache with the realization that my sisters stopped liking me once I grew up. When I took my first steps toward becoming an individual with my own personality and interests, likes and dislikes. From my conversations with friends, this isn't *that* unusual—except most siblings come back together and rediscover common ground as adults. Eliana and Maeve never bothered. So, no, I won't hold my breath that everything will be different because of this trip.

Eliana wipes her mouth with a napkin, her tacos demolished, and leans back in her chair. "Honestly, I'm pretty sure my marriage died when Clara was born. So, close enough."

"What's the deal with Chad, anyway?" I ask, not only because I'm curious but also because I can't do this with Maeve right now. Pretend like there's anything worth nurturing between the three of us when, in reality, we'll all float our separate ways after this trip is over. If we're not arrested or clubbed in the head with a log, that is. "Why's he out for blood?"

Eliana drums her fingers on the table, the silence stretching out and, annoyingly, piquing my curiosity. "I messed up. And Chad found out."

"Oh my god, did you cheat on Chad?" Maeve leans forward eagerly and grabs Eliana's forearm. "Because we'd respect you more if you cheated on Chad."

"Chad's a chud," I say in agreement. Yeah, I'm enjoying this way too much. But after the last sixteen hours, I deserve this one, singular joy.

Eliana yanks her arm back from Maeve, her face flushed. "Yes, okay? Are you happy?" She brushes back invisible hairs from her cheeks. "Before we separated . . . I saw someone."

"You mean you fucked someone," Maeve corrects, and says this so loudly the elderly couple in the corner glance over with scandalized expressions.

Eliana swats our sister in the arm. "Be quiet! And yes, I cheated on Chad. Sexually."

I snort at her phrasing. "Don't get me wrong, I am all for this, but why? I thought you and Chad were happy."

"We hadn't been happy in years," she says casually, as if her sharing this kind of intimate, personal life detail with me is normal. "Chad . . . look, marriage is complicated, but do you know what the death of a marriage is?"

"No sex?" Maeve suggests.

"No," Eliana says with an annoyed sigh, "when one partner stops respecting the other. And Chad stopped respecting me *years* ago. I'm not saying what I did was right, but I don't regret it either. I had an affair with someone I met at work last year, and Chad found out only a few weeks ago. He acted as if I'd *castrated* him. Now he's swinging for the fences with the custody case. But I won't be surprised if he changes his mind after this weekend. Chad's never had the kids this long without me before. They're going to destroy him." The corner of her lips tugs in a smile.

"Are your kids assholes or something?" I joke, and Eliana's smile vanishes.

"No, my kids aren't *assholes*," she says. "Which you would know if you ever saw them."

I lean back in my seat and cross my arms, trying very hard not to feel guilty. But the last time I saw my nephew, Connor, was when he was four, and his sister, Clara, was two. I think. They weren't with my sister at the hospital when our mom had shoulder surgery, so I'm not sure. It's been years, though.

Sure, I'll like the photos of the kids on Eliana's Instagram, and she sends a coordinated-outfit holiday card every year that I hang on my fridge until the New Year due to guilt before throwing it away, but I don't *know* them. That's partially my fault, but Eliana isn't blameless either. She's never opened her life up to me. Until this trip, she's been a closed door that I could never crack.

Before I can muster up an apology or reply, Eliana pushes up from the table, gathering her leftovers on the red plastic tray before carrying them inside.

"Yikes," Maeve says, dangling one arm over the side of her chair to scratch Buffy's head. "The kids are a touchy subject for Eliana. But, between you and me, Connor is kind of an asshole. Clara's a sweetie pie, though."

I snort-laugh, which is so inappropriate, but inappropriate is what I am now, and I'm embracing it. And Maeve giggles, too, a soft blossom of wrinkles crinkling at the corner of her eyes.

"What's so funny?" Eliana returns to her seat, avoiding eye contact with me as she picks up the phone.

"Oh, nothing," Maeve says in a singsong, smoothing both her palms down the length of her dress. "Now, does anyone have any guesses as to Guy's password? My money is on sixty-nine, sixty-nine."

# CHAPTER NINE

*July 5 / Afternoon*

Guy's password wasn't 6969. Or 6699. Or his birth year—Eliana's practical, yet boring, guess—and Maeve lost the ten dollars she decided to bet our sister over her horny suggestion. But the phone warned us that it'd lock after one more failed attempt, so we cut our losses and turned it off. Maybe we'll get a strike of inspiration later and guess the correct password. As frustrating as it might be, we may never get into Guy's phone, and it feels like we've barely made any progress into figuring out what happened last night.

What was Guy tangled up with that led to someone clubbing him in the head? Did the killer have it out for Guy, or did they stumble across him?

"Hopefully someone at camp saw or heard something last night that might be useful," I say with a resigned sigh and tuck the phone into my backpack.

"Or one of them did it," Eliana says with a quirk of her brow. "Oh, Maeve, you totally missed the shit-on-Guy-a-thon the night before you arrived. Everyone in our family hates him."

"Hated him," I correct, and slurp the remainders of my iced coffee.

"Surprising who exactly?" Maeve slides her heart-shaped sunglasses—which I had no idea any adults actually owned, let alone wore—from her bag and onto her face. "Guy Moran has always been trash. Didn't he try to drown Remi once?"

"I forgot about that," Eliana says, a disgusted expression twisting her face.

"The fugitive definitely did it," Maeve adds. "What's that called? Occam's razor? The simplest explanation is usually the right one."

Our sister glances sideways at her. "Didn't you fail out of your freshman year philosophy course?"

"Doesn't mean some of it didn't stick," Maeve says. "What? I'm not in charge of how my brain stores information."

I laugh and glance around the patio before leaning in closer to my sisters and adding, "Maybe we'll get lucky and this fugitive is good at dumping bodies, and he won't be found for weeks or months. Or ever."

Okay, that's definitely my hopeful delusions talking, but hundreds of people are never seen again after they enter a state park. Why couldn't Guy be one of them?

"We should look for the car," I add. "Getting rid of any sign that Guy was at the state park will give us more time."

The waitress returns with our cards, and we all shut up, smiling as if we're not talking about committing crimes and procuring dead bodies. You know, normal lunch conversation. We all scribble our signatures on our individual receipts, then collect our belongings and leave.

When we're in the minivan, Eliana picks up as if we were never interrupted. "Remi has a good point about the car."

"Should I be offended that the most you've ever agreed with me is over how to deal with a dead body?" I joke, and my sister rolls her eyes at me in the rearview mirror.

"We should assume that the body will be found by someone, eventually, even if we can't get to it. But on the off chance it's not found before we all leave tomorrow, then we need to set ourselves up for success." Eliana clips her seat belt and turns on the minivan.

"Meaning?" Maeve rolls down the window, leaning her elbow against the door.

Buffy noses her way through the small gap between Maeve's seat and the side of the vehicle in an attempt to stick her head out the window, and I'm gifted with a face full of dog butt.

"Meaning we erase any sign of Guy Moran from Fallen Lake," Eliana says in a clipped, calm tone. I envision this as an additional bullet point on her list. "The phone was a good start, but if we find his bag, or even the car? Even better. We dump it."

"Ooh, we should remove the plates too," Maeve says excitedly, like she's happy to contribute.

I stare between my sisters and out the windshield from the back seat as we curve toward the lake. "When are we supposed to do this exactly? We don't even know what kind of car he drives. Also, Aunt Lindy and Salli said we need to help them decorate when they get back from Tahoe."

Am I the only one who remembers we're on a family vacation and the fact that the Finches will only be gone until the afternoon? Everyone is bound to be back at camp by the time we return.

Eliana cracks her neck side to side. "Let's help decorate and, while we're prepping for the party, talk with everyone. Hear their stories from last night, gather all the info we can. Then we can say we have an errand to run for Mom and Dad. We'll leave, look for the car, and deal with it before the party. Then, later tonight, once everyone is passed out from Aunt Lindy's signature cocktail, we find the body and get the sleeping bag."

This plan isn't foolproof. It's actually miles away from foolproof, given we looked for the body all morning and couldn't find it.

"Fine," I say distractedly. "Are we still calling the cops when we find the body?"

Eliana hesitates, shrugs one shoulder. "I mean . . . we probably should. But I guess I'm not feeling so charitable toward Guy right about now. He's dead, and it's not our fault. Will calling the police *actually* make things any better? We should think it through, is all I'm saying."

I circle my arms around Buffy, tugging her back into my lap. My head throbs with a headache even though I'm properly stuffed full of meat and gluteny carbs. "I'll think about it. I can't wait for this vacation to be over."

Eliana grunts—something between a laugh and a sigh. "You know, when we decided that the kids would stay with Chad this weekend, I imagined that I'd have this relaxing vacation. I brought *five* books with me. And I'm spending my time dealing with a dead body, not reading the newest Emily Henry."

"I had to use most of my vacation time for this trip." I shift Buffy's weight onto my other thigh; she has pointy dog-butt bones. "And I'll probably use all my sick time for the mental breakdown I'm planning on having. Good thing Warp has nice health insurance."

"Is that why you stay at that awful job?" Eliana asks.

"Huh?"

"Your job," Maeve pipes up, "sounds like hell on earth, Rem."

"'Hell on earth' is a bit harsh." I turn toward the window and watch the lake blur by. "You get used to it."

"No one should get used to *death threats*. Or doxing." We slow down at a stop sign, and Eliana glances at me. "Mom said you were doxed last year."

I grimace. Because, okay, the doxing was bad. After the new patch released for Warp's biggest game last August, a few die-hard fans were upset by the reworking of the skill trees. Since I'm the lucky one who interfaces with the community, they targeted me. They found out my name. And my phone number. And my address. Then they posted *everything* online.

A year later, and the memory still nauseates me. Nowhere near as bad as Gamergate or anything like that, but it *definitely* wasn't in my job description. I had to change my phone number and moved in with Stephanie until my lease ended and I could find a new apartment. Even if immature gamer bros have the attention span of angry goldfish, nothing is ever gone from the internet. All that information is still out there, but the more haunting thought is, What's keeping it from happening again?

If I took Tasha's job offer, *doxing* wouldn't even be in my vocabulary anymore, let alone looming in the background of my everyday life. I'd be a user interface designer, not a human punching bag. But no job is perfect, and who's to say I wouldn't have equally awful problems at my new job? What I said to Mr. Hot Park Ranger earlier wasn't a lie. I don't like change, and I'm pretty sure it has a bad rap for a reason.

I'm weirdly tempted to tell Eliana and Maeve about Tasha's job offer. About Seattle and how, if I took the job, I'd live in the same city as one of my sisters for the first time in over fifteen years. But, for whatever reason, I just can't bring myself to tell them. Maybe because I'm afraid, deep down, that I actually want to take the job. And I don't want anyone—*especially* not Eliana—making me feel worse about my inability to make a life decision that's more than a lateral move.

"Hey, it could be worse," I say, and ignore that voice inside my head. The minivan slows as Eliana turns in to the campground parking lot. Despite it being the day after the Fourth of July, the entrance is busy, and we join the back of the check-in line. "I could be an *accountant*. Tax season is as bad as doxing."

Eliana sighs, flips me off.

I shift Buffy on my lap and am staring out the window, thinking about how to successfully interrogate my family about what—if anything—they heard last night, when I notice the official-looking vehicle parked in the lot on the other side of the check-in kiosk.

Even with my glasses, I can't quite make out the wording on the side, but there are lights—*police* lights—on the roof of the sedan. "Has this weekend risen to stress-induced hallucinations, or do you see that cop car too?"

Maeve pinches her cheeks.

Eliana swears, then leans out the window to get a better view.

I sink deeper, deeper down in the back seat.

"They have to be here about Guy. It's the only logical explanation. We were too late. They found him."

"Oh, calm down," Eliana snaps from the driver's seat. "We don't know what's going on. Besides, it's just the highway patrol. They write traffic tickets. If this was about Guy, wouldn't the *actual* police be here?"

"I don't know what their jurisdiction is!" I rest my chin on top of Buffy's head, and she snuggles against me. Like the good unofficial emotional support animal she's become, Buffy knows when I'm moments away from losing my cool. Because maybe Eliana's right—if Guy had been found, this place would be a circus. But it's still law enforcement. Law enforcement that wasn't here earlier.

Maeve twists to look at me in the back seat and frowns at my lack of composure, then turns her gaze out the window again. Her expression lights up. "Ooh, isn't that your ranger friend, Remi?"

"Who? Leo?" I shift my miserable head and peer out the window.

Leo's striding across the parking lot toward the rangers' kiosk.

Before I can move my sluggish, anxiety-ridden body, Maeve leans across Eliana and yells out the window, "Leo!"

"Maeve!" I throw an errant crayon that must belong to one of Eliana's kids at her head. She swipes it out of the air, and the crayon lands in the center console of the minivan.

Outside the minivan, Leo hesitates, then walks over. Since I can't disappear into the void in this back seat, I force myself upright and roll down my window, saving Leo from interacting with my sisters.

The confusion on Leo's face softens as he spots me. "Hi, Leo," I say apologetically.

Leo slides his sunglasses off his head and fiddles with them. "Hey, Remi," he says, still slightly confused as he looks at the two women in the front seats.

"Sorry, these are my sisters, Eliana and Maeve," I say and hate that Maeve did this. Even though I've been single—by choice—for a year, she's treated my lack of obsession with dating and finding my soulmate as a personal affront. She takes after our mom in that way: a hopeless romantic.

Leo introduces himself, then readjusts his weight on his feet. "Apologies about the wait. Busy day!"

"No problem," Eliana says diplomatically, but Maeve leans across our sister again, and I hope she isn't giving Leo an eyeful of her cleavage. Not like I have any claim over Leo—the dude is out of my league, vastly—but Maeve's flirtatiousness has always been too aggressive for my liking. See: Maeve almost making out with my college boyfriend.

"We wanted to ask what was going on," Maeve says, her voice lilting up in a way that makes her sound way more like an airhead than she actually is. "Is everything okay?"

"We're curious," I rush to tell him, and wonder how bad this makes us look. We are too interested in what's going on here, and the blood rises to my cheeks, my face splotching red.

"Not a problem," Leo says politely but continues to fidget with his sunglasses. "Actually, this is about the fugitive I mentioned earlier, Remi. CHP was alerted when our system flagged that wanted vehicle. They're helping us out until a detective from down south can take over. It's all standard procedure, nothing to be worried about."

I'm stuck between relief and panic. Relief over the fact that this isn't about Guy. His body hasn't been found. But an actual police detective is coming to camp. "When?" I blurt out before common sense can catch up with me. "When is the detective coming?"

Leo gives me a quizzical look. "Uh. An hour or two," he says, and hooks his sunglasses over the collar of his shirt, studying me in a way that is both pleasant and completely terrifying. Unlike my sisters, I am not a good liar. I am an open, anxious book. "Why? Is something wrong? I might be able to help—"

"We're bored," Eliana interrupts, smoothly and calmly. "Remi got us hooked on this creepy true crime podcast, and I swear, we're seeing murder *everywhere* now."

Leo barks a laugh, his suspicions fading. Or he's easily disarmed by my sister, who is *freakishly* good at lying. "Well, it's nothing quite as serious as that. And there's no reason to believe you're in any danger. Just . . . keep your wits about you. Officer Ericson will ask you a few questions and check your license plate; then you'll be free to head back to camp."

"Thank you, Ranger Zebrowski," Eliana says with a beatific smile. "We will definitely keep our wits about us. Thank you so much for the info."

"Happy to help." Leo nods at my sisters before turning back toward me.

I'm opening my mouth to say something—but my window rolls up before I can think of something, *anything*, to say to this man.

Eliana moves her finger off the button control on her door and turns to look at me in the back. "Sorry, but you are really bad at lying. I had to save you—and ourselves—from yourself."

"When did it become a negative quality to be a bad liar?" I wave lamely at Leo through the tinted window. He looks supremely confused but returns the gesture, then shoves his hands into his pockets and walks into the kiosk. "Maeve, why did you call him over here? Aren't we trying to keep a low profile?"

"To get information," Maeve says, and throws her hands. "What? That was informative! Also, Leo is cute, and you two keep . . . running into each other. How very kismet."

"You yelling his name across a parking lot isn't us 'running into each other' or 'kismet,'" I say, both embarrassed and exhausted by my sister. Also, I'm annoyed and won't admit it, but maybe Eliana did save me from myself. My previous conversation with Leo wasn't all that smooth, either, and knowing myself, if I spend too much time around the dude, our entire sordid crime might come spilling out of my lips. There's a reason that detectives in cop shows are super hot—it's so the criminals are disarmed into spilling all their dirty, murderous secrets.

The info Leo gave us makes it easier for me to breathe, though, as we pull alongside the check-in kiosk. The detective will be an issue for future Remi to deal with. I hug Buffy, hoping the ranger will talk to one of my sisters and not me, the human disaster in the back seat.

"Hello, my name is Officer Ericson, and I'm with California Highway Patrol." The woman is Black, her hair pulled into a no-nonsense bun that matches her serious expression. "A vehicle connected with a hit-and-run entered this campground last night, and we're stopping each guest to alert them and ask if they've seen anything suspicious over the last twenty-four hours."

"Thank you for letting us know," Eliana says as all my words get trapped in my throat, where they threaten to choke me to death. "And nope, nothing suspicious. Is there anything else we can help with? Look out for?"

"A detective handling the case will be arriving within a few hours to take over," Officer Ericson says, echoing Leo's vague estimate, "and they'll have more information. You're sure you haven't seen any suspicious vehicles? Odd behavior?"

Maeve shakes her head, curls slapping her cheeks. "Nope."

"Okay then." Officer Ericson taps at her tablet, then walks around to the front of Eliana's minivan to check her license plate before returning to the rolled-down window. "You ladies stay safe and enjoy your vacation." And with that, Officer Ericson ushers our car forward.

Eliana wastes no time, shifting her car into gear before driving into the campground. "We have a few hours," she says, both her hands grasping the steering wheel as if she's going a hundred miles an hour, when in fact, she's adhering to the campground's fifteen mph speed limit, "until this detective shows up."

"There's not a chance in hell we'll be able to find Guy's car and his body before then," I moan from the back seat.

"Stop being a defeatist, Remi," Eliana snaps.

"I'm being a realist." I struggle upright and move my dog onto the other bucket seat. "Two hours max? To interrogate our family? To find a body and a car? And decorate for our parents' vow renewal? We can't sneak off."

"Same plan as earlier." Eliana slows for a grouping of kids to cross the road, headed toward the beach. "But we put the car on the back burner and focus on finding Guy's body before the party. A detective snooping around, even if it's not for Guy, could be . . . *tricky* for us. Hopefully someone at camp will have some info to help us find him—"

"And if they don't?" I interrupt, wondering how *I'm* the defeatist. This entire plan is bonkers. Maybe I should leave. Kiss Mom and Dad on their cheeks, apologize, say my apartment's on fire, then drive back to San Jose. The thought is tempting, but even I am not that much of a dick.

"Then we'll just have to find him all on our own," Eliana says as she speeds up. "We don't have any other choice."

# CHAPTER TEN

*July 5 / Afternoon*

The pure joy on my parents' faces when they see the three of us climb out of Eliana's minivan together makes me want to hang my head in shame. Because the truth is, we *have* gotten along the past eighteen or so hours, but our parents have absolutely no idea why. They'd be mortified that it took an accidental murder and missing body to bond their three daughters together. And, even then, we're still taking shots where we can. Nothing is different between us, no matter how much Maeve might want it to be.

Because, at the end of the day, we're the same people. The same sisters.

I think of my comment about Eliana's kids and grimace. Not my finest moment, but to my credit, I *was* trying to joke around. That's the issue between Eliana and me, I guess. We rarely understand each other. More reason to believe that, even after all of this is said and done, we'll go back to exactly the way we were.

I plop Buffy onto the dirt and clip her leash to my belt, then glance sideways at my sisters. All too aware that our parents are watching, and the scattered Finches are swarming our reserved campsites. "What's the plan? Do we split up? Tag-team someone?"

Eliana loosens her hair from its bun and massages her scalp, the swoosh of her waves somehow flawless. "Let's split up. Remi, you talk to Aunt Lindy and Mom. Maeve, you try Grandma Helen and Bill. I'll work on Dad and Salli. But hurry. The faster we can turn this campground into a magical lovefest and interrogate everyone, the better." And with that, my oldest sister strides off in the direction of Salli's camp.

Maeve walks toward Grandma Helen's tent trailer, and I linger before forcing myself toward my aunt's site. Aunt Lindy's campsite is as eccentric as its inhabitant. A cooler is splayed open on her picnic table, in clear violation of the campground's bear safety rules, and a ground squirrel is currently trying to abscond with a snack-size cheese wheel, lugging it over the side of the ice chest. Her tent, which she definitely borrowed from Salli, looks as if she put it up drunk, in the dark, or both. Half the stakes aren't secured into the dirt properly, the tarp is both too long and not wide enough, and I'm pretty sure she forgot an entire tent pole, since the roof sags in the middle.

For my aunt's sake, I really hope it doesn't rain.

"Hey, Aunt Lindy," I call out as I walk around her tent, spotting my aunt sprawled in the hammock strung between two sturdy pines. Her bare foot hangs over the edge, and her slip-ons are neatly tucked against the base of the tree. As I approach, my aunt doesn't move, and for one panic-stricken moment, I worry that she's dead.

I have spent way too much time dealing with Guy Moran when my go-to thought is *dead* after someone doesn't immediately reply to me. Aunt Lindy has always been a deep sleeper—no doubt a side effect of the heavy drinking she's so fond of—and I stop beside the hammock, then gently shake her foot. "Lindy?"

Aunt Lindy snorts herself awake, legs flailing as she grips the sides of the hammock and nearly capsizes herself. "Oh! Oh, Remi, dollface, where did you come from?" My aunt wiggles her way upright and swings her legs over the hammock, tucking her feet back into her shoes. "Sorry, you gave me a fright." She smiles, and her soft, leathery skin wrinkles. Our aunt has long hair that's a similar strawberry blonde as our dad's, streaked with grays and faded highlights. She tucks the flyaway hairs behind her ears, which sag beneath the weight of heavy turquoise earrings.

My palms moisten because I have no idea how to ask my family about Guy Moran. About last night. Then my brain clicks on. Maybe I can use the whole fugitive story as an interrogation icebreaker. "Didn't mean to scare you, Aunt Lindy," I say with my sweetest, most innocent smile, the one I cultivated as the youngest. "Eliana, Maeve, and I got back from lunch—"

"I thought you went on a hike," my aunt interrupts and stands, using the side of the tree to steady herself. She frowns, wipes some sap off her fingers, which have several small scratch marks, the longest of which cuts into her palm.

"We went out to lunch. After the hike." My mouth twitches, but my aunt's turned, walking to the main part of her disorganized campsite. The fact that Lindy knows about our "hike" means our parents were definitely talking about us at mini-golf, and the thought makes my skin itch. "Anyway. Um. Did you hear about the fugitive in camp? We spoke with a ranger at the kiosk."

Aunt Lindy wanders—seemingly aimlessly—around her campsite before removing a massive container of Red Vines from her bear-proof bin. She holds the tub out to me, and I slide out a piece of licorice. It's soft, almost mushy, from the heat. "Right, right. Yes, we saw all the hullabaloo when we got back from Tahoe!"

As a stress eater, I help myself to some more licorice and perch on the bench seat of her picnic table. Unlike my parents' campsite, there's no sunshade and there's also no table cover. Just a propane lantern, the open cooler, and a coffee percolator. "The officer asked if we'd heard anything last night. The whole thing is kind of creepy, don't you think?"

Aunt Lindy chews on the piece of licorice absentmindedly, her gaze straying over my shoulder. "Creepy, yeah." Then her expression tightens, and she focuses her gaze on me. "Wait. Why do you think it's creepy?"

I shrug. "A fugitive in the woods? I wonder what he *did*, you know."

"Or she." My aunt points at me with her flaccid licorice, ever the feminist. "Everything was dead quiet when we got back here last night. I don't know what the rangers think we could've heard."

"So, you didn't hear anything?" I ask this as casually as possible, but my stomach twists in discomfort. Stress-eating licorice was a bad idea.

My aunt's gaze holds mine, her large hazel eyes fringed with pale lashes. "Nothing at all. But between you, me, and the trees, I was a little buzzed last night, as the kids say," she says with a throaty laugh; then her thin lips sink into a frown. She reaches into the container for more licorice.

"What happened to your hand?" I ask, and she withdraws her scratched-up hand from the Red Vines container.

Aunt Lindy wraps her other hand around the scratched one, turning her palm as if inspecting it for the first time. One of her sharp acrylic nails is broken at the tip. "Oh, you know, I fell on our way back after the fireworks."

"And only scratched up your hand?"

Aunt Lindy shrugs, helps herself to another piece of licorice. "Broke a nail too," she says as she munches on the candy. "Pity there aren't any good nail salons in this town."

"You really should bandage that up. Want me to ask Salli for her first aid kit?" Because if my aunt didn't bring a single item of camping gear, there's no chance she has a Band-Aid or antiseptic wipes on her person.

Aunt Lindy waves this away with her hand. "No, I don't want to bother her. Remi, it's not a big deal, just a scratch. Don't let Salli's hypochondria rub off on you," she says. "The whole thing is embarrassing. I don't need everyone knowing how clumsy I am. Makes me feel . . . old."

I think of the flesh-eating bacteria podcast and my aunt's open wound, then shudder. "Okay, I'll drop it," I say, then add, "Wait. How did no one else see you fall? Weren't you all together, after the fireworks?"

"Oh, it wasn't when we came back. I misspoke," Aunt Lindy continues. "After, when everyone went to bed. I wanted to stretch my legs before I went to sleep, so I walked around. That's when I fell. What's with all the questions, doll?" My aunt laughs breathily, then offers me a final go at the Red Vines container before replacing the lid.

"Nothing," I say, and take yet another licorice even though my stomach hurts. This is so obvious. I'm suddenly a teenager again, lying that *one time* to my parents when I went to a concert in San Francisco. My parents started laughing once they realized what I was trying to do, that their sweet youngest was trying to pull the wool over their eyes. They weren't even mad, just proud that I was trying to be independent. "You should just be careful, especially with a fugitive wandering around the woods."

"Remi." Aunt Lindy folds her arms over the lid of the container, which is in her lap, and smiles. "I'm fine. Like I said, I had a little too much to drink, so I tried to walk it off and tripped, that's all. You really ought to stop listening to all that true crime garbage. It's bad for that sweet little head of yours."

I'm not entirely sure if I should take offense at "sweet little head," but I fold an entire licorice into my mouth, then say, "I'll work on finding some new hobbies. Anyway, I wanted to let you know I can help out with party prep early. Eliana, Maeve, and I need to run an errand for our parents before the party, so we want to get a jump on the decorating."

My aunt claps, and I flinch like the guilt-ridden mess I've become on this family vacation. I didn't kill Guy Moran, but I moved his dead body last night and burned the weapon used to murder him in a firepit. I'm definitely drifting into Chris Pratt territories of bad. "Lovely! I'll grab the lights. They might need a *light* detangling."

Okay, I can't claim that my interrogation of Aunt Lindy was successful, but as I carry the bundle of tangled solar-powered bulb lights to Salli's campground, I think over what my aunt told me. If she went on a walk after everyone went to bed, it's possible she was wandering around the woods the same time Guy took off on foot. If we didn't hear anything helpful—when we were feet away from the body—I doubt that my aunt did on her drunken midnight stroll. The fact that she didn't is simultaneously comforting and frustrating.

But I believe Aunt Lindy. She's not exactly calm under pressure. Maybe that's where I get that particular personality trait from, now that I think about it. Once, Lindy got lost in a Costco and freaked out so epically that she was banned from the entire chain. They cut up her membership card and everything. Not the murdering type.

Both of my parents are taking a power nap in Atlas, so I'll have to wait until later to question my mom, and I hope that either of my sisters has been more successful with their targets. Maeve disappeared into Grandma Helen's tent trailer, so I have no idea how that's going, but Salli and my oldest sister are chatting intensely as I walk up.

"Can I join you?" I ask and gesture to the nearest empty chair with my free hand.

"Sure," Eliana says with a distracted nod. "Salli was telling me that she thinks she heard something last night."

I lift my gaze from the tangled ball of lights in my lap. "Wait, really?"

Salli clutches her knitting project—which I secretly hope is a dog sweater for Buffy, as it's way too oblong of a sweater to fit a human child—to her chest as she leans forward. "Yes! Around midnight. I swear I heard a . . . *dragging*," she says in a whisper, even though there's no one else around to overhear her.

Eliana and I exchange a glance across the firepit, and I wonder if she's thinking what I'm thinking. Whoever moved Guy must have dragged his body, not being strong enough to carry him, and taken him past Salli's campsite.

"Midnight?" I ask Salli, and she nods aggressively; her glasses slip down her nose with each movement of her head, and her bauble chain thwacks the side of her neck.

Guy attacked me around ten fifteen, and we found him at ten forty-five or so. All I know is we crawled into Eliana's sleeping bag closer to eleven. Whoever moved the body didn't waste any time, and the fact that *I* didn't hear anything gives me pause. Had I fallen asleep by then, stuck in a dreamland loop of Guy Moran drowning me? Or was I still tossing and turning beside my sisters, too distracted by my own thoughts to hear what was happening fifteen feet away?

"Anything else?" I tug at one of the bulbs, then frown as all I succeed in doing is tightening the rat king of bulb lights.

Salli scoots her butt back in her chair and rests the knitting on her lap. "I don't think so but . . . I'm so embarrassed to admit this, but I had too much of Lindy's punch last night." Her cheeks redden and she shrugs sheepishly. "Things are a little fuzzy."

What the hell did Aunt Lindy put in that punch?

"But you remember that you heard this at midnight?" I ask, almost certain that I sound way too interested in this mysterious dragging sound, but I'm too eager to care.

"I think so." Salli taps her sharp metal knitting needles together. "What do . . . what do you think happened? Do you think I heard him?"

"Or her," I say, echoing my aunt. "The fugitive could be a woman. Women can be . . . criminals."

Eliana widens her eyes at me and shakes her head tightly. *Shut up, you freak.*

"Very good point, Remi." Salli nods, resumes her knitting. "Women can do anything men can do."

I can't help it. This conversation is way too ridiculous, in ways Salli can never know, and I snort, failing to cover up the noise with a cough. My sister looks as if she's going to smack me with the s'more stick resting against the firepit and up this weekend's body count to two. But Salli's too focused on her knitting to notice our wordless conversation.

"Thanks for the chat, Salli." Eliana pushes to her feet and juts her chin toward our grandma's campsite. "C'mon, Remi, let's go find Maeve. We have a lot to talk about . . . with the decorations."

I've gotten absolutely nowhere with the lights, but I say goodbye to Salli and fall in step with my oldest sister.

"Did Aunt Lindy hear anything? See anything?" Eliana asks beneath her breath, her shoulder bumping into mine as she leans in conspiratorially.

"Nope. Like Salli, she says she was drunk. Didn't hear anything," I say, and Eliana pauses, halting me with her hand on my arm. "What?"

"We're not just asking them if they heard anything, Remi," she whispers. "We need to figure out if they were . . . involved."

"Okay, there was one weird thing," I admit, and then regale my sister with a description of our aunt's scratched-up hand and her drunken walkabout that could, possibly, coincide with our altercation with Guy. "But you can't possibly believe our drunken aunt was involved in a murder? Not when a *literal* fugitive is wandering the woods. Remember when she got banned from Costco?"

Eliana snorts. "I forgot about that."

"I believe her," I tell Eliana, "and Salli too. Why would she tell us about the noise if she'd been involved?"

"Okay, okay, we can tentatively cross off Salli and Aunt Lindy," my sister says, and pulls her phone from her pocket.

"Please tell me you don't have a suspects list on your phone."

My sister taps at the phone's screen. "Save your judgment for someone who deserves it, Remi. I'm keeping us on track." After she strikes out Lindy's and Salli's names, she stows her phone. "Even if it wasn't Aunt Lindy or Salli, we need to keep an open mind. People can surprise you. You heard how everyone talked about Guy our first night. They hated him."

"Which means a bunch of other people—who are way more capable of murder—probably hated him too," I point out, and my sister's expression softens. She agrees with me, even if she's too prideful to admit this. "But I'll keep an openly suspicious mind while we interrogate the rest of our family."

"That's all I ask." Eliana starts walking again and makes a beeline for our grandma's site.

I hurry to keep pace with her.

"Jeez, slow down," I say. "Not everyone has soccer-goddess legs."

Eliana tosses me a smug look. "How *do* you get around on those things?"

"Funny," I say flatly, and finally catch up as we reach Grandma Helen's site.

Eliana walks up to the tent trailer and is lifting her fist to knock on the door when a low, painful moan comes from inside the trailer.

"Oh my goodness!" Grandma Helen shrieks as Eliana and I burst into the trailer, and she drops the tin mug in her hand onto the linoleum floor. Tea splatters onto my hiking boots, and I run face first into my sister's shoulder as she skids to a stop. Turns wildly to her left, then right, trying to locate the noise we heard outside. Bill's splayed out on his stomach on the tent trailer's pop-out bed, and Maeve is kneeling over his body.

"What's going on?" I scoot away from Eliana and nearly slip on the tea on the floor. "Is he okay?"

"What?" Bill grunts, turns his head on the comforter to look at us. "I'm fine, I'm fine. Your sister said she could fix my back. Threw it out last night."

Maeve smiles over at us, oblivious to our nervous energy. "Doing what, I wonder?" she jokes suggestively, and I shudder at the thought of my grandmother having sex. But my heart rate is calming. No one is seriously injured. Bill cried out because he threw out his back, and, if I had to guess, my sister is making it worse.

"Sorry." Eliana swipes her loose hair back from her cheeks. "It sounded like someone was . . . hurt."

"No one is hurt," Grandma Helen says snippily, and her cheeks are a flustered pink as she grabs a rag off the small kitchen counter, then leans over to wipe up the mess. "What are you girls doing in here? Have you heard of knocking?"

I shift guiltily on my feet. "We were looking for Maeve. Sorry, Grandma." Then I look at Bill. "You know that Maeve's not a licensed massage therapist, right?"

"I took a course." Maeve presses her elbow into Bill's back. He groans and buries his face into the mattress. This trailer is way, way too small for five people, especially with our grandma passive-aggressively wiping up the tea *she* spilled, muttering beneath her breath about our lack of manners.

"Yeah, which still doesn't make you a licensed massage therapist," I say, and wince as Bill grunts again in pain.

"I was just asking Grandma when she and Bill went to bed last night," Maeve says with absolutely no tact. At all. "But you two interrupted us."

Grandma Helen straightens up, tosses the damp rag into the sink. "It's none of your business."

"One, I think," Bill says, and I wonder if he's just trying to answer my sister's questions as quickly as possible so she'll stop torturing him with her bony elbows.

"Nonsense," Grandma Helen says, and proceeds to pour herself a new cup of tea. "We went to bed immediately after we got back from the fireworks show. Remember, Bill? We never stay up that late. Lindy's punch, I swear, must've had paint thinner in it."

"Of course," Bill says with another painful gasp of air. "Silly me."

Grandma Helen lifts her teacup to her mouth and sips. "What are you three up to, anyway?"

"We heard something weird last night," Maeve says before Eliana and I can speak up, "and we're trying to figure out if it was the fugitive."

"Why," Grandma Helen says slowly, "would the fugitive be . . . prowling around our campsites? That's preposterous. Don't you girls have something better to do? Like help decorate for the party tonight?"

"Fine, fine. We'll go." Maeve adjusts her elbow and digs into Bill's back for another moment before releasing the poor man. "Hope you feel better!"

Bill gives us an unenthusiastic thumbs-up—still prone on the mattress—and our grandmother shoos us out of her tent trailer, locking the door behind her.

"Jeez, you think Grandma would be a little more chill if she was getting laid," Maeve mutters, and readjusts her dress.

Eliana massages her brow, then motions for us to walk toward our campground. "Please never speak about Grandma Helen and Bill having sex, ever again. My emotional state is fragile enough as it is."

"Agreed," I say, and cluck my tongue to get Buffy's attention; she trots beside me.

"Prudes." Maeve points to the both of us, and we begin walking back to camp. "We should all be so lucky at Grandma's age."

I snort, but the sad reality is that my grandma gets more action than I do. *Wow.* Now that's a depressing thought. We reach our camp and sit at the picnic table, where we work on detangling the bulb lights.

"Was it just me," Eliana says, deftly untangling a knot, "or were Grandma Helen and Bill acting suspicious? Maeve and I left the show a little early to beat traffic—the parking lot was packed—but everyone else should've gotten back around ten thirty. There's a big difference between that and one in the morning."

Maeve fumbles with the task, her acrylic nails a hindrance. "Sure, but Grandma is clearly just embarrassed about her sexy times with Bill." She waggles her eyebrows.

"What," Eliana says coolly as she glares at our sister, "did I *just* say?"

As the youngest, it's comical to watch Maeve harass Eliana. Eliana should know better—she made herself an easy mark. The survival tactic

I learned at a young age was never letting your siblings know what actually upsets you; it only gives them ammunition.

Maeve ignores our sister and continues, "They didn't say anything else helpful before y'all showed up. Grandma spent, like, five minutes trying to set me up with Bill's grandson. What about you two?"

As we finish straightening out the lights—which are actually four separate strands matted together—we catch Maeve up on what we found out. Other than Aunt Lindy's scratched palm and the dragging tidbit we got from Salli, our investigations have led to dead ends.

Either we suck at interrogating our family, or no one heard—or did—anything last night. The dragging . . . it makes sense. We already knew the body had to have been moved, and the fact that someone dragged Guy instead of carried him isn't exactly a revelation. The three of us together could barely lift him.

Aunt Lindy had a perfectly good explanation for her scratch marks. And as for the discrepancy with when Grandma Helen and Bill went to bed . . . that's understandable. Even though I shudder to think of it, my grandmother is definitely having sex with Bill, but she's prudish enough that she'd rather die than admit that to her granddaughters.

How Aunt Lindy and my dad came out of that woman is beyond me.

"Finally." I pull the last knot loose and set the lights in the center of the table. "We still need to talk to Mom and Dad. Are they up yet?"

Eliana shakes her head. "Salli said Mom asked her to wake her up at *three*," she says with a heavy tone of derision toward napping. I take quiet, personal offense, as napping is one of my favorite hobbies. "We'll have to wait until closer to the party."

I drag my fingers through my hair, snagging in a tangle. "If literally no one else heard anything, I doubt they did, especially in Atlas. That thing is a fortress."

"Let's decorate, then start the hunt?" Eliana begins to gather the lights, looping them around her arm.

"The *man*hunt," Maeve says with a giggle, and then she stops, eyes widening. "Oh my god, I totally forgot to tell you what I found earlier!

I did a little Instagram digging, and Guy drives a Ford F-450. We can look for it while we're on our manhunt." She pulls her phone from her bra and unlocks it, then shows off the screen.

My stomach twists at the screenshot of Guy standing in front of a very large, lifted truck. "Photo's from three days ago. There's a chance he took a different car, but it's unlikely," Maeve says. "The entire post is one long brag about his new rims and how he couldn't wait to try them out. Can you even try out rims? Aren't they, like, *cosmetic*?"

"Nice find, Maeve," I tell my sister, genuinely impressed. Even if 90 percent of my life is online, dealing with message boards and Discord servers and replying to emails, I pretty much avoid social media in my day-to-day life. Maeve's obsession with it freaks me out. "Eliana, I know you said we should put the car on the back burner, but there's no reason we can't keep an eye out while we're on our manhunt."

"Sure," Eliana says, "but what good is us finding his car without the keys?"

"Oh, I can hotwire a car." Maeve tucks her phone back into her bra. She rearranges the straps, then looks back up at us. "*What?*"

Eliana stares at her, emotionless, and sets down the lights. "Do I want to know how you know that?"

"Probably not," Maeve says with a mysterious smile. "And you're welcome, for finding such helpful information."

"Thank you, Maeve," Eliana says tightly, then grabs something out of her purse. She flattens out a map of the campground, identical to the one Leo gave me the day I checked into this nightmare of a family vacation. "Salli's campsite is on the edge of the Buckeye campgrounds, right? Whoever took the body probably dragged him in this direction. If I had to guess, whoever took the body dumped it here"—she points to a field behind Salli's campsite—"in the lagoons near the lake"—another tap of her fingernail to the map—"or this trail here."

"Seriously, if Chad ever disappears, you're my first suspect," Maeve says, and Eliana ignores her.

I squint at where she's pointing: the remote trail in the Buckeye campground. "Wait. That's where I was earlier today when Leo stopped me. The trail is closed."

"Exactly," Eliana says, and folds the map into quarters before putting it back into her purse. "What better place to dump a body than one with no foot traffic because it's closed down?"

Maeve taps her fingernails on the picnic table. "Why was Leo there if the trail was closed?"

"I don't know," I say with a flustered shrug. "He was just walking around."

"Aren't rangers supposed to patrol areas where campers are? Why would he be out there if no one else was supposed to be?" Maeve asks with a dramatically arched brow.

I'm transported back to my childhood, when Maeve would throw murder-mystery parties every Halloween, where someone would dramatically be "murdered," and Maeve, along with all her theater-kid friends, would spend the evening solving the murder while high off edibles and stolen handfuls of my hard-earned Halloween candy.

"Rangers are supposed to keep people safe," I say, even though I have no idea what the job description for a park ranger would even begin to look like, but I'm winging it. "Leo was probably making sure that campers were keeping away. He said it was a safety hazard."

Eliana waves us off and gathers up the lights. "We'll be careful. Now, come on. Let's make this crime scene a Fleetwood Mac music video."

# CHAPTER ELEVEN

## *July 5 / Midafternoon*

Maybe it's my delusions talking, but what if what happened to Guy Moran was a freak accident? A coincidence, nothing to do with us. Like Maeve said, the simplest explanation is often the most likely one, and no one in our family heard a thing.

Okay, yes, everyone was drunk off Aunt Lindy's infamous punch, and Salli did mention the dragging, but still, as I'm mulling over the facts, the more convinced I'm becoming that Guy ran into bad news on the outskirts of camp. Not like we tested the log for blood and hair DNA, but given the wood chips in Guy's wound, that was probably the murder weapon. We didn't help the situation with the whole firepit kerfuffle—which was a complete accident; people trip all the time—but we didn't deliver that final blow.

Whoever killed him didn't want the body found, so, after we'd moved it, they disposed of it like a proper criminal.

I mean, it makes *sense*.

That's what I keep telling myself, anyway, as I take a shower while my sisters finish decorating the camp. Maeve and I helped Eliana hang the bulb lights before our sister waved us off, stating that our technique was too messy. What level of technique is needed to hang lights is beyond me, but for once, my sister's controlling ways didn't bother me.

I've been dying to shower since last night, and while the showers at Fallen Lake Campground leave everything to be desired, my composure returns as I feed the meter quarter after quarter to continue the stream of tepid water. My shower sandals squish beneath my feet as I turn around, letting the water pour down my spine. Tip my head back into the stream and close my eyes as the water follows the curves of my body.

Last night, I carried a dead body through the woods, but the real ick clinging to my skin is courtesy of when Guy was still very much alive. The saliva and dirt and scuff of blood-flaked skin on my elbow from when I fell. My skin stings from various nicks and scrapes as the shower washes last night down the mystery-hair-clogged drain.

I didn't bring nearly enough soap. Actually, I'm not sure enough soap *exists* in the entire world. I drag both palms over my face to push back my sopping wet hair off my cheeks and open my eyes to stare at the ugly, beige shower tiles. The sign with the shower-meter rates hangs crooked from a rusted nail.

I should cry. So why can't I? This shower stall is prime breakdown real estate. No sisters to mock me for having basic human emotions, a hobby of theirs when we were younger. The splatter of water will drown out my sobs. But, for whatever reason, I can't bring myself to tear up. I think I'm worried that, once I start crying, I might not be able to stop.

I don't think I've really . . . processed what happened with Guy last night. Him, you know, *dying* kind of stole the show, which is several different layers of messed up. I've been more focused on a missing body than the attempted assault. It's been easier to think about the big questions, the mystery, of what happened to Guy Moran than to confront the simple facts of what happened last night at camp. I scrub my skin harder with the washcloth Eliana loaned me, because she's the type of organized person who actually thought to bring towels on a camping trip, whereas I forgot sunscreen and—as I recently discovered while grabbing fresh clothes—enough clean underwear.

I'm not sure how old I'll need to be to finally become an adult, in control of my life. I sincerely doubt I'll turn thirty and, *poof*, feel like an adult, but that'd be nice. My mom always used to say that you never feel older—that you're the same person you were when you were younger—and I never used to believe her. But sometimes I swear I was just in high school, an anxious girl with a permanent stomachache who, embarrassingly enough, wanted people to like her more than she liked herself.

Last night wasn't my fault; I know that. And yet I can't quiet that voice inside my head that tells me I shouldn't have said yes to the beer. I wish I hadn't. Because I've always hated Guy—so why did I say yes? If I'd had the choice to hang out with an angry beehive or Guy Moran, I would've chosen the bees every time. One day around my family had me feeling like a teenager again, like the incompetent mess-up that everyone puts up with because we share the same last name. Not that last night was my family's fault either. The only person to blame for Guy's behavior is himself. But it's that mindset, the mental trap, I fall into whenever I'm around my family. I had absolutely *nothing* to prove to Guy Moran—to anyone—but I was desperate to be someone other than the version of myself I become around my family.

The stream sputters into a trickle, then dies out. I've used all my quarters for the trip—five dollars' worth, mined from the cracks between my driver seat and center console or stuck to the bottom of my cup holders in a thin film of coffee—and I reluctantly dry off with another one of Eliana's borrowed towels, then tug a yellow cotton sundress over my head and tie my flannel around my waist.

The bathroom is empty and humid, the warped mirror that runs above a row of sinks fogged. I inspect my reflection as I get ready. Not even two full days in Fallen Lake, and my freckles have exploded across my nose and cheeks, and my forehead's peeling with a sunburn. There are bags beneath my eyes, and I have no doubt this vacation will cause a few untimely grays to pop up in my dirty-blonde hair. My glasses are smudged, and I clean them off on the hem of my flannel before tossing my products back into my toiletry bag and heading outside. The shower—and shower thoughts—helped, and I feel renewed. Not capable, because I am not a capable person, but slightly less close to the breakdown I've tiptoed around all day.

The showers are a fifteen-minute walk from our campsites, but the road back is bustling with cars and fellow campers. My "I might get murdered" meter has ticked to low, but I have Eliana's pepper spray in the pocket of my dress. Just in case. Buffy is back at camp with my family, and while she did a bang-up job finding the murder weapon, I should probably leave her behind when we look for Guy's body. I'm not wild about Eliana's idea of walking the off-limits trail later, but she wasn't wrong. If I were going to dump a body, I'd dump it somewhere with no foot traffic. Unlike the rest of this campground, which is crawling with people.

Reluctantly, my mind wanders back to Maeve's comment about Leo. Was it really that strange that he was wandering the closed-off trail? Why do I feel this weird, almost panicky instinct to defend a man I barely know? Probably because he's hot, nice, *and* flirted with me. A holy trinity I rarely encounter in my daily life. The realization is shameful, low-key pathetic, but not at all surprising. Guess it's good to know yourself, though.

The sun warms the back of my legs and arms, dries the strands of my hair, as I walk by the side of the road. The campground is busy, which means if Guy's body *is* somewhere obvious, it should've been found by now. Maeve might be right—Eliana is way too good at this, and if Chad disappears, I won't be upset, but I might side-eye my sister.

"Remi, hey," a familiar voice calls out, and I nearly twist my ankle in a squirrel divot as I turn toward the voice; my nerves are shot, and while I know Guy Moran is dead, I'm still worried he'll show up, like the villain in a horror movie who's never really dead the first time. But my panic fades into something more pleasant as I place the voice with a face: Leo, Mr. Hot Park Ranger. He's driving one of the ranger vehicles, a hard-topped UTV that he slows to a crawl to match my walking pace.

"Nice ride," I joke, and he grins.

"Thanks, I can get her up to thirty miles an hour," Leo says, and he glances at my bags, the wet towels draped over my arm, my hair dripping down my shoulders. "Are you walking back to the Buckeye campgrounds?"

I nod and readjust my bags in my arms. "Yep."

"Where's Buffy?"

The fact that Leo remembers Buffy's name catches me off guard, in a good way. But we only officially met earlier *today*—even if it feels like weeks ago—and basic memory-retention skills shouldn't be a turn-on.

"I left her with my family," I say. "I have the completely rational fear that a bear might eat her if I leave her outside unattended."

"Black bears are omnivores." Leo glances from the road back to me every so often. "It's unlikely they'd chow down on a dog."

"You said 'unlikely,' *not* 'impossible,'" I point out, and he laughs.

"Hey, do you want a lift back to your campsite?" He slows the UTV to a stop now and cants his body toward me, head tilted slightly to the side.

I bite the inside of my cheek because I'm smiling. But should I be smiling right now? I'm pretty sure Maeve was just leaning into her flair for the dramatic, but what *was* Leo doing back on that trail? Why did he remember me from the day I checked in? What if it isn't kismet, like Maeve joked. What if Leo is tracking me?

The thought is preposterous. *Ridiculous*, really. Too bad my anxiety loves a good paranoid spiral.

"Oh, I'm fine walking," I tell him, wave off his offer. "You don't need to go out of your way."

"Not out of my way at all," Leo says, and jerks his thumb over his shoulder to the back of the UTV, which has a small dump bed stacked with firewood. "I'm dropping off firewood at the Campfire Center."

The Campfire Center is a small outdoor amphitheater for kids' wilderness education and storytelling, and it's not far from our campsites. His story checks out. Nothing about Leo—his body language, his tone, his energy—raises my hackles, sets me on edge, rings that small alarm bell of danger that I often confuse for the dirge of anxiety. I have to admit that, during a trip that has almost exclusively consisted of bad, awful, terrible things, my run-ins with Leo have been the smallest, brightest light. Also, it's refreshing to have a conversation that doesn't revolve around a dead body.

I shouldn't take rides from strangers—my mom instilled that basic stranger-danger rule inside me from an early age. Then again, Guy *wasn't* a stranger—I'd known him my entire life—and he didn't hesitate to hurt me.

Last night, my gut was screaming at me that something wasn't right, and I ignored it. But looking at Leo, seated in the UTV in his park ranger uniform and with his dorky compass watch, and kindness that seems genuine . . . nothing feels *wrong*. Running into Leo earlier—and now—wasn't suspicious. It's just a coincidence. Coincidences exist. And maybe I should listen to Aunt Lindy and lay off the true crime podcasts if I've become this wary, this paranoid, about the kindness of strangers.

I'd like to think I've learned to spot the difference between a good man and a bad one, but I have Eliana's pepper spray in case I'm wrong, and I climb into the seat beside Leo. "Okay, yeah, thank you," I say, and he shoots me another grin.

The UTV is similar to an off-road golf cart. The seats are worn and cracked, and the footwell is brown with the fine campground dirt I've found beneath my fingernails and most bodily crevices since I arrived.

I settle my belongings on my lap, and Leo slowly drives forward.

"So, um, any updates on the whole fugitive situation?" I ask before I can stop myself. But I'm so curious, it's burning an ulcer in my stomach, and if anyone might know something, it'll be Leo. It's been over an hour since we returned to camp, and if the detective has arrived already . . . well, that will really put the pressure on.

Leo slows down for a group of kids crossing the road. "The detective from Sacramento will be here in the next hour, I think," he says.

"Good thing, too, because none of us really know how to handle something like this. We, uh, found the fugitive's truck earlier."

My eyes widen as I process this information, and I stare ahead at the road so Leo can't see my expression. Sacramento is one of the closest larger cities to Fallen Lake, so it shouldn't be surprising that's where they're headed from. But the fact that the fugitive's car was found . . . maybe that's a win for us. Is it possible that the detective will leave or be so distracted by the car, we can swoop in and find the body? "What does that mean?"

Leo shrugs one shoulder. "Most of us rangers think he dumped the car in the park and left—not the first time it would've happened—but we're not cops. The detective will probably want to take a closer look at everything when they arrive and go from there. I hope they wrap this up soon, though. It's really freaking a lot of the campers out."

I lift my hand to my mouth and chew on my nails, even though they're already nubs. Okay, the detective isn't here yet. Good. We have an hour to find Guy. That's plenty of time. Especially if we've narrowed down the dump sites. I mean, I'm almost certain Guy's body is in my sleeping bag, which means I can't let this go.

But my little delusional hope keeps popping up: What if no one ever finds him?

What if . . . we forget this entire thing ever happened?

"Remi?" Leo says, and I have no idea how long he's been trying to get my attention.

"Sorry." I motion around my head. "I spaced out. What'd you say?"

"I asked how long you've lived in San Jose?"

The change in topic makes me worry I've spaced out for way longer than I realize, and I try to focus on the man beside me, not my poor attempts at talking myself into leaving Guy Moran's body—covered in my DNA—in the woods to rot. Because that'd be reckless, even if my anxiety is all over it like a cat on a chenille couch. "Since college graduation. I went to Cal Poly, then got a job at Warp two months after graduation. My turn: How long have you worked for AmeriCorps?"

Leo squints, as if doing the math. "Five years. I jumped between jobs after high school, never went to college. School was never really my thing. But I've always loved camping, hiking, and AmeriCorps seemed . . . honorable?" He laughs, blushes. "I like the idea of doing something good rather than needlessly contributing to the capitalist system."

I bite the inside of my cheek to keep from smiling. Because I can't like this guy, this genuinely *good* human being. I shake my head. Guy's body is missing, and now is not the time.

"Okay, now that I'm mentally playing that back," Leo says, "I regret saying that. I sound like an idealistic douche."

"Don't worry, you sounded the appropriate amount of idealistic. Not douchey at all."

"Phew," Leo says with a blush, and I swear I'm not imagining it, but he's slowed down as we've talked. Like he's trying to drag out the ride back to my campsite. And as much of a hurry as I'm in, I'm not mad about a few extra minutes with Mr. Hot Park Ranger. "Hey, uh, hopefully this isn't too forward, but I'm glad I ran into you again."

"Why?" The question plops out of my mouth like an awkward fish.

"Why do you think?"

Man, he's not making this easy on me. "You want to go pro at Pictionary and are looking for advice from the experts?"

"I hear there's good money in competitive board games," Leo jokes, and my skin flushes pleasantly because under no circumstances should I flirt with Leo right now. But maybe the universe owes me a solid after last night.

"It's a dicey industry," I say, and desperately wish my flirting game weren't as stale as the cookies Salli brought.

Leo laughs at my extremely not-funny pun. "I'm serious. I liked talking to you earlier."

I wrestle with my smile, but it's too strong to hide. "Yeah, well, I liked talking to you too."

Leo's grin widens. "She admits it."

"She does." I tuck my wet hair behind my ears and stare out the front of the UTV.

We're quiet for a moment, only the sounds of the campsites on either side of the road filling the air between us. Was I ever good at this? Talking with men? I really don't think so, and I'm completely out of my depth. But compared to all the *other* ways I've been out of my depth or out of control over the last twenty-four hours, I don't hate the feeling. It's a spark of good in so much bad. Not to mention, the stakes are much, much lower.

My therapist has talked about perspective for years. She'll be so proud.

"Okay, so, I've spent the last two minutes trying to think of a clever way to ask for your number," Leo says, interrupting my thoughts, "and I've got nothing, and we're almost at your campsite, so I'm just going to ask."

I lift my brows at him. "For my number? Like my phone number?"

Leo's cheeks flush, and he stares straight ahead at the road. "Yup."

"I'll text you," I tell him. "What's yours?"

Leo rattles off a number with an area code I don't recognize, and I tap the digits into my phone. For a beat, I consider saving his contact info as Mr. Hot Park Ranger but type out *Leo* instead. Once I've saved his contact information, I text him my name and an emoji of a dog.

A phone chimes from Leo's pocket, and he smiles. "Thanks. Anyway, uh, hopefully that wasn't the most awkward way someone has asked you for your number?"

"No, that honorific goes to the guy who hit my car with his bike so we could exchange information," I tell Leo and delight at the way he laughs. "I'm not joking. It happened to me in college." I conveniently leave out how I went on three dates with the guy, even *after* learning this knowledge.

"Low bar then," Leo says, and I chuckle. Then he adds, "Since I ruined your hike earlier, I was thinking I could take you on one tomorrow morning?"

My anxious insides soften because this guy is sweet. Way too sweet. Or maybe I'm that disillusioned. Even before this trip, I've always been comically unlucky with men. Maybe it's a lifetime of low self-esteem due to having two wildly beautiful and successful sisters. Or because I only had one boyfriend throughout high school, who broke up with me after graduation and catapulted me into two years of bad rebounds in college. According to my therapist, I subconsciously gravitate toward shitty guys because I don't view myself worthy of unconditional love or something. Not depressing at all.

The likelihood of this hike happening is slim to none, but I cling to the fantasy. Sure, I hate hiking, but if it was a hike with Leo? I could get on board with the great outdoors. "That could be fun."

My phone buzzes and I check the screen. A message in my sister group chat, which until this trip had collected such a thick layer of digital dust, I'm surprised it hasn't dissolved from disuse completely.

ELIANA: We're done decorating. Are you still in the shower? We need to go look for that super-secret anniversary gift for mom and dad before we're too late!

*Subtle, Eliana.*

Eliana and Maeve said it was fine if I showered while they finished decorating our parents' campsite, and I haven't even been gone for half an hour. My shower lasted a sum total of *five* minutes. I don't need Eliana reminding me of the stakes here, and her micromanagement makes my skin itch.

ME: Leo is giving me a ride back. I'll be there in TWO minutes. Calm thyself.

**MAEVE: Leo, huh?! KISMET!**

"Everything okay?" Leo asks and slows down to allow a ground squirrel safe passage across the road.

I lock my phone, turn it face down on my lap. "Do you have siblings?"

"Nope, only child." Leo drives forward now that the squirrel has made it to the other side of the road.

"Consider yourself lucky," I say and watch as a trio of teenage girls in bathing suits, carrying towels and a small cooler, walk along the side of the road, toward the beach. "My sisters and I have never gotten along. We've spent a lot of time together this trip. More time together than we have in years, since we were kids. There are these rare blips where we get along, but then I'm back to feeling like the annoying little sister they once left at a 7-Eleven."

Leo laughs—then winces. "Oh, you're *serious*. They left you at a 7-Eleven?"

I hang my arm out the side of the UTV, the sun on my skin. "Oh yeah. They sent me inside to buy Slurpees, then went to the mall without me. I drank three cherry Slurpees and got an hour-long brain freeze while I waited for them to come back. This was before I had a cell phone, and I was too nervous to ask the cashier to use theirs."

"I'm now reconsidering my childhood wish of having a sibling," Leo says.

"You're a smart man, Leo Zebrowski," I tell him, and shove my complicated sisterly feelings deeper inside. Because I'm too embarrassed to say that all I've wanted is to be acknowledged and *liked* by my sisters. Pathetic. "But to answer your question, everything is as okay as it possibly can be for a family vacation."

This trip is turning me into *such* a liar.

# CHAPTER TWELVE

### *July 5 / Early Evening*

The Finch Family Festivities are in full swing by the time Leo drives me back to the Buckeye campsites, and like an embarrassed teenager, I almost ask him to drop me off at a nearby empty campground instead. Not because I'm ashamed of my family—not exactly—but because I *know* my family. And I'd really love to avoid Maeve's inappropriate innuendos or Eliana's silent, judgmental face. She claims it's resting bitch face, but after twenty-nine years, I know better. It's intentional. Not to mention Aunt Lindy's lack of filter or how Salli will ask *literally anyone* to look at the mole on her shoulder because she's worried about its irregular borders.

But I miss my moment, and Leo pulls the UTV to a stop alongside #34.

Mercifully, our campsite is empty, but my return does not go unnoticed. Over at Aunt Lindy's picnic table, Aunt Lindy and Salli are hard at work re-creating Mom's wedding-flower crown while blasting Fleetwood Mac, and Salli pauses her branch-weaving to put on her glasses, squinting over at us. She pokes Aunt Lindy, who cranes around to look over her shoulder.

"Thank you for the ride," I say to Leo and gather up my belongings.

Leo glances over at the bustling nearby campsites. "Of course. Y'all having a party?"

"Yeah, for my parents' fortieth wedding anniversary," I tell him as I climb out of the UTV. "There will be sheet cake and signature cocktails."

"Fancy." Leo smiles, a crooked and very nice smile. "So, we're on for the hike?"

"Depends on how much sheet cake I eat and signature cocktails I drink," I joke, because there's a 90 percent chance that I might be in jail tomorrow if Guy Moran's body is found snuggled up in my sleeping bag. I shouldn't lie to Leo, but it's nice pretending that I'm a totally normal person, on a normal family camping trip. Not to mention, I've always aspired to be one of those people who *like* hiking. It seems like a nice, peaceful hobby. "I'll text you," I tell him, and that part I actually mean.

Then I wave and walk toward the bustling campsites—the croon of Stevie Nicks floats over as she sings about never breaking chains—and I ponder if I was ever *not* awkward around men. Luckily, Leo didn't seem to notice my social ineptitude, which makes me wonder about his social skills, but the dude is hot enough that I don't question the situation. Besides, it's been far too long since a man I've found attractive has flirted with me.

I walk over to Eliana's tent—she dismantled mine earlier, saying we could tell the group that it had a hole in the mesh window—and chuck my toiletry bag inside. Then I track down Buffy, who's snoozing beneath Aunt Lindy's hammock, her head on her paws. While I was gone, my sisters finished setting up the lights and hung eco-friendly streamers from the trees. The table at my parents' campsite is decked out with a lace tablecloth, unlit candles, and fresh flowers. A secondary card table and extra chairs have been set up beside my parents' firepit, since my uncles and the cousins from Nevada are supposed to arrive before the party.

Aunt Lindy turns down the Bluetooth speaker as I approach, a bright-orange sunflower in her hands as she weaves its stem around a flexible wooden band. "What happened to your gentleman friend?" she asks in a husky, low voice. "No introductions?"

"He was *very* good looking," Salli says seriously and holds out the boutonniere she's making for Dad, adjusting a small pink bud.

I sigh at the two women. "The park ranger—not my gentleman friend—offered to give me a ride back to the campground, which was very nice of him, given the whole fugitive-on-the-run situation," I explain, then narrow my eyes at them. Because *why* did they assume Leo was my gentleman friend? "Were you talking to Maeve or something?"

Aunt Lindy winks, and her false eyelash droops, unpeeling from her lid. *"Maybe."*

"You might need a little more eyelash glue, Aunt Lindy," I say, and she grabs a spoon off the table to check her reflection, fussing with the wonky eyelash.

Naturally, Maeve is telling our family members about me and Leo. Not like there *is* a me and Leo; I barely know the dude. But I doubt that's how Maeve told the story. Can't wait to put out that fire all night. With another sigh, I walk over to Buffy and untie her from the tree.

Buffy stretches to her feet, her tail smacking side to side. I scrub her chin and smoosh my lips against her head, then ask my aunt and Salli, "Hey, is my mom awake from her nap?"

"Nope, she had *quite* the night yesterday." Salli winds a length of twine around the base of the boutonniere and ties it into a bow, then smiles at her work. "Tahoe was a bad idea. The mini-golf wiped her out."

"I told Juliet"—Aunt Lindy blinks a few times, the eyelash in place, and returns to her flower weaving—"that mixing those shrooms with the punch was a bad idea."

I straighten up, Buffy's leash in hand. Open my mouth to ask about the shrooms—then promptly shut it, because I decide that I don't want to know. *Nope.* My parents doing drugs in a state park is something I really don't need to concern myself with today. As my therapist always says, pick your battles.

"Eliana, Maeve, and I need to run an errand before the party," I say vaguely. "Can I leave Buffy with you later?"

"Sure thing, jelly bean." Salli smiles and sips her iced tea before batting at Aunt Lindy and grabbing the flower crown from her hands, lecturing her on technique.

Back at my campsite, I prepare Buffy's lunch and set the bowl in Eliana's tent, unzipping the windows so the entire thing doesn't stink of dog food, but this way Buffy can eat without having to fight a ground squirrel over it. After she's set up with her bowl of mushy prescription dog food—she's allergic to almost everything—I back out of the tent to find both my sisters waiting for me.

"Where have you two been? I got back five minutes ago." I tuck my hair behind my ears and stare at my sisters. "Wait. What's wrong? You're looking at me weird."

Both of my sisters are dressed for the party. Eliana in a crisp button-down and bold statement jewelry, her hair twisted to the nape of her neck. Maeve swapped her clingy sundress for an even more camping-inappropriate jumpsuit and chunky sandals.

"I started thinking about what Maeve said earlier," Eliana says, and I groan. Because I should've probably seen this coming. "Why *was* Leo on that trail? And now we're supposed to believe that he just happened to be driving by while you were walking back from the showers?"

Maeve nibbles on her bottom lip, then says, "Sorry, Remi. I was joking around earlier, but Eliana kind of has a point. It's weird."

"Weirder than a guy flirting with me?" I ask flatly because I should know better than to let my sisters conspire without me. Sure, I was suspicious of Leo, thanks to Maeve's comments, but the entire claim is ridiculous.

Eliana smiles apologetically. "I mean, he is *really* hot."

I glower at my sister. "Thanks, Eli."

"What? I'm just saying, we can't get bamboozled by some dude's good looks and charms."

"Leo's not involved," I say, and for whatever reason, this hardens into fact inside my head. Call it my gut instinct, but my sisters' paranoia can't convince me otherwise. "I keep running into him because he works here. It's not that strange."

"How can you be so sure?" Eliana asks, and she attempts to quirk her brow, but all the neurotoxins pumped into her muscles limit the movement. "Remi, we don't know who killed Guy. We need to be smart!"

"Leo didn't kill Guy *or* dump his body," I whisper, and force my tone to be even and firm. "He's in AmeriCorps and picks up litter and stopped for a squirrel to cross the road earlier."

"Aw," Maeve says, and Eliana smacks our sister on the arm. "Ouch, Eli!" Maeve pouts and rubs her arm.

"You really trust him?" Eliana's staring at me so intensely I fight my childhood defense mechanism of shriveling up into a ball.

I try to stand my ground. "Leo's given me no reason not to. So yeah." This is apparently the hill I'm willing to die on with my sister. But, you know, hopefully I don't actually die on this hill. "Can you just trust me on this one? Leo's nice, and, yes, he's way out of my league, but that doesn't mean he's a *murderer*."

Eliana purses her lips to one side, thinking. Then she nods. "Fine. But if he ends up being the killer, then I won't hesitate to tell you I told you so."

"Sure, Eli." I duck back into the tent for Buffy, who's cleaned out her bowl and sits beside my suitcase, licking her chops. After hooking her back up to her leash, I zip the tent shut and then grab my backpack from the picnic table. "Now that you're done accusing Leo of being a murderer, I can tell you about the updates he gave me. The detective is an hour out, coming from Sacramento. The rangers also found the fugitive's car in the campground. He didn't mention anything about a body being found too."

Eliana spins her minivan keys around in her finger. "Leo told you all of this?"

"Yep," I say, and sling my backpack over my shoulder. "He's been more than willing to share what's going on with me, so if he is a murderer, then he's a really bad one."

Eliana digests this, nods. "Valid point."

"Let me drop off Buffy with Aunt Lindy; then we can head out," I tell my sisters and begin to walk, then pause to add, "Oh, and before I forget, apparently our parents were high on shrooms last night, as well as drunk, so I doubt we'll get anything out of them."

Eliana's weary expression no doubt mirrored mine when I heard about the shrooms, but Maeve looks utterly thrilled with this tidbit of information. But I hurry Buffy over to my aunt's campsite and don't linger to hear Maeve's commentary. I hand over the treat bag and leave Buffy in the shade with my aunt, then wander back to our campsite. Then I stop, nearly tripping over a gigantic rock in the path. Because, parked beside my junky sedan at Campsite #34, is a Sacramento Police Department cruiser.

"What's going on?" Mom reaches our campsite at the same time I do, and we both stop and stare at the police car. Her voice is thick with sleep, and she's clearly just rolled out of the RV's bed—pillow creases indent her freckled cheek—but her eyes are narrowed in suspicion. My parents . . . they don't love the police on a fundamental level, and I'm not feeling very fond about them right now either.

Dad joins us and places a hand on my shoulder. I jump at his touch, heart rate pounding. "Rem, why is there a cop car at your campsite?"

"I'm guessing this is about that fugitive on the run?" My mouth is parched and dry, and I wonder if my parents can sense, through parental intuition or whatever, how panicked I am right now. Leo said the detective wouldn't be arriving for an hour! Clearly, that piece of information was wrong, and I am *this* close to turning and running into the woods.

Maybe I could survive out there for a few days until this all blows over.

Swallowing the cement lump in my throat, I force myself into the campsite—because I'd die in the woods; who am I kidding—and join my sisters. Mom and Dad hang back, and I hear them murmuring to one another, but they're too far away for me to hear the words.

Eliana smacks me when I reach her. "You said an hour!"

I bug my eyes out at her. "That's what I thought! We're on the same team, asshole."

"Shut up," Maeve hisses beneath her breath, then smiles charmingly at the woman approaching us. "Hello there, Detective! How can we help you?"

The detective is a little older than Eliana, in her early forties. She's Latina, with glossy dark hair in a high ponytail and wide brown eyes that are almost doe-like. *No, do not be disarmed,* I tell myself. This lady, right here, is my enemy. At least until I clear my DNA off Guy's body, that is.

"Hi, I'm Detective Diaz." The woman seems startled by Maeve's friendliness. "I'm here on behalf of the Sacramento Police Department. We're looking for a fugitive who we believe fled the city and entered the state park last night."

"Right," Eliana says, picking up where Maeve left off with a friendly, affable tone. "We heard about that from Officer Ericson earlier. I hope you caught him."

Detective Diaz fiddles with the walkie-talkie on her belt, which hangs beside a gun. A real-life, actual gun that can shoot people. "Not yet, I'm afraid, but the rangers found his car on the premises earlier today. The truck was parked in an overflow lot not far from here, so we're going around to the surrounding campsites and asking if anyone saw the truck or its driver," Detective Diaz continues, her gaze bouncing between the three of us. Then she spots our hovering parents in the background and smiles politely. "We found some of his belongings on the trails and believe he took off on foot. Anyway, I have a flyer, if you don't mind taking a look. It also has my contact info, in case you remember anything or see him."

The woman opens the folder she's carrying and hands us a flyer.

The piece of paper has what looks like a printout of a police database entry.

Custody Information
Name: Guy Moran
DOC Number: 3456911
Supervision County: El Dorado
Crime Type: Vehicular Assault

A tiny photo of Guy is beside the criminal profile. Below, a number for Detective Diaz.

I'm sweating. The cool, slippery sweat trails from my armpits down my ribs, and I look anywhere except at Detective Diaz's face. Open book. I'm an open book, and I can't let her read me. Because holy shit, *Guy* is the fugitive they've been looking for this entire time.

That means a fugitive didn't kill Guy. Someone else did.

And the police are here, at camp, *looking* for Guy.

I might be sick.

Mom and Dad join us and peer over our shoulders at the sheet of paper we're collectively holding out in front of us. My stomach twists into a tight, unrelenting knot as I wait for my mom to gasp when she recognizes the name. For my dad to groan, in that Charlie Brown way of his, when he realizes what Jim Moran's son has gotten up to now. But neither of those things happen.

"Sorry, Detective, but we didn't see anything last night and have never seen the man," Mom says, her tone cool yet polite. "Do you need anything else from us? My husband and I are having a vow renewal party for our wedding anniversary, and we need to get ready."

Detective Diaz shakes her head, a strand of glossy hair escaping her ponytail. She quickly tucks it behind her ear. "Nope, you're free to go. Have a nice evening and congratulations."

Mom and Dad thank her and hurry off to their campsite. My entire body is frozen in place. Why did my parents lie to Detective Diaz? Yes, they hate the police, and they didn't see anything, but they *know* Guy Moran. What is going on?

"You can keep the flyer," Detective Diaz says as Eliana tries to hand it back. "I'm in town until this evening but have to return to Sacramento. I'll be back tomorrow, though, to follow up on the case. But please, reach out if you remember anything or come across something in camp. You can also talk to the park rangers, who will be here twenty-four seven, okay? If it helps calm your nerves, we don't believe the man is an active threat."

Detective Diaz must think our behavior is due to fear over the loose fugitive, not guilt. Sweet, sweet guilt that is currently oozing out of my pores. Because Diaz doesn't know that Guy is dead, that any crime beyond the one printed on this wanted flyer has been committed.

Eliana smiles and folds the flyer neatly down the middle. "Thanks. We'll be sure to reach out if we remember something."

"Great." Detective Diaz's gaze lingers on me, like she can tell I'm the weak link, the most likely to break. But then her walkie-talkie crackles and she excuses herself, walks back to her vehicle.

The three of us turn to our parents, who're huddled together by their lacy, decorated table. The cruiser pulls away from our campsite and curves around the bend, and Eliana sprints over to them.

Maeve and I follow.

"What was that?" She shoves the flyer in their faces. "Can you not read? The fugitive is Guy Moran!"

"What did you do?" Maeve's voice is an awed whisper, her bejeweled fingers held in front of her mouth.

I focus on not throwing up, and stare at my parents. My hippie-dippie, weed-smoking parents, who are pacifists. Usually.

"Oh, sweeties, don't be upset. We were only trying to help." Mom walks over to us, pats Eliana on the cheek. "We took care of Guy. No need to worry. Everything's A-okay!"

# CHAPTER THIRTEEN

*July 5 / Early Evening*

The campsite is dead silent as we stare at our parents.

"What," Eliana says, "does that mean? You took 'care' of him?"

"Quiet down," Dad hisses and widens his eyes comically behind his thick glasses. "We hid the body last night."

My mouth is cottony and dry, and I almost choke on my own spit before saying, "What? *You're* the ones who moved the body?"

Eliana's body sags against the nearest tree. "You didn't kill him?"

Mom's face whitens and she squeaks. "No, oh my god! But . . ." She exchanges a confused glance with our dad. "We thought you did. That's why we moved the body! To protect you girls."

Mom says this triumphantly. Like what my parents did was good and helpful.

I fainted once, in middle school. We were in rehearsals for the school play, and our drama teacher had warned us about locking our knees. But I had no idea what that meant, and—bam—my body hit the floor. That Drowning Pool song was popular at the time, and a bunch of kids in my class would chant *Let the bodies hit the floor!* when I passed them in the halls. It was hell.

Anyway. I remember the sensation. The way my body flushed warm and my vision went blurry and orange, how my hearing fuzzed like static. The first time it happened, I thought I was having a panic attack;

they're so similar, at the start. Fainting is better because you get to be unconscious, whereas panic attacks are ten to thirty minutes of torture. I'm not entirely sure on which path I'm headed but, as my vision blurs violently, I lurch into the nearest camp chair and hang my head between my legs.

The sensation passes.

Maybe I should've let myself pass out. Because how is this my life? My parents are the ones who moved Guy Moran's body last night! They say they didn't kill him, which means . . . oh god, were *we* actually responsible? But if so, where'd that bloody stick come from?

I slowly lift my head and look miserably at my family, who're all staring at me with concern in their eyes. "I'm fine," I croak. "Just dead inside. Carry on."

Mom tuts and brings me her Nalgene bottle, which I dutifully sip from.

"Tell us everything," Eliana commands, and I stare at the firepit—so similar to the one Guy smacked his head on—as my family drags camping chairs to either side of me, forming a tight semicircle.

"Hold on," Dad says, and he pets his mustache with his forefinger and thumb, twirling its ends. "We need to get a few things straight, girls. You didn't kill Guy?"

The three of us shake our heads in unison.

The water has helped, and I lick my chapped lips. "Guy fell and hit his head, but he was okay. Ran off, into the woods. Then we went after him because we thought he might have a concussion."

"What happened? How'd he fall?" Dad glances between the three of us.

Eliana turns to me, her brow slightly quirked. As if saying it's up to me, how much I want to share. "Guy made a pass at me," I say and don't look at my dad. "I told him no. He didn't listen, then Eliana and Maeve pulled him off. He fell. It was an accident."

Mom's breath catches, and she swears. "Remi, baby girl," she says, and wraps her arms around my shoulders. Shame and embarrassment roll over me like a fog, and I try to shake her off, but my mom doesn't let go. "I am so sorry."

I lift my gaze, only to see tears in my dad's eyes. "Dad, I'm fine! Look," I say and gesture to myself, "totally okay. Unharmed."

He swipes his thumb beneath his glasses. "I'm just sorry, sweet pea. Your mom and I figured something bad must've happened, for you to kill him—"

"Which we didn't do," Eliana interrupts. "It's very important to me that you both understand that."

Dad brushes this off. "Yeah, yeah, you know what I mean. We figured it must've been bad, but it's different, hearing it."

Mom finally releases me, then says, "You went after him? After what he tried to do, Remi? You're much kinder than I would've been."

Given where my socially ingrained politeness has led me on this family camping trip, I can guarantee I'll make some very different decisions in the future. Not like I envision myself ever being in a similar situation to this one. At least, I hope not.

Fuck being polite and kind and nice to men who don't deserve it.

"Dad, why'd you think we killed Guy?" Maeve perches on the edge of the decorated table, mussing the tablecloth. Eliana reaches out and steadies a wobbly unlit candle.

"You girls must've thought we were asleep, but we came over to say good night, when we heard you three huffing and puffing. Then we saw . . . well, we saw you three carrying Guy, then you put him in Remi's tent. We couldn't hear your conversation, but after you went back to Eliana's tent, we couldn't help ourselves. We looked inside, and once we saw him . . ." Dad looks each of us in the eye. "What else were we supposed to think?"

Eliana fills in the blanks for our parents. The thunk we heard, the body we found. The bloody stick Buffy unearthed this morning and how we burned it up. "What I want to know," Eliana's saying now, "is why you two thought it would be a good idea to move the body?"

"Well, we thought you killed him, and we didn't want any of you getting into trouble," Mom says hurriedly and glances between us with wide, innocent eyes. Like we're the illogical ones here, not her and my dad. "Also, the three of you were . . . you were getting along—sharing a tent, even—and it was so nice to see!"

My left eye twitches. "You did all of this because it forced us to get along?"

"And all the other reasons," Mom rushes to say. "We didn't want our weekend ruined, cops everywhere. Good lot that did. Of course Guy had to be wrapped up in something illegal. I told you, Ernest, that new leaf Jim talked about Guy turning was a load of applesauce!"

Maeve snorts, and I'm not sure if I should laugh or cry over the absurdity of this situation. Both, maybe.

"And is there any chance you took Guy *out* of the sleeping bag and disposed of it before you dumped his body?" Eliana asks.

Mom and Dad exchange a little glance, and Mom says, "No?"

"That was Remi's sleeping bag," Eliana says. "We need to get it back. It's covered in her DNA."

Mom's brow bunches up. As if she's just now thinking about this. "Oh dear," she murmurs, and taps her forefinger to her chin. "That . . . we didn't think of that! Everything just happened so fast."

"You need to take us back there," Eliana insists. "We need to get the sleeping bag off his body, and, honestly, let's just call Detective Diaz once we find him. We'll make it look like an accident, like he fell on a trail. If they're that concerned about finding him, it's possible they won't ask too many questions. He is a wanted criminal, after all."

I don't hate Eliana's plan, and I admit, part of my anxiety quells at the thought of getting my hands on that sleeping bag. It's a plan, at least, and nothing soothes my anxiety more than a plan. "Fine by me."

"Hello, Finches," a loud, cheerful voice booms, and a car door slams from behind us.

We all whip around in our chairs to see my uncles, Damien and Andrew, standing beside a blue hatchback. While Andrew unloads the back seat, Damien walks over with his arms open wide. "Happy anniversary, sis," he says to my mom.

Mom turns to us. "After the party, okay? We'll go and take care of everything. We did a great job hiding him—" She cuts herself off midsentence as Damien steps into hearing range, and she pops out of her chair, dashing over to hug her brother.

"Dad," Eliana pleads helplessly. "This isn't something we should put off! Tell us where you put him, and we'll go on our own."

Dad smiles tightly as he gets up from his chair and says in a low voice that only we can hear, "No. Girls, you need to listen to your mother. That cop, Detective Diaz, she knows our plans for the evening. It could look suspicious if the three of you are wandering around on a trail when you're supposed to be with us. Your mother and I will go back for the sleeping bag later, once it's dark. Let's try to have a nice evening, okay?" And with that, he walks over to our uncles.

"This," Eliana says in a tight whisper, "is absurd. Are they serious right now? They want to have their vow renewal first? What is wrong with this family?"

"Good question," I mutter. "And if anyone should be mad, it's me. That's my sleeping bag they hid him in."

"Maybe they actually did a good job hiding him?" Maeve suggests with a hopeful lilt. "Isn't this better than not knowing where he might be? Mom and Dad might be . . . kooky, but they're serious when it comes to protecting us."

I sip from my mom's water bottle until it's empty, then shrug. "I guess it's better. Not much better, just marginally better. If they're not going to help us, though, then we'll have to survive dinner and the vow renewal party. It's probably smarter to go out after dark, anyway. Diaz might be gone by then."

"How are my favorite nieces?" Uncle Damien joins us by the firepit, smiley and high energy like always. Ten years our mom's junior, Uncle Damien is in his midfifties and works as a veterinarian in Bakersfield. Unlike our mom, Uncle Damien can be described in one word: *stability*. He's almost boring, in a way, and that's probably why I've always gravitated toward him the most out of my extended family. He finds calm within the chaos of the Finch family, which gives me hope I can too.

A flurry of greetings and hugs takes place, which is only amplified as Salli and Aunt Lindy walk over to the campsite, carrying Mom's flower crown and dad's boutonniere. Aunt Lindy plops the crown on Mom's head, then scurries off to retrieve the Bluetooth speaker, and Salli hugs Uncle Damien, showing off the growth on her neck, asking him for his medical opinion, even though he's a veterinarian, not a human doctor.

When Aunt Lindy whips out the vow renewal signature cocktail, Birds of a Feather, whatever hope we had of refocusing our parents on Guy Moran's missing body is gone.

Not like I should be surprised. Not much stands between my parents and a good party.

Dinner with the Finches is always a loud affair. Pretty much any event involving us has the dial turned up to eleven. Parties. Graduations. Wakes. You name it, my family overdoes it. This is probably why, when I was a kid, my friends couldn't fathom why I disliked my family. According to outsiders, they were *fun*. But for someone like me, someone with social anxiety, any kind of family event with the Finches is a recipe for disaster. Add in a missing body covered in my DNA, and it's a miracle I have any appetite left at all. The Prozac helps with my social anxiety. A lot, actually. But the social anxiety I have around my family is a special kind of hell no medication can cure.

The main picnic table was crowded, so my sisters and I are eating at the extra fold-out table pushed at the end. It's a foot shorter than the picnic table, and we have to sit in camp chairs, and the old fabric sags, so I basically have to eat holding my plate over my lap.

Other than the cousins from Nevada—two old biddies in their seventies with suboptimal hearing who have no interest in talking to us—we have the table to ourselves. But for once, we don't talk about Guy. I have to trust my parents on this one. They hid him, in a very misguided attempt to save us. Because they thought *we'd* killed Guy.

If I were a different kind of person, maybe I'd be moved by this act of . . . kindness? The ultimate act of parental protection. But all my mom and dad did was bungle up an already messy situation, and I can't help but feel frustrated. If they'd left Guy's body in my tent, this entire nightmare would be over. We'd have called the police this morning, reported the accident. Detective Diaz probably would've shown up anyway, chasing her fugitive to the very end, but I wouldn't be *involved*.

I try to be like Maeve and look at the bright side. The body isn't missing—it's missing adjacent. We have a plan to get the sleeping bag after the renewal. After nearly twenty-four hours of hapless free-falling, I can see the next few steps ahead, breathe a little easier. I can't change what my parents did or how they intervened—I can only make sure that all of us get away with it.

Because they implicated themselves too.

What I'd give for a normal family.

My phone vibrates on the table, and I flip it right side up. The food, while all vegan, was cooked by Grandma Helen, who can make almost anything taste incredible, and I shove another vegan "chicken wing" into my mouth as I read.

> LEO: Hey, I have to work early because of all the chaos with the fugitive and need to cancel our hike. I'm really sorry

I squint at the message. In the chaotic haze of the last few hours, I'd forgotten that I'd agreed to go on a hike with Leo. An unexpected crush of disappointment hits me, but this is for the best. If everything goes as planned, I'll be out of here as early as humanly possible tomorrow. Lingering—even if to go on a hike with a hot park ranger—probably isn't in my best interests.

"What do we have here?" Maeve peers over Eliana, who's seated between us. She gasps theatrically. "You didn't tell us you exchanged numbers with Mr. Hot Park Ranger. And made a hiking date? How *cute*."

I swipe my phone off the table. "Boundaries, dude. Don't read my texts." This time tomorrow, I'll be at my apartment in San Jose. Far, far away from my chaotic sisters and a dead dude in my sleeping bag. Up until this moment, I hadn't focused much on getting home—too many obstacles and unknowns have been in my way. But after dinner and the renewal party tonight, we'll get the sleeping bag and, I don't know, burn it or something.

Then I will be *free*.

Eliana is hunched forward with her plate on the fold-out table, like she's determined to be proper at this campground dinner. She even has a napkin on her lap. "I thought you hated hiking."

"I do." I turn my phone face down in my lap. "But I don't know, I figured it could be slightly not awful with Leo. Why are we talking about this? Oh, Maeve, thank you for telling everyone he gave me a ride. Salli and Aunt Lindy were acting as if I'd been proposed to or something."

Maeve snickers. "What? They asked where you were. It's not my fault our family is nosy."

"Well, it's a canceled date now, so not much to talk about," I say tightly, and pick up another vegan chicken wing. "I'll probably never see Leo again."

"You could hang out with him tonight," Eliana suggests.

Luckily, these fake chicken wings are boneless, because some of it gets lodged into my esophagus as I choke in response. "What? No. We're . . . *busy*."

"Not all three of us need to go with Mom and Dad tonight. If we could find out a little more about what Diaz knows, it wouldn't hurt," she says. "Leo will probably be way more willing to talk to you."

"Yeah, use your feminine wiles, Remi," Maeve says.

"Feminine wiles," I deadpan. "Grandma Helen, is that you?"

"Did someone say my name?" Grandma Helen yells from the main picnic table, and Maeve snorts.

"Text him!" She pokes my arm insistently.

"No," I say because the hike was a pseudo-date at best. A hangout. One that I wasn't really expecting to happen. My entire body breaks out in a light nervous sweat at the thought of texting Leo, asking him to see me tonight instead. "What happened to you two being suspicious of him?"

"I've always been Team Kismet," Maeve points out, "not Team Killer."

I shoot a sharp glance at the cousins from Nevada, but they're not listening.

"If you trust him, then so do we," Eliana says simply.

My sisters are giving me a headache. "Thanks, but no thanks. It's not happening. Not with everything that's been going on, and last night . . ." I trail off, both due to the subject matter and the fact that we're not alone. We can't talk about Guy here.

Maeve's smile falters. "Oh, I didn't think . . . no one's going to force you to text Leo, Rem. Whatever you want to do is up to you. It's your choice. We can handle the stuff with Mom and Dad if you want to see Leo. But only if you *want* to."

Either Maeve is acting surprisingly kind or she's on board with Eliana's plan to use Leo to spy on Detective Diaz. Both options make my stomach squirmy, and I sip my glass of lemonade so I won't have to answer right away.

"We don't even know that he's free tonight," I say evasively. Because, okay, I don't hate this plan. My entire vacation has been a total disaster, and the thought of spending an hour or two with someone I'm not related to—and not talking about a dead body with? Heaven. It sounds like *heaven*.

Eliana nudges my arm with hers. "Then text him and find out." Lowering her voice, she adds, "Don't worry, we'll find the sleeping bag.

We'll call you if anything comes up or if we need help, but we've got this. And if you happen to get anything useful out of Leo about Diaz? Even better."

After a beat of hesitation, I unlock my phone and text Leo. Not because Maeve is pushing me, or because Eliana wants me to snoop for information. But because I want to.

# CHAPTER FOURTEEN

*July 5 / Evening*

The vow renewal was surprisingly sweet, my parents holding hands between the lit-up trees, reaffirming their love for one another, forty years later. My parents have survived four decades of marriage, three daughters, and as of this weekend, moved a dead body together. I wonder what that must feel like. Not the moving a dead body part but finding *that* person. Your person. I've never been close. But for once, I watched my parents' relationship with admiration and longing, maybe even a little bit of hope, rather than disgust over their frequent public displays of affection.

When I pulled Mom aside after dinner to tell her my updated plans, she was wary about me going off with a stranger, especially after what happened with Guy. But Eliana and Maeve backed me up, said they met him and trusted Leo, and even if this is Eliana's elaborate plan to get more info on Diaz, it felt nice—if not unnatural—to be supported by them. After I agreed to share my location with the group chat, Mom kissed me on the cheek, told me to have fun, to be safe.

Now that I no longer have dinner or the vow renewal to keep my mind occupied, I'm slipping into anxiety land as I wait for my ride. Leo replied back, almost immediately, that he was free. He said he'd pick me up after the vow renewal and mentioned a place in down-town Fallen Lake that has drinks, since I already ate. While it's kind of weird—abandoning my family as they help clean up my mess—it's also nice. I've shouldered a lot of the blame and the guilt for what happened to Guy Moran.

I didn't kill him.

I don't know who did—and I probably never will—but it wasn't me.

I didn't move his body. Not the second time, at least.

All I wanted, from the get-go, was to call the police.

A black sedan pulls alongside my campsite, and I glance over my shoulder at the celebrations. My uncles, parents, and Salli are seated around the firepit, which flickers with young flames. They all hold blue-tinged Birds of a Feathers, and while I'm worried about my parents getting too sloshed to remember where Guy Moran is tucked away, Eliana promised me she'd keep an eye on them. Buffy's set up in Atlas for the evening, snoozing on the daybed.

Between the loud music, Aunt Lindy getting drunk before we cut the cake and shaking her ta-tas in tune to Starship, and how the rangers will, undoubtedly, be called before the end of the night, I don't feel guilty as I duck into Leo's car.

The inside of the car is tidy. A pine cone–shaped air freshener hangs from the rearview mirror. A tin of Altoids sits inside the otherwise impeccably clean cup holders. And Leo smiles at me from the driver's seat, as if he's actually delighted to see me, which is honestly not a reaction I'm used to from the guys I date. Not like this is a date.

"Hey, Remi." Leo's dressed in regular street clothes—no khaki-green uniform—and looks even better in a flannel jacket and jeans, his dark hair curling around his ears.

My fingers fumble over my seat belt buckle. "Hi. Thanks for rescheduling." I cringe. *What?* Why do I sound like I'm talking to my therapist that one time we changed our weekly meeting from a Tuesday to a Wednesday because I had a dental appointment?

"I should be thanking you, since I bailed on our hike." Leo puts the car into drive and curves down the road, the chaotic Finch festivities fading in the rearview.

"Okay, I need to be honest about something," I say. "I hate hiking."
Leo glances sideways at me. "What?"

I nod emphatically. "Yeah. I took Buffy on a walk earlier to escape my family. I'm not a hiker. Hate it." Okay, that was partially honest. I do hate hiking, even if the reason for my excursion isn't exactly as I said.

Leo cracks a grin. "Why'd you agree to the hike then?"

"Why do you think?" I smugly toss his words from earlier back in his face.

"Fair enough," he says with a chuckle and reaches one hand up to smooth back his hair.

As we drive out of the campground and journey downtown, Leo and I make small talk that *doesn't* make me want to shrivel up and die inside. Leo tells me about growing up in Iowa—awful, apparently, lots of corn—and how he got involved with AmeriCorps after joining the Iowa and Minnesota branch of the Conservation Corps in his early twenties. He even enthuses about his favorite types of trees, which is adorable. I don't bring up Detective Diaz because I'm not wasting this night dwelling on Guy Moran. Eliana might be annoyed, but she'll live.

By the time we park in downtown Fallen Lake, I'm 50 percent less nervous than when I got into the car. Leo holds open the door to a small saloon-style bar for me, and I step inside. Back home, I don't go out. I'm not a big drinker—beyond the whole antidepressants-and-alcohol-interaction thing, I deeply dislike the feeling of being drunk—and the concept of bars stresses me out. Too loud, too many people, *drunk* people.

This one isn't full of tech bros like in San Jose. It's campy, with skis and snowshoes mounted on the walls between what I hope are faux stuffed deer and bear heads, Christmas lights strung between their antlers even though it's July. A long scuffed bar runs along one side of the room, and a couple of booths against the other. It's not too loud, a mix of locals and tourists chatting over the noise of a wall-mounted TV playing a baseball game.

"This okay?" Leo glances at me, brows lifted in apprehension. "The options are limited, especially for a Sunday. Small towns and all."

I hoist myself onto a barstool and perch my feet on the higher rung. "Yep. This is perfect."

Leo slides onto the stool beside me and flags the bartender with two raised fingers. I order the only nonalcoholic drink on the menu that isn't soda—an old-fashioned—and Leo orders a whiskey. His leg presses into mine as he adjusts on the barstool, leaning closer to me to ask, "Sorry if it's rude to ask this, but do you not drink?"

"Not rude. And I sometimes drink . . ." I trail off, considering lying to him or not providing any explanation. But I say, "I'm on medication for anxiety. Alcohol doesn't mix well with it, so I usually stick with libations that won't make me want to fall asleep."

"Gotcha. It's fine that we're at a bar, though?" He has this worried little furrow to his brow that I want to press my thumb against, smooth out. "I was serious about limited options. It was this or the Dairy Queen."

"While I appreciate a good Blizzard as much as the next gal," I say, thanking the bartender when he brings my drink, "this is fine. Seriously. I'm here for the company, anyway."

The worried scrunch disappears as his cheeks flush, and he smiles. "Just tell me if you change your mind and start craving ice cream."

I test out my old-fashioned, which isn't half bad. "I will."

Leo picks up his whiskey and glances down at the bar top, and I stare at his profile for a moment. Strong jaw, slightly aquiline nose, a soft feathering of wrinkles around his eyes. A few wisps of silver-gray pepper his dark hair. His leg presses against mine—his jeans rough against my bare leg—as he sips his whiskey, and something flushing and furious warms my stomach.

Leo *is* interested in me. I'm not misreading this entire situation. Not like I have amazing self-confidence—I'm not as stunning as Maeve or conventionally beautiful in that Barbie kind of way like Eliana—but I'm not ugly. It's just that Leo's . . . way out of my league. He's gorgeous in a way that I find uniquely fascinating. Maybe he doesn't leave the woods often and I'm benefiting from isolation beer goggles.

"Thanks for this," I tell Leo, and sip my drink. "My vacation has been utter crap, and it's nice to get away from my family for a little while."

His smile tugs at the corner. "You've said that a few times, about how you're not having a great vacation. What's so bad about it?"

I bite back a groan. Of course Leo is thoughtful and remembers my constant stream of complaints and wants to know *more* about me. But I can't tell him the truth. Well, not the whole truth. Will this be a complete vibe killer? Yeah, probably, but I also don't want to lie to Leo. I should probably lie to him, but I don't.

"Beyond spending so much time with my sisters—which, to be fair, hasn't been as horrible as I imagined—I had a . . . run-in with an old family friend. He was really, um, aggressive and pushy with me. Nothing *happened*, but it shook me up a little."

Leo's smile all but vanishes now. "Are you serious?"

I nod into my drink, sip it, and briefly wish it were full of alcohol to obliterate my mind right now. "Yeah. I'm okay. Obviously. It was just weird."

"Weird? Remi, that's more than weird," Leo says, those gray eyes locked onto mine. "Are you really okay?"

Even if Leo doesn't know half of it, I consider his question. Beyond everything that happened after my sisters showed up, I'm not sure how well I've processed Guy's attack. I keep reminding myself that it could've been worse if Eliana and Maeve hadn't shown up. So much worse. But that doesn't mean the feeling of losing all my control—during what could have really only been a minute or two—hasn't haunted me. Of someone's hands on me who didn't have permission. The shame of how I almost gave in because I didn't think I could stop him.

As women, we have so little say in our lives. At the very least we should be able to say who can and can't put their hands on us, touch us. But I am okay, I think. Or . . . I will be okay. I'll tell my therapist about Guy, talk it through. Jury's still out on how much else I will tell her. Not really sure what all those confidentiality laws mean when an accidental death is in the mix. "Yeah. *Yeah*," I say with a wave of my hand. "I'll be fine."

Leo's eyes search mine, and I can't tell if he believes me. But his leg shifts away from mine beneath the bar top, and I wonder if I've made a mistake sharing what happened. I don't want Leo to act differently around me. If anything, I want Leo to help me take my mind off what happened with Guy. Because, if I'm being honest with myself, that's why I'm here.

Like what Maeve said—it's my choice. I chose to be here. All of this is because I wanted it to happen, and I have no doubt that, if I change my mind at any step, Leo's the kind of man who will listen to me. And if he's not, I never returned Eliana's pepper spray.

"Leo, I'm fine," I say a little firmer now. "I wouldn't be here if I wasn't."

I shift my hand on the bar toward his, running my fingertips over his palm, the callouses and cuts, the weight of his gaze on me. Leo's leg presses against mine again, and then his fingers slide through my fingers, holding my hand. Such an innocent gesture that only provokes that flushed, furious feeling inside my body.

"Tell me if that changes, okay?" Leo tilts his head to the side, an errant curl falling into his gray eyes. "I'll take you back or call you an Uber if you want to leave. Just let me know."

The gesture is so kind—yet so simple—that I have no idea what to say. Then I joke lamely, "You have Uber in Fallen Lake?"

"Last I checked, we had three drivers," Leo says with a lift of his brows, as if this is something to brag about. The tightness in my chest is loosening, and the vibe isn't dead. If anything, the incessant, anxious buzz that's been humming in the back of my mind since I agreed to this date fades softly.

"The family friend . . . This guy isn't still hanging around, is he? He's gone?"

An inappropriate laugh catches in my throat. Nursing my drink, I nod and avoid looking Leo in the eye. "Mm-hmm. Yeah. He's gone."

"Good." Leo seems pleased with the answer and releases my hand to pick up his whiskey.

"Thank you, for the offer, but I don't want to leave," I say, and Leo's smile is back.

"Me either," he says, then asks the most obvious non sequitur of all time: "Okay, so, I know what you do for a living, but what do you do for fun? Back in San Jose?"

"I work a lot," I admit, and while I'm grateful for the change in topic—the deliberate nudge toward moving the night forward—I worry about how pathetic I might sound to this man. "Since the pandemic, I've worked from home, which is one reason why I got Buffy. My apartment was pretty lonely, and I can't keep a houseplant alive, so."

"You can't keep a houseplant alive, but you thought you could keep a pet alive?"

"Buffy is still alive, isn't she?" I widen my eyes meaningfully. "The evidence is right there. Anyway, I work a lot. My best friend got married earlier this year, and she's been way busier, so I've kind of . . . hermitted. Been pretty hyperfocused on my job."

"The job with the death threats and kids sending you profanity-laced emails?" Leo sips his whiskey, his eyes on mine.

"That's the one." I lift my glass in a faux cheers. Tasha's job offer picks at the back of my brain. Leaving San Jose, working in UI design . . . never having to deal with another disgusting teenager's email again. This weekend has to be rotting my brain, because for a half second, I almost consider it.

Leo's studying me. "What's up? You look very . . . ponderous."

A flush heats my face. "Ponderous? Nothing's up, just thinking."

"Right, sorry, if I was nosy," he says, tipping back some of his drink. "This whole date needs a huge-ass disclaimer. I haven't been out with someone in like eight months."

"First of all, this is a date?" I ask, and Leo nods, one resolute tilt of his chin. "Okay, cool, cool. Good to know. And I have you beat. Last date I went on was a year ago." I sip my old-fashioned and stare across the bar, the rows of bottles shining beneath the Christmas lights. Because how pathetic am I? It isn't a contest.

"You really are a hermit," Leo says with a cheerful laugh, no tinge of judgment or pity. All in all, not the worst reaction.

"I know what I like," I say after a moment. As unsure and self-conscious of a person as I am, this is true. Maybe one of my few decent qualities as a person—I know myself, for better and, usually, for worse. Stephanie says my standards are too high, but I got tired of bad dates that were carbon copies of one another, the unsolicited dick pics, how one dude asked if I was into toes. Not even feet. *Toes.* "And I wasn't seeing anything I liked."

"I'm really enjoying your use of past tense in this conversation," Leo says with a lopsided grin, and that flushed feeling sinks lower, between my thighs.

"Me too, honestly," I say, and my breath catches in my throat as he rests his hand on my leg. He does this so slowly, as if giving me every opportunity to push his hand away, but I don't.

"Not like I wouldn't go for a Blizzard right now," I say, lifting my gaze to his, "but other than the Dairy Queen, is there somewhere else we can go . . . ?"

"I have lodging at the park." Leo's cheeks are flushed, and I swear I see the thud of his heartbeat in his neck, the low bar lighting casting shadows against his skin. "If that's what you meant? We can just go there and talk, I wasn't implying—I swear I'm not usually this awkward, but you make me . . . nervous."

I tip back the rest of the old-fashioned, secretly delighted that I have the power to make someone else nervous. "I make you nervous?"

"Extremely. I don't know why, but you do." Leo grins, then finishes off his whiskey. He tucks a twenty beneath his empty glass, then slides off the barstool. I follow.

Outside the bar, beneath a striped awning, I stop him, curl my fingers around the collar of his jacket, and pull Leo's lips against mine. He wraps his arms around my waist, mouth opening as he deepens the kiss. His mouth is cold, tastes like whiskey, and I'm relieved, breathlessly relieved, because nothing about this moment reminds me of last night. The barbed memory doesn't rise to the surface like a bruise. Instead, there's something healing about kissing someone I want to kiss. About removing the power Guy had over me when he forced his mouth onto mine.

I pull Leo even closer. *Sink* into him because he's a good kisser. Slow and purposeful. Not too much tongue, which is an underrated talent. Leo eases away after a minute and presses another soft kiss to my lips before capturing my hand in his and leading me wordlessly back to his car.

# CHAPTER FIFTEEN

*July 5 / Night*

Never would I have thought that a single-room log cabin in a state park is where I'd have my first one-night stand. Because I don't do this. Remi Finch doesn't have one-night stands or make the first move. I'm the girl who waits to be kissed, who frets over every single decision in a relationship, who is often told she's too much or, more commonly, not enough.

Maybe it was Maeve's subliminal horniness or the fact that everything about Leo reminded me that I hadn't had sex in a year. Or maybe it's because of what almost happened with Guy last night; I don't know, but as Leo's body curls around mine, his head tucked against the bare slope of my shoulder, I don't have any regrets. None whatsoever.

The way Leo touched me was kind and slow and purposeful, always with permission, his mouth hot against my ear, asking if what he was doing was okay. And it was. Very, very okay. For a brief moment, as he pressed into me, I wondered if I was doing this for the wrong reason. If this was the best way to cope with what had happened the night before. But then Leo said my name, and it shocked me back into the present, back into my body, and I stopped thinking altogether.

"Do you want to stay the night?" Leo murmurs now, his lips grazing my shoulder.

I shift, roll onto my back, and look at him. The small bed inside the ranger's cabin barely fits the both of us, but it's cozy, our legs tangled beneath the thick wool blankets. "Okay." I brush his dark curls off his face. Then I remember what my sisters and parents have been up to while I've been here, tucked away in Mr. Hot Park Ranger's bed. I reach over Leo and grab my phone off the bedside table, checking the screen. No texts or calls. The search must be going well.

I switch my phone's ringer on, just in case, then burrow against Leo, rest my head on his chest. His skin is warm, his heart thudding too fast, his hand hovering over my hip for a moment until he curves his fingers around my body.

"For the record, I've never . . . done something like this before," Leo admits after a moment of silence, and I lift my head to look at him. "Never slept with a stranger. Had a one-night stand, if that's what this is."

"Never?" I ask, unable to mask the surprise from my voice. Probably because I thought most single people lived much more exciting and risqué dating lives than me. It's entirely possible I watch too much TV.

"No." He squints at me. "Why do you look so surprised?"

My cheeks warm. "I mean, you're . . ."

"I'm what?"

"I've called you 'Mr. Hot Park Ranger' inside my head for most of the day," I say as an explanation, and Leo barks a laugh. When he laughs, he laughs with his whole body, his stomach contracting beneath my palm, the corners of his eyes crinkling.

"Not sure if I should feel objectified or flattered."

"Both?" I suggest, and he laughs again. And I really, really like making Leo laugh. There's something weirdly satisfying about it, about someone finding me *funny*. "But good to know. Neither have I. This entire thing is . . . very unlike me." In more ways than one.

"I've been putting off asking you this," Leo says, "but when do you check out?"

"Tomorrow morning."

He groans. "Seriously?"

I nod, conflicted because—as much as I've wanted to flee this state park and run back to San Jose—I'm really enjoying myself right now, enjoying Leo. "Yeah. I have to be back at work Tuesday."

"At your terrible job?"

"Yep, at my terrible job." I bite the inside of my cheek. "Sorry, I probably should've told you that sooner."

"I'm not sure if we're doing the one-night stand thing right," he says, and my face falters. "Not in a bad way! It's just . . . I don't think I should feel sad about you going back to San Jose."

"Sad, huh?" Maybe it's messed up, but the fact that Leo's sad warms my stomach. But my natural state is deflection, and I say, "Pretty sure that's the sex talking."

"It *was* good sex," he says with a grin. "But I don't know, I like you."

"You don't know me," I say, and try not to think about Guy Moran, the sleeping bag, any of it. Sure, I didn't kill Guy, but everything that's happened over the last twenty-four hours is morally gray at best. Whoever I end up with in my life—if I'm so lucky to find someone and not die alone with six cats—can never find out about what happened with Guy.

Especially not a law-abiding, recycling, brakes-for-squirrels park ranger.

"I know enough." Leo grins, and rational thought is getting harder and harder to cling onto. He leans around me to grab his boxers off the bed, then stands and pulls them on. "Do you want something to drink? I can make us tea."

Something about Leo making me tea in his boxers at midnight is so weird and adorable that I find myself saying yes. When, in reality, I shouldn't stay the night. I should leave. Put some distance between us— go help my sisters burn that sleeping bag in our firepit—because the super-annoying thing is, I kind of like Leo too. I don't want to, because I'm leaving tomorrow, and this was supposed to be a fun distraction. And while it's been both, I might mourn what could've, possibly, been.

Trust me, I'm extremely aware that I'm never going to sleep with someone this hot ever again.

Leo puts the kettle on and grabs a sweater off the back of his dining chair, tugging it on over his head. My dress is crumpled on the ground, so I grab Leo's discarded shirt and pull it on over my breasts, then shimmy on my underwear beneath the covers. He plops down beside me again, leans his back against the wall. "Okay, so. You admit that your job is terrible. Why don't you quit?"

I sit upright and cross my legs, wrinkling my nose at the question. "It's not that bad."

Leo lifts one brow. "You're lying."

"Okay, it sucks," I admit with a laugh. "But I like the people I work with, and it's not *all* terrible."

"This job offer—would you be doing the same thing you do now? I can't remember what the role is called, sorry. My brain filed it as 'human punching bag,' but I'm pretty sure that can't be right."

"Community manager," I say, but he's not wrong about the human-punching-bag thing. "And nope. I'd work on designing UI."

"Which stands for . . ."

"User interface. They're how players find information and interact with the game. Think menus, bags and inventory storage, HUDs," I explain, and this is when I realize Leo has never played a video game before. He looks like a lost puppy. "Not a gamer, I take it?"

"I don't even have a TV, let alone a computer," Leo says with a self-deprecating chuckle, and gestures around the small cabin, which is bare bones. "But I think I understand."

"It's not very glamorous," I say, "but I went to school for graphic design. Tasha's job offer would have me working on the UI design for her new game. A far cry from the purgatory of glorified customer service."

As I say this, something unsettled takes over the warmth that's spread throughout my body since I climbed into Leo's bed. Because I *do* hate my job. Like, a lot. Ever since I went remote, I rarely see any of the colleagues I like, and the pay is decent, but since when is that worth the misery?

Warp was my first job offer after college, and I took it. Too panicked by the idea that another might not come along. Twenty-two-year-old

Remi told herself she'd move up in the ranks at Warp, find a way into the graphic design or art departments. But I let each and every opportunity pass me by, too intimidated by office politics and pressure and the likelihood of failure.

"I hate you for making me consider this." I pull the nearest blanket around my body like a cape. "But working in graphic design would be awesome."

"Then take the job," Leo says with a grin.

"It's not that simple."

"Pretty sure it is."

I have a laundry list of excuses. Moving in general is a life stressor that I'd like to avoid—so is starting a new job. Two life stressors in one seems like a bad idea for someone like me, especially given how this vacation was the exact opposite of the rest and relaxation I needed. I've never lived outside California, and I have no idea how I'd survive in Washington. Sure, I like the rain and am a self-confessed hermit, but what if I turn into a seasonally depressed hermit?

Even if Eliana and I have tolerated one another well, moving to the same city would probably mean spending more time with her. And her kids. What if I'm a terrible aunt? What if Eliana doesn't want me moving closer to her?

Guy tried to assault me last night, and I've spent the last twenty-four hours petrified of the thought of somehow going down for his murder, only leaving Fallen Lake in the back of a police cruiser. All the possibilities in my life will become impossibilities, and this will be it. My life ending before anything *real* and lovely and exciting ever happened. I'm still that kid, kicking out and gasping for air, lamenting a life that hasn't happened yet. A life I'm too afraid to make happen.

If this weekend hasn't been a wake-up call to change my life before someone changes it for me, I don't know what is.

"You're not allowed to be hot *and* give good life advice," I mutter beneath my breath, and Leo laughs again—a noise cut off by the squeal of the kettle that makes me jump.

Leo slides off the bed and pours us each a cup, then returns to his spot beside me. He carefully passes me the mug of tea, and I sit upright beside him, leaning against the exposed-log wall of the cabin. "I may not know you, Remi Finch, but I know that everyone deserves a job that doesn't make them miserable."

I clutch the mug of tea with both hands, Leo's body pressed firmly against mine. "Yeah," I say with a sigh and sip the tea, "you're probably right. I think . . . I think I'm going to take the job." Even as I test the words, saying this out loud to Leo, it doesn't quite feel real. But, at the same time, it feels *right*.

Leo gently bumps his shoulder against mine. "I can't take all the credit. It's the power of the great outdoors. Something about the trees, the fresh air . . . it really helps you connect with yourself."

I nod in agreement, even though it was more the realization I might go to prison that's made me reassess my life choices up until this moment. But all of this *technically* happened in the woods, so Leo might be onto something.

"I like you too," I admit after a moment. Because I never said it earlier and I *want* to, which again, is very unlike me. Vulnerability and me normally don't get along, but Leo's surprised me. Did I think he was just a hot park ranger earlier? Yes, definitely. But the dude's got layers. Even if there can't be anything between us, maybe this experience will help me break out of my dating-comfort shell. Not all men are terrible. Most men, sure, but not all.

Leo slides the mug out of my hand and places both mugs on the bedside table. Then he kisses me, cradling my face in his palms. I shift into his lap, my arms around his neck, and lose myself in the sensation of his tongue against mine, his hands on my hips.

Ding.

My phone chimes with a text message on the bedside table, and Leo stills, but I ignore the interruption, kissing him deeper, and his attention switches back over to my mouth, my body.

Ding.

Ding.

Ding.

Ding.

"Sorry," I say, and grab my phone off the table, leaning back to glance at the screen.

ELIANA: The search didn't go as planned. Mom and Dad couldn't find it. We looked for two hours. I'm covered in mosquito bites and branch scratches and while I feel good about our sisterly gesture of letting you go off with your hot ranger friend, we need you back here ASAP!

ELIANA: Hello?!

MAEVE: Reemmmiiii hi don't ignore us

MAEVE: We know Leo's hot but this is BAD. Even Eliana is freaking out. Omg, you'd love it, she's spiraling

MAEVE: But seriously this is no bueno. 911. Red Flag Emergency. Halp.

I slide out of Leo's lap, my gaze glued onto my phone. Processing. They didn't find the body. Meaning they didn't find the sleeping bag. All the evidence is still out there, linking us to Guy Moran's death. All the warmth—from Leo's mouth and the tea and the blankets—vanishes as I lock my phone.

"Um," I say, scattered mentally as I try to find my dress, my bra. "I need to go."

"Is everything okay?" Leo's brows are notched with concern, and he watches as I scramble around his bed until I find my bra kicked beneath the comforter.

"Yeah," I say with a forced grin and pull off the shirt I co-opted, shoving it at his chest. With shaking hands, I swoop and scoop my breasts into my bra, then tug my dress down over my head.

Leo swings his legs over the bed and stands up. "Whoa, slow down. What's up?"

I lean down to grab my flannel, but Leo's stepping on it, and I rip it from beneath his foot. "Sorry, just . . . family stuff. I'm really, really sorry, Leo. Trust me, I'd stay here, if I had the choice." I stuff my arms through the sleeves in my flannel, my fingers fumbling with the buttons.

Leo's standing in the center of the cabin with a befuddled look on his face, his curls mussed from my fingers, dressed only in his sweater and boxers. "Let me drive you back." He grabs his jeans off the kitchen table—not sure how they got there—and pulls them on.

"No, it's okay. You stay." Every time I open my mouth, I'm making this worse. Because Leo senses my panic—it's oozing off me. "It's not a far walk."

"Sure, but there's a fugitive in the park," Leo says with an exasperated laugh.

The problem is, if Leo drives me, he'll keep asking what's wrong. I'll crack. I *know* I will. I'll tell him the entire sordid mess and he'll realize that I'm not the woman he thinks I am, and the likelihood that he calls Detective Diaz on my family is high. Way too high.

"I have pepper spray," I say, and force myself to calm down. To not raise any more of Leo's annoyingly attentive alarm bells. "Seriously, it's late. You said you had to work in the morning."

The car keys are already in Leo's hand. "Let me drive you, Remi. It's not safe."

I nearly laugh. Because the woods are safe. Guy's dead! The threat hasn't been a threat for twenty-four hours, and oh god, I'm nervous sweating again. "I'll be fine. I can take care of myself. See you around, okay?"

Then I lean in and kiss him one last time before darting out the door.

# CHAPTER SIXTEEN

*July 6 / Midnight*

Five minutes into my run and I'm regretting not saying yes to Leo's ride. Because I am *not* a runner. My shins hurt and my breath is tight in my lungs, a reminder that I left my inhaler at camp somewhere. Since I only have exercise-induced asthma—and I do not exercise—I rarely need it; it's a glorified medical prop these days. And even though there isn't a fugitive prowling around the campgrounds, that doesn't mean it's not creepy as shit out here. The shadows are too deep, stretching into nothingness, and I swear to god an owl is following me, branch to branch, hooting ominously.

I jog, a pathetic flailing of my limbs, alongside the main road, darting past sleeping campgrounds, and rely on my shoddy memory to guide me back to Campsite #34. When I first left the rangers' cabins, I texted my sisters that I was on my way. I should've had them pick me up. If I end up being eaten by a bear, I won't be surprised. It would be a fitting end to this vacation.

After ten minutes, I slow to a walk. It's cold out, the temperature dropping sharply, and the sky is cloudy, dark; barely any moon is on display. My chest wheezes, and I take long, slow gulps of air. Trying not to panic, but how can I not when my parents lost Guy Moran! How do you *lose* a dead body?

Guilt rams into my already tight chest, replacing the anger over my parents somehow misplacing a dead body. Because I wish I didn't have to deal with this. I want to turn around and crawl back into Leo's bed. I want to email Tasha to say that yes, absolutely yes, I'll accept her job offer. I want to pack my car and drive back to San Jose in the dead of night and pretend like this entire camping trip never happened. I want to bail, to avoid, but I can't. The fact that I want to, though, makes me feel like a bad sister, a bad daughter.

My phone buzzes in my bag, and I slide it out, wincing at the bright screen in the woodsy darkness.

**LEO: Can you at least let me know when you get back to camp safe?**

My heart lurches, low behind my belly button. This entire situation is a *mess*. I don't regret sleeping with Leo, but I wish the circumstances were different. Although, if the circumstances were different—if Guy hadn't gone and gotten himself murdered—then I'd probably never have ended up in Leo's bed in the first place. How ironic.

"Remi!" A voice hisses my name, and I lock my phone, stuffing it into my bag.

I squint toward the nearest campsite, my chest deflating with relief as I realize I've made it. Campsite #34. My sisters and parents are all sitting—in the dark, like that's not suspicious—at our picnic table, and I hurry over.

"Thanks for finally joining us" Eliana says coolly, as if she hadn't encouraged me to go out with Leo in the first place.

"Can we not do this right now?" I find my inhaler on the outdoor pantry shelf and take a puff. "What the hell happened? You lost the body?" This last bit I release in a fervent whisper, glancing in the dark between my two parents.

Mom presses her thin lips together, exhales. "Well. I would've sworn that we hid Guy in the fields near the Jellystone Trail. But when we looked, we couldn't find a thing!"

I press my eyes shut for a brief moment, collect myself. From studying the campground map, I remember that the Jellystone Trail was highlighted as one of the most popular and kid-friendly trails in the entire park. "Isn't that trail, like, super popular?"

"We couldn't carry him very far," Mom says defensively. "Seemed like a good idea at the time. The grass is tall in the fields, I'll have you know."

In that moment, Aunt Lindy's comment resurfaces in my mind. The shrooms. Oh my god, my parents were stoned last night when they moved the body. I don't know why I hadn't thought of that before now, but of course they were high! Forget my parents doing mushrooms on my prom night; this is worse. So much worse.

Eliana catches my gaze, and we share a rare, exasperated moment. "We looked everywhere, Remi. All around the trail, through the fields. We looked for two hours. Nothing."

I rest my head in my hands, slumping forward. "This is terrible."

Mom pats me on the back. "Remi, it'll be okay."

"How? If you had left Guy in the tent, none of this would've happened," I say, and my mom flinches, even though I didn't raise my voice. Then I turn to my sisters. "I wanted to call the cops last night! I don't know why I listened to you two, but I did. I folded to the sibling peer pressure and went along with your plan, even though it was a bad idea. Even though it made us look guilty, when we didn't kill him. And now someone's going to find Guy's body—inside *my* sleeping bag—and I'm going to go to prison."

"We were only trying to help." Mom shifts beside me, no longer comforting me, but curling into herself. "We made a mistake; I can admit that. But we wanted to help you girls."

I squeeze my eyes shut, wondering why I don't have normal parents, a normal family. "What're we supposed to do?"

"You leave in the morning," Dad says. "Pretend like nothing happened. And maybe no one will find him."

I flirted with these exact same delusions earlier and even said as much to Eliana at lunch. But that was before Detective Diaz. That was before Guy's wanted flyer. Before I knew that our parents had moved the body. Nothing—nothing at all—has gone our way this trip, and denial won't get us out of this situation. "We need to keep looking," I insist. "I'll help. I'm not tired, I can go—"

"We looked everywhere around the Jellystone Trail," Eliana interrupts, and I study my sister. She's exhausted, shadows beneath her eyes. "Face it, Remi. We don't know who killed him, and we don't know what happened to his body. Dad's right. We all should leave in the morning and hope for the best."

"Easy for you to say," I say with a frustrated laugh. "He's not in your sleeping bag."

Eliana's eye twitches, either from exhaustion or irritation; I'm unsure. "No, but I touched his body. My DNA might be on him too. *All* of our DNA might be on him. Your life isn't the only one at stake."

"Then we should keep looking," I say, wondering why no one else agrees with me.

"We tried," Maeve says, her voice cracking. "Mom and Dad swear that's where they hid him. And he wasn't there. What else are we supposed to do?"

Anger and frustration and fear all twist my stomach into knots. "I don't know," I admit, and I don't like the feeling that's sweeping over me now. Hopelessness. The body is gone. Again. Guy Moran tormented me in life, and he's somehow still tormenting me in death. How fitting.

Deep, out in the darkness, thunder rumbles.

And then it begins to rain.

The five of us stare out at the trees, listening to the loud patter of rain on the sunshade above our heads.

"Remi," Mom says gently. "It's almost one in the morning. Now it's raining. We can't figure this out tonight, no matter how much you want to. Go to sleep, baby."

I'm dangerously close to breaking down in frustrated tears, and I try to hold them back. "Most parents wouldn't have moved the body. Why'd you have to do that? Especially when you were higher than a pair of giraffe's balls! You made everything *so much* worse."

Mom's eyes widen in hurt. Dad's mustache twitches.

Maeve cackles. "'Higher than a pair of giraffe's balls'? Oh my god, I'm stealing that."

"We've never been most parents, Rem," Dad says with a sigh as he gets up from the picnic table. "But we love you girls, and we try. Maybe we made a mistake, moving Guy's body, but we wanted to help. The least we could do for inviting him on this trip." He pats my shoulder once—quick and emotionless—before walking out into the rain, toward Atlas.

"Buffy's in Eliana's tent." Mom moves slowly, groaning a little as she stands. And that's when I notice how filthy they all are. Bug bites and branch scratches marring their arms. "We'll see you in the morning."

"They really were trying to help," Eliana says once we're all alone. "But I freaked out on them earlier too. I was so mad that they *forgot* where they put Guy."

"Oh yeah, she yelled at them," Maeve says with the reverence of someone who goes to hockey matches just to watch the fights.

"Not my finest moment." Eliana tugs the sleeves of her sweater down over her hands, hiding her bug-bitten fingers, dirty nails. "But what I'm trying to say is they heard it enough from me. Lighten up on them, okay? They were really trying to help us, as absurd as it sounds."

I sigh, my shoulders rolling forward with the oncoming shame. Because I'm the worst daughter. I let my frustration and helplessness and panic get the better of me. Did I even thank them for searching the woods for two hours without me? Maybe my parents were onto something when they chose Eliana and Maeve as their favorite offspring. I clearly suck.

"I'll apologize in the morning." Then I rub my brow, a move so similar to my oldest sister's go-to stress move that I worry about the potential amount of Botox in my future, given how much I furrow my brow.

The thought haunts me.

A branch cracks from behind us, somewhere in the darkness, and I flinch. Even though the threat is gone—*has* been gone—I'm chronically on edge. As if I'm expecting an axe murderer to jump out from behind the trees. Then another twig cracks, and we all turn to look into the inky darkness behind us.

Eliana turns on her phone's flashlight and illuminates the person standing there.

And from his absolutely horrified expression, Leo has heard our entire conversation.

Maeve shrieks, a high-pitched yelp. She grabs her sandal off her foot and chucks it at Leo.

"What the—" Leo ducks as Maeve's sandal flies over his head, disappearing into the darkness.

"Let me handle this." I jump up from the table, my heart hammering so chaotically I swear it echoes against the tree trunks around us. "Leo, what're you doing here?" I ask, when the question I want to ask is how much he heard. But I'm fearing the worst.

Leo glances back at the sandal, as if he should retrieve the object my sister tried to chuck at his face. "You never texted me back, and I was worried about you," he says faintly. "Guess I should've listened when you said you could take care of yourself."

The trees shelter us slightly from the rain, but we're getting soaked more by the second. Leo doesn't seem to notice. He's just looking at me, and I don't know what to say. I'm too busy replaying the conversation with my family, wondering how much we said out loud. All of it, I think.

"Um. Okay. I know how bad all of that sounded, but I didn't kill Guy. None of us did."

Leo shifts on his feet, brow all scrunched in concern. "Is Guy the family friend? The one who . . . got aggressive with you?"

"Yeah." I wrap my arms around myself and force myself to look at him. "Just tell me. Are you going to call the police, Leo?"

Leo wipes the rain from his face, as if suddenly realizing he's drenched. He gently grabs my arm, leads me over to the shelter of the picnic table. My sisters watch us approach, hawkeyed and suspicious; Maeve holds her other sandal in her hand, and I shake my head at her. I'm too nervous to sit, though, and hover beside Leo.

Wishing I knew him, just a little bit more, to read his face in this moment.

"Well," Eliana says flatly, "is your boyfriend turning us in?"

"I'm not entirely sure what I'd turn you in for," Leo says after an achingly long moment of silence.

"Probably removal and concealment of a body," Maeve pipes up as she slips her remaining sandal back onto her foot, her bare one tucked beneath her. At our confused glances, she shrugs. "What? I googled it."

Leo blinks at my sister. "Sure, okay. For the record, I didn't mean to eavesdrop on y'all. As I told Remi, I was worried about her—she ran out of my place after getting some text messages and was acting really weird—so I drove over and parked, walked up, but you were talking. And . . . I should've said something, but I didn't know what to say. Not really the conversation I expected to walk in on."

Eliana laughs humorlessly. Then asks, "Are you turning us in or not? Cut to the chase, lover boy."

Leo slumps onto the picnic bench and drags his hand through his wet hair. "I'm not saying what you did last night was right, but . . . I get it, I guess? Remi told me earlier about what Guy did, and I can't say I'm upset he's dead. But what's with the sleeping bag you kept mentioning?"

"We put him in it," Eliana says, face pale as she recalls the memory. "We didn't realize he was dead until *after* we'd moved him into Remi's tent. We panicked, knowing how bad it looked. So, we came up with a plan. We were going to tell the cops that we discovered Guy passed out in Remi's tent the night before and didn't realize he was dead until the next morning. We never expected our parents to move the body."

"Then forget where they hid it," Maeve adds.

Leo lifts his gaze to meet mine. "The sleeping bag is *with* the body?"

I nod, chewing on my nails again. Unable to speak. Because Leo looks so disturbed, which is probably the correct emotional reaction to have in this moment. But I want to rewind, back to an hour earlier, when he said he *liked* me. To when I thought we had the sleeping bag in our possession again, that everything was under control. Or close enough.

Leo processes this. "Look, uh, I won't tell anyone. Because I agree: it'll look really bad if they find him with your belongings. I believe you, but the police might not. No offense or anything, but you all seem shady as hell talking about what happened."

Maeve snorts, and Eliana smacks her arm.

My body deflates with relief. "Thank you, Leo."

He nods, plucks at the wet sleeve of his sweater. "Can I talk to you alone?"

"Sure," I say, and my sisters thank Leo for his indifferent silence. Then Maeve grabs her projectile sandal from the forest ground among the trees, and they walk off toward the bathrooms.

I slide onto the bench beside him. "Thank you. Seriously. I'm pretty sure I owe you my life. Any chance you want a kidney? My 401(k)?"

Leo takes my hand in his. "I'm not going to sit here and pretend that I'm sad the person who assaulted you is dead. But Remi, if I'm understanding what happened right, Guy was murdered. Someone killed him. And if you found the body at your campsite . . . it could be someone you know."

"Everyone hated Guy," I admit, and chew the inside of my cheek. "We kind of asked around, tried to find out what people heard last night. But no one heard anything. My parents say it wasn't them, and

I'm not sure why they'd lie. They only moved the body because they thought *we* did it. And to be fair, we kind of thought we might've until we found the murder weapon."

Leo stares at me. Right. I hadn't told him that part yet. "You found *what*?"

"A bloody stick. Buffy, um, actually found it. When we were walking earlier." I wince as Leo puts the pieces together—realizes why I was on a hike to begin with—his cheeks losing all their color. "Eliana made me burn it because I touched it. But after that, we knew someone else had killed him. Guy obviously had a lot of enemies, beyond my family."

"Just . . . be careful," he says, and squeezes my hand once before letting go. "I mean it. I'd never forgive myself if something happened to you in this park, when I could've stopped it."

"So noble," I joke, as if what he's saying isn't melting my heart. Then I add, more seriously, "I'll be careful, Leo. And I'm probably going to hit the road early tomorrow. Hope for the best. Not sure what my other options are unless my parents have a spontaneous recall of where they hid Guy while high on shrooms."

Leo stands, tucks his hands into his pockets. "Shrooms?"

I stand too, suddenly so aware of how tired I am, how sore. "I wish I were kidding."

"I'd say keep in touch, but I have a feeling you're not going to want to remember much of this trip once you get home, will you?"

"I'm probably going to try and repress the entire weekend. But for what it's worth, I had a really nice time tonight."

Leo smiles, and it's crooked, and it's sad. "Promise me you'll still quit that awful job?"

"I've already mentally drafted my resignation letter, don't worry," I tell him, and the smile becomes a shade less sad. He ducks his head down and kisses me, but the kiss is too short, too brief, and then he waves and walks across the street, toward a parked car none of us noticed earlier.

# CHAPTER SEVENTEEN

### *July 6 / After Midnight*

The three of us lie side by side on Eliana's California king air mattress.

I readjust the lumpy pillow beneath my head, but I'm pretty sure a lack of comfort isn't the reason why I can't fathom falling asleep. How am I supposed to sleep knowing Guy Moran's body is just . . . out there? Unresolved, hanging over me for the rest of my life?

"Only our parents would manage to lose a body," I say, staring up at the dome of the tent above us. "And to think, earlier tonight I actually thought everything might be okay. I was a fool."

"You believe them when they say they didn't kill him?" Eliana rolls onto her side and peers at me over Maeve, who's holding her phone above her face and scrolling with one thumb. I'm waiting for the moment when she accidentally drops it on her face.

I grunt at all the unknowns piling up around me. "Why would they lie?"

"Murdering someone is *way* worse than concealment of a body, from a legal standpoint," Maeve says, the light of her phone making her face glow. She has a single star-shaped pimple patch on her chin.

"You really need to stop googling prison sentences," I say with a sigh. "You don't believe Mom and Dad did it, do you?"

"No. Mom and Dad are softies," Maeve says. "They're also bad liars—it's probably where you get it from, Rem."

"But if not them, who?" Eliana asks.

My mind flits back to earlier today. The dragging noise Salli heard must've been Mom and Dad hauling Guy's body over to the Jellystone Trail; the timing checks out. Grandma Helen and Bill squabbling over when they went to bed and Aunt Lindy's scratched palm were easy enough to write off when we thought a fugitive had killed Guy, but now I'm not so sure. "You think Grandma and Bill were just acting weird because they didn't want anyone knowing that they boned last night?"

Eliana makes a disgusted noise from her side of the air mattress, but our sister says, "Don't you?"

Grandma Helen is closer to ninety than eighty—even if she's one of those genetic marvels who thrive in their octogenarian years, she's not a killer. I'm fairly certain a strong wind could blow her over, and Guy was over twice her weight. Bill has a bad back, and I can't imagine him killing Guy, someone he didn't even know.

"Yeah, I guess," I say after a moment. "What about Aunt Lindy?"

"Those scratches aren't exactly a smoking gun." Eliana kicks her feet beneath the sleeping bag and blankets as she tries to get comfortable. "Honestly, Aunt Lindy was probably sneaking out to have a smoke and tripped, which is why she was acting so cagey."

I grunt in agreement. I hadn't thought of that, but it makes complete sense. "What happened to you being suspicious of *literally* everyone?"

"I'm exhausted, that's what happened," Eliana says. "I'm trying to make peace with the fact that we probably won't know what happened to Guy."

My stomach squirms. "But we didn't kill him."

Eliana hesitates, then says, "We didn't kill him."

Maeve yawns, then locks her phone, tucks it under her pillow. "You wanna tell us how earlier went? I'm so tired of talking about Guy Moran. The dude has been such a dark shadow over this entire vacation, and I'm over it."

While I'm also tired—exhausted, honestly—of talking about Guy, I don't know how to talk to my sisters about anything personal. We've skirted around most personal topics this weekend, with Eliana's rare blip of sharing about her affair, divorce, and custody battle. When I was in middle school, both of my sisters were in college. They weren't around for me to ask questions about boys and dating or for them to warn me not to overpluck my eyebrows. Which I did. They have never recovered.

But, as much as I begrudge to admit it, my sisters did a nice thing earlier. They could've made me come along with them on the world's most morbid scavenger hunt, but they didn't. They mucked around in the woods with my parents for two hours, while I actually enjoyed myself for the first time on this vacation.

"Um." I smooth my hands out on the sleeping bag. "Nice, I guess. Yeah, it was nice."

"Nice?" Maeve repeats with derision. "That's all you're going to say? Like, if we forget the part about how he overheard us blabbering about Guy Moran with Mom and Dad, it was kind of sweet Leo was worried about you."

"To be fair, I freaked out when I got your text messages and basically ran off into the woods," I say. "It'd be weird if he wasn't worried."

Eliana snorts. "No, it wouldn't have. Most men don't give a shit, Remi."

"Your jaded-divorcée impression is uncanny," I joke, and—I swear to god—Eliana laughs. Just a tiny bit, then covers it up with a cough.

"Very funny," she says dryly, but I hear it in her voice, the hint of a smile.

I rub my eyes, then flop my arms back on the air mattress. When's the next chance I'm going to have to share and connect with my older sisters? They never made an effort, but it's not like I've been breaking down their doors for the past seven years, trying to build a relationship with either of them.

For the last near-thirty years, I think I expected a relationship with my sisters to be organic, like you see in television shows and movies.

And maybe it is, for some people. But for others, it's a relationship like any other. I've spent so long feeling disappointed that this magical sisterly bond didn't exist between us that I neglected trying to build one in the first place.

"Until tonight, I hadn't had sex in a year," I admit, and Maeve actually *gasps*. Like I'm someone giving a confessional on her favorite trashy reality-dating shows. But I soldier on. "After my ex cheated on me, I went on a few dates, but they were all terrible. So many unsolicited dick pics. All I do is work, eat takeout—my local Thai place can recognize me by voice on the phone, which is horrifying—and I only go outside to walk Buffy. Rinse and repeat. And I think I was doing a decent job of pretending like I was happy, that my life was fine, until this trip.

"Everyone in this family is so . . . happy and content," I continue, working through my thoughts as I talk. "And I think I've always felt a little broken, since I've been miserable for most of my life. Maeve, half the time I hate you because everything rolls off your back. Like, it bothers me how *unbothered* you are. And Eliana, I honestly thought your life was perfect until a few days ago."

"My life is far from perfect," Eliana says listlessly from the other side of the tent.

"Mine's pretty great," Maeve says, and I hear the swish of sleeping bag fabric as Eliana shoves her arm. "But the fact that I don't let things bother me . . . Remi, that's *intentional*. It takes work. Part of it is my personality, sure, but I'm confident in who I am, the direction my life is headed in. When you feel good about those things, I don't know, it's easier to not sweat the small stuff."

"You make it sound so easy," I say with an exhausted, humorless laugh. Confidence. What a concept. But I've never considered that Maeve chooses when to engage, when to walk away. That this is a conscious effort, not a natural-born gift. Maeve actually might be the happiest and most well adjusted out of all three of us: a more shocking revelation than Eliana's affair.

"Oh, it's not," Maeve says. "But worth it, in the end. With a job like mine, you have to build up a thick skin; otherwise people will eat you alive."

Maybe I've been miserable because my life has been the culmination of too many panicked, anxiety-driven choices that were always the safe bet. Not moving far away after college. Taking the first job offer to land in my inbox. Shutting myself off after my ex-boyfriend cheated on me and caused an HR scandal, even though sometimes I felt so lonely I wanted to cry.

"I'm, um, quitting my job when I get back to San Jose," I admit, and the act of telling my sisters—not just Mr. Hot Park Ranger—makes the decision even more real. Even harder to back out of. "Do you remember my friend from college, Tasha? Last year, she secured funding for her own video game company; there's an article about it in GeekWire and everything. The company just launched, and she offered me a job."

My heart hammers, slick and nervous in my chest, and I have to remind myself that sharing big, important news with your family is normal. Even still, I'm worried about what my sisters will think. I'll need way more therapy to figure out why I care about their opinions so much.

"Really?" Eliana asks, and this might be the first time I've surprised her in a good way.

"Congrats, Rem," Maeve says, her foot kicking mine beneath the sleeping bag in excitement. "Mom and Dad must be so happy. They hated that job."

"Yeah . . . they don't know yet."

Maeve turns her head toward me on her pillow, her eyes wide. "You told us *first*?"

"Technically," I say before Maeve can get too emotional over this insignificant amount of bonding, "I told Leo first. Well. He actually convinced me to do it, and while it's weird to take life advice from a random dude I slept with, the decision feels . . . right."

"You told the random park ranger about your big life change before us?" Eliana frowns.

"To be fair," Maeve says, "Leo is very, very hot. I'd give him my social security number if he asked."

"He has that effect on people," I say, and stare at the dome of the tent instead of my oldest sister. "The job is in Seattle."

Eliana exhales, a whoosh of breath. "Oh," she says, and I can't read her tone to save my life. Then she adds, "That's great, Remi. I'm happy for you. And I guess it could be kind of nice, seeing you more than once every few years."

I smile a little because that's the best reaction I could hope for out of Eliana. "Thanks. I'm . . . excited."

"How's Maven Maeve?" Eliana asks our sister, and I'm relieved the spotlight is off me. But I did it. I shared, I was vulnerable with my sisters, and I survived. "You haven't brought it up at all this trip."

Huh. Maeve is usually chattering about sponsorships or new products she's testing or the latest article she wrote for her site. Sure, we've had a lot going on the past twenty-four hours, but other than her comment about worrying about losing her sponsors, she hasn't mentioned her company. At all.

Maeve fiddles with her silk eye mask. "If we're all opening up and being honest tonight, then it's because neither of you respect my job. You act like I make Instagram Reels for a living."

Eliana glances over at me in the dark. Because Maeve isn't wrong. As someone who loathes social media, I've been flippant about my sister's job. Eliana, who has always been loftily stuck up compared to the rest of our family, has never hidden her snide comments or eye rolls when it came to Maeve's career either.

"Owning a company like Maven Maeve isn't as fancy as working as an accountant for some swanky law firm, or as cool as working at a video game company, but this was my dream. Neither of you have ever taken me seriously."

"Sorry, Maeve," I say after a squirming moment of guilt. "You know me, I hate social media. And it's, like, your life."

"Trust me, I know," Maeve says with a huff. "Your entire Instagram is photos of Buffy, doughnuts, and screenshots of that *Realms* game. It *pains* me. Your aesthetic is tragic."

Eliana snorts, and our sister shoots her an icy look.

"You know I make more money than you." Maeve says this factually, not cruelly. "And I don't have to wear power suits."

"I like my power suits," Eliana mutters, and the sleeping bag shifts as she yanks it up around her neck. "I look *good* in power suits."

"You do know how to rock a shoulder pad," Maeve admits.

"I'm sorry, Mae," Eliana says.

"Apologies accepted," she says breezily, and if this were anyone else, I'd be suspicious I wasn't forgiven. But Maeve is . . . *Maeve*. She doesn't hold a grudge, and it's a skill I should probably learn, considering I'm still holding several from high school. "But to answer your question, I'm selling Maven Maeve to a lifestyle company. I'll still stay on, keep my brand, but I'll have more support and flexibility. The sale doesn't go through until July eighteenth, though, so I'm trying to avoid any . . . scandals. Or, you know, prison. I'm no Martha Stewart. I don't think I can make prison jibe with my personal aesthetic."

I snort, because if anyone can pull a Martha Stewart, it'd be Maeve.

Maeve yawns again, then adds, "Who knows if it wouldn't have mattered—it's not like we killed him—but this sale is a *huge* deal. My lawyers told me to be on my best behavior. I should probably thank you, Remi, for not calling the cops, even though all that did was get us into more trouble."

"I think we're at the point where we can blame our parents for what happened," I joke, and my sisters laugh. Not at me, but with me, and it's a nice change of pace.

"Yeah," Eliana says, "but they were trying to help. As misguided as they were."

I make a contemplative noise, smooshing my pillow again. The older I've gotten, the easier it's become for me to realize that my parents are just . . . people. They're going through life the first time, just like I am, and while I often wish I had more normal parents—parents who didn't do shrooms or eschew modern psychiatry or send me long emails about my menses and iron levels, since the last time they saw me *I looked a little pale*—they aren't bad parents. Or bad people.

Should they have left Guy where they'd found him? Most definitely.

But I also should have done a lot of things differently this trip.

People in glass houses, et cetera, et cetera.

"Okay, but really, how *was* the sex with Leo?" Maeve asks after a moment of nice sisterly silence.

"Probably recency bias, but really good," I say without an ounce of shame, of regret. "So good it's a little depressing, since I'm never going to see him again. But the whole thing has made me slightly less terrified of dating." Although, I do wonder what the men in Seattle will be like. More tech bros, like in San Jose? I shudder at the thought.

"Look at you," Maeve preens, "looking on the bright side!"

"It's like two in the morning. I'm sleep deprived and delirious. Fear not, I'll be back to my pessimistic self in the morning."

Maeve shoves my arm, but it's playful, without malice.

"I'm going to try sleeping," I say, although I have no idea if that's an attainable goal.

Everything feels too much right now. Too much unknown. Too much hope. Too much dread. Too much anticipation for the morning to come, to flee back to San Jose, to run. As I curl up on my side, I'm surprised by my heavy eyelids, my quiet brain. Almost as if talking to my sisters has helped. Go figure. As I drift off into sleep, I can't get Leo's voice out of my head, his warning about how Guy *was* murdered, and how it could be someone I know.

# CHAPTER EIGHTEEN

### *July 6 / Early Morning*

I need to apologize to my parents.

But first, coffee.

My sisters are asleep when I slip out of the tent with Buffy tucked under my arm like the world's cutest football. The campsite is foggy and muddy from last night's rain, and I frown as Buffy gleefully jumps into several puddles on her way to her favorite bush. As she does her business, I pull on a sweater over my pajamas and pick at the sleep crust inside the corner of my eyes.

A light is on inside Atlas, and I hope that means my parents are awake. And if they've made coffee, well, that's a bonus. No idea where Eliana keeps her percolator or beans, and after decades as her sister, I know better than to wake her up. As Buffy and I walk over to my parents' campsite, I glance at our other sites, but everyone is still asleep. No doubt due to Aunt Lindy's cocktail. Damien and Andrew's car is gone—they stayed at a local hotel for the night, and I feel guilty over the thought of leaving before I'll get the chance to say goodbye—and the cousins from Nevada drove home after last night's festivities. Just the original group is left.

I rap my knuckles on Atlas's metal door, and footsteps shuffle on the other side before it creaks open. Mom peers down at me. Her hair is braided in its usual rope, but it's littered with bits of flower and twig from her flower crown, and her eyes are bloodshot. She's wearing her glow-in-the-dark bug sweater and stirrup pants. Silently, she steps back and opens the door wider, letting me and Buffy climb inside.

Atlas is an old RV, from the 1980s, and has that musky, vintage smell you'd find in the cushions of a secondhand store. It also carries the faint skunky undertone of weed, and it's decorated in small hallmarks of my parents' personalities. One of Salli's hand-knit blankets is thrown across the back of the bench seat. The small bookshelf is stuffed with philosophy books, tomes on mushroom foraging, and blank-spine journals, no doubt filled with my mom's travel ramblings. A postcard from every state they've visited since Dad's retirement is taped to the cabinet in the kitchen, the corners curling from the heat and steam of the stove.

I slide off my shoes and unleash Buffy; she bounds toward my dad, who pokes out his head from the bedroom at the end of the RV's lone hallway.

"Hope it's not too early," I say awkwardly.

"Not at all, sweetheart." Dad walks slowly into the main room, stretching as he goes, my chaotic dog at his heels.

My eye catches on the percolator of coffee on the stove. My mom follows my gaze, and the corner of her mouth softens. She pours me a cup, and I sip it greedily. Then I sit at the booth-like kitchen table, my legs tucked beneath me. "I want to apologize for last night," I say, and jump right into it. I'm exhausted and sleepy and probably a little traumatized from this entire weekend, but I'm sincere, and I hope they can tell. "You two were trying to help, and I can't fault you for that."

Mom slides into the seat across from me, holding her own mug of coffee. "We're sorry, Remi. I honestly can't believe that we forgot where we put him! That's so unlike us."

Yeah, that's a lie. My mom forgot me at a *lot* of farmers' markets growing up. But now is not the time. "Anyway, I want to apologize for getting so upset last night. It's been . . . an emotional few days. And I don't blame either of you for inviting Guy. What he did, tried to do, wasn't anyone's fault but his."

Dad's placid, sleepy expression falters into one of anger. "I've never had a good feeling about that kid. I wish I'd done something earlier, said something to Jim. Or put more distance between our families. I never thought it'd escalate the way it did."

"You swear neither of you . . ." I trail off, let them fill in the blanks. The murderous blanks.

"No," my mom says, and shakes her head quickly.

"You haven't told anyone else in the family?" I ask, unsure if I should tell them that Leo knows about their drugged body snatching. If anything, it'll stress my parents out more, which they, admittedly, don't deserve.

Dad guffaws. "Are you kidding? Of course not. No one in this damn family knows how to keep a secret."

*Now isn't that the truth,* I think.

"And we're all on the same page about keeping it that way?"

"Sweetheart, we're not telling anyone what happened." Dad pours himself a cup of coffee but doesn't take a sip, just looks down at me at the table. "I'm not saying we're happy with this weekend or what happened, but the fact that you girls are getting along has been a very nice turn of events."

I squint at them, my weird and overly optimistic parents. Always finding the bright side in the deadliest of storms. "There was some mutually assured destruction involved, but yeah, it hasn't been completely terrible. Um. I have some news that I've been meaning to tell you. I haven't officially accepted it yet, but I got a job offer. I'm quitting Warp."

Mom stares at me across the small table, almost like she finds this *more* improbable than one of her daughters killing Guy Moran. "Are you serious? Remi, oh, what joyous news!" She throws out her arms, the sleeves of her bug sweater sliding down her wrists.

Dad pats my back so hard I almost spill my coffee all over myself. "We're so proud of you. Scoot over, Juliet, I want Remi to tell us about her new job."

And I do. I tell them about Tasha—whom they remember fondly from college, since she often tagged along with me on Thanksgiving breaks and winter holidays; she wasn't close with her family—and Soft Cat Interactive. My parents know even less about video games than Leo does, but thanks to my near decade in the industry, they understand the basics of my new job, working on UI design for a brand-new single-player adventure game. They're overjoyed when they hear I'll be moving to Seattle, closer to Eliana.

Camp awakens outside Atlas not long after we're done chatting, and Mom busies herself with making breakfast. Dad hugs me, says he's proud of me, then heads outside. Before I join them, I slip my phone out of my hoodie pocket to text Tasha. It's early but technically a workday—I took Monday off to travel home—and she'll be awake. Even though my nerves are downright riotous, I have to remind myself that Tasha offered me this job for a reason. Is it casual-friend nepotism? A thousand percent. But Tasha wouldn't offer me the job if she didn't think I was right for it.

Tasha and I lived together all throughout college, and senior year is when we met Stephanie, whom I became closer with due to sheer proximity, since Tasha had moved to the East Coast for grad school. Tasha knows that I never leave a dirty dish in the sink but will, without fail, dump my wet towels on the bathroom floor, and how I struggle to fall asleep if the TV or a podcast isn't on. She knows about Eliana and Maeve, and all the subpar dudes I hooked up with in freshman year, and the fact that I'm a ball of anxiety disguised as a functional human being.

My hands shake as I send the message.

ME: I'm in if the job offer is still on the table

The morning campground energy is buzzy. People tearing down their tents, loading their cars with dirty tarps and coolers sloshy with melted ice. And I allow myself to become slightly hopeful. I haven't seen Detective Diaz all morning, no police cruiser trawling the roads around camp, and it's easy enough to trick myself into thinking everything will be okay. Who knows how much of my DNA was on that sleeping bag, anyway. Maybe I'm . . . overreacting, as I'm wont to do.

Tonight, I'll sleep in my own bed.

Tomorrow, I'll quit my job.

And in a few short weeks, I'll be in Seattle.

Tasha said the job offer was most definitely still on the table, and she promised to send me a drafted contract by the end of the week. My apartment lease in San Jose is up at the end of September, and I might be able to find someone to sublease it, if I wanted to start right away. Which I actually want to do. For the first time ever, I'm *excited* about my job.

I haul my suitcase out of Eliana's tent, my backpack tossed over my shoulder. As I emerge, Eliana and Maeve are busy packing up the camp chairs Salli lent us. Eliana's also driving home today but is staying the night in Eugene to break up her drive over two days. Maeve doesn't fly out until tonight; our parents are dropping her off in Reno on their way out of town. We will all scatter, just like I expected, but I don't hate that there's something in my heart other than indifference toward my sisters.

After I toss my suitcase into the trunk of my car, I walk over to them. "I'm gonna say goodbye to everyone, then head out. Staying any longer feels like tempting fate."

"You better not drop off the face of the earth again." Maeve folds a chair and leans it against a tree. "Stay in touch, okay? I can come visit the both of you after my sale is finalized and everything settles down."

Eliana swipes back her hair from her forehead, smiles. "Sure, that'd be fun. And . . . obviously, we're not telling anyone about this weekend, right? I think that goes unsaid."

"Yeah, according to anyone outside of our parents, this weekend never happened," I say. "And Leo, I guess. But once we leave here, we don't tell a soul. No boyfriends or girlfriends or spouses or street performers or therapists or random subreddits. Promise?"

Maeve holds out her pinkie. "Yep. Let's pinkie promise."

"You're a thirty-four-year-old woman," Eliana says. "Seriously?"

"Seriously. C'mon, pinkies in." Maeve wiggles her little finger.

I laugh and hook mine around hers.

Eliana shakes her head at our sister but does the same. "If you hear anything about you-know-who, let me know," she says. "And I'll do the same, but hopefully what happened during this trip will stay here."

"It's been like a way less fun Vegas," Maeve says.

We agree to keep each other informed, but I'm with Eliana. Hopefully there won't be anything to inform each other of. I hug both my sisters goodbye, thanking them again, then pop over to my parents' campsite.

"Hey," I call out as I approach. "I'm heading out."

Mom and Salli are seated around my parents' smoldering campfire with mugs of coffee, and Dad and Bill are engaged in a backgammon showdown at the picnic table. When I reach them, the flurry of goodbyes commences, and the Finches have never understood the value of brevity; there's crosstalk and laughter among my family members as I try to make a hasty exit.

After Mom hugs me for way, way too long, Salli bustles over to us. She holds a lump of fabric toward me. "I made Buffy a sweater! Good thing, too, it's cold in Seattle. You really ought to look into a happy lamp, you know. Seasonal affective disorder is an epidemic."

I hold out the dog sweater, which is immaculately made. "Thanks, Salli. This is perfect." We hug, and she smacks a kiss to my cheek. She smells like medicinal ointment, and it's comforting.

"Where's Aunt Lindy?" I ask my mom as Grandma Helen wanders over from her tent trailer, which has been cranked down into a small, tidy rectangle that she can tow with Bill's SUV.

"No idea, but if she doesn't show up, I'll tell her you said goodbye," Mom promises, and I feel bad about leaving without saying goodbye to my uncles and Aunt Lindy, but I'm dillydallying enough as it is.

"Remi," Grandma Helen says warmly as she wraps her arms around me, pats my hair. "Don't worry, chickadee, there's a man out there for you. Don't give up."

"Thanks, Grandma," I say sarcastically as I step out of the hug, but the old woman doesn't pick up on my tone.

I wave goodbye to Bill, then hug my parents again. We don't say much, just hold on to one another, but it's the closest I've felt to either of them since I was a little kid. They caused a gigantic mess when they moved Guy's body, but they did it out of love. Not many people can say their parents would do that for them.

"Let us know when you get home," Mom says. "Drive safe, baby girl."

Promising that I'll drive safer than Grandma Helen on her way home from church, I walk back to my car.

"Back in you go," I tell Buffy as I open the back and attach her to the safety harness. Then I climb into the front seat and run the air-conditioning, which is pathetic and lukewarm at best, while I route myself home. My phone chimes, no doubt Tasha—she's been bombarding me with excited GIFs for the last two hours—and I preview my route. Five hours with traffic. Not the best, but anything's better than staying in Fallen Lake.

The drive back out of the campground is quick, and it's entirely possible I'm speeding. It's quiet today, most of the campers having checked out yesterday. I'm sure a bunch ended their vacations early when they heard about the fugitive drama.

My phone trills, ringing, and I glance at the screen, my phone mounted in its car holder.

Leo Calling

A clean break with Leo is probably best. I might—okay, most definitely—like him more than someone should like a one-night stand. The fact that we clicked so well last night is almost annoying. I'll be mad at myself later for this, but I also want to hear his voice. I answer the call.

"Hey, Leo," I say, and hit the speaker button on my phone. I'm nearly to the exit, the trees thinning out as the road snakes closer to my freedom.

"Did you get my text?"

"No, I'm on my way out of camp right now. Are you at the front?" My stomach pits. His voice isn't warm; he didn't even say hello. "What's wrong?"

And that's when I curve around the final bend, jerk my car to the side of the road.

Leo sighs and his breath is static. "They found a body, Remi," he says, and I stare at the park entrance, at the flashing lights. "You can't leave the park. They're locking it down."

# CHAPTER NINETEEN

*July 6 / Morning*

I rest my head against the steering wheel, unable to hear anything except the frantic, feral beat of my own heart. Am I surprised? No. But I'm mad. Mad that I was foolish enough to believe for one single moment that things might be okay. I should know better by now. In the grand scheme of my life, things rarely go my way. Guy Moran wasn't even my mess to clean up, and somehow I've ended up as the most likely suspect to go down for his murder. Did I accidentally get cursed by an old crone in a previous life? Open too many umbrellas indoors? What, exactly, did I do to deserve this?

As much as I want to blame everyone else—my parents, my sisters, Guy for being an awful trash bag of a human being—I blame myself. I *never* stand my ground, and I should have. I should've called 911 when we realized Guy was dead. Or when I found the murder weapon. I had *ample* opportunity to step up, to do the right thing, and I folded like a cheap suit at prom.

Fifty or so yards ahead, two CHP officers are placing barricades over the one exit in this entire state park. There's no way I'm driving out of here. Doomed. I am doomed.

"Thanks for the warning, Leo, but I—"

"Remi, have you been listening to me?" he interrupts. "I might have an idea. Where are you parked? Never mind, I think I see you."

I tear my gaze from the barricades as I notice Leo on the road, walking alongside the dirt shoulder toward my parked car. He's dressed in his ranger uniform, the sleeves of his button-down rolled to his elbows, and he lifts his hand in a friendly, if apathetic, wave as we make eye contact. He lopes over to my car, and I unlock the passenger side. He ducks inside and folds his long legs up to his chest as he adjusts. My car has never felt so small.

"You weren't kidding when you said you were on your way out of camp," Leo says, glancing into the back seat at my suitcase—he pauses to pet Buffy, who wiggles in excitement over seeing Leo—then turning toward me. "You didn't hear a thing I said on the phone, did you?"

"It's entirely possible I blacked out after you said the campground was locked down," I say, and focus on Leo, not the barricade and police. "Sorry, you have a plan? What plan?"

Leo drags a hand through his curls; he has shadows beneath his eyes, and I wonder how much sleep he got. But even crumpled and wrinkled, he's still beautiful. "I might be able to get you up to the body."

"What? Why didn't you lead with that?"

"I basically did," he says with an exasperated laugh. "Not my fault you stress black out."

"Sorry," I say, my heart ping-ponging around inside my chest, unsure if it should speed up or slow down. "This is a lot, and you're just trying to help. What's the plan?"

Leo hesitates, as if he's second-guessing himself, then says, "They found the body up on the Historic Fallen Lake Loop. The rain last night caused a mudslide, and he, uh, slid down the hill into the center of the trail. A hiker found him this morning and couldn't get cell service out on the trails, so they told us. We alerted Detective Diaz, who's on her way, but due to the rain, the location of the body is impossible for a car to reach. They'll have to helicopter him out. You have about an hour before this place is crawling with Sacramento police officers."

The Historic Fallen Lake Loop isn't near the Jellystone Trail, where my parents said they put Guy, and I hesitate. "Are we sure it's him?"

"White male, midthirties, wrapped up in something that appeared to be a sleeping bag," Leo says with an apologetic smile, and my brief hope that this was an entirely different body fades. "But he hasn't been officially ID'd yet."

I stare at Leo, thinking back to what Eliana said last night. How most men don't give a shit. "Why're you doing this? Why are you helping us?"

"Why do you think?"

"I'm serious."

"Because . . . you're not a bad person, Remi. *Guy* was, and you didn't kill him," Leo says, his voice all soft and earnest. "Your decision-making is definitely questionable, but it sounds like you and your sisters—your parents even—were all trying to protect each other. I wouldn't be okay with myself if y'all got in trouble, especially if there's something I could do."

I swallow, my throat tight and itchy. "Oh."

Inwardly, I kick myself. *That's* my response? The best thing I could think of? This ridiculously hot man is saving my ass, and all I came up with was a one-syllable noise. No wonder I'm single.

"Yeah," Leo says with a laugh. "And I don't usually . . . look, I meant what I said last night. I like you, even though your family is truly one of the most chaotic groups of people I've ever met."

"And you've only met, like, half of them," I say, because Leo saying he likes me hits a little different in the light of day. You know, when we're both wearing pants. But now is not the time. In fact, it's the most inconvenient time, of all time, to talk about our feelings. "I like you, too, Leo, but the body?"

"Right, sorry," he says. "They've cordoned the area off while they wait for the helicopter to come in from Sacramento. I can swing by your campsite in about ten minutes and take you there."

"And my sisters?" I ask because I'm terrified of dealing with Guy's body without them. My parents, however, need to stay back at camp. They have done enough, and if they get near Guy Moran's body again, who knows what chaos they'll unleash next.

"Sure. I'll be in a ranger's truck. It's a hike, though, so be prepared." Leo bites his bottom lip, then asks, "You're just going to get the sleeping bag? Not disrupt the scene in any other way? The report doesn't have all the details yet, so if the bag is missing, we *might* be okay, but no one can know you were up there."

"Just the sleeping bag," I promise, and, while this is *not* the time, I don't push Leo away when he kisses me. His lips are chapped, and he tastes like fresh coffee with cream, and I wonder if I'll ever find another person whose touch can calm me down as much as his.

"Ten minutes," Leo says as he slips back out of my car and hurries toward the front entrance of the park with his hands in his pockets.

I sit for a moment, my face hot, a conflicted soup of emotions inside my chest. Feelings for Leo, panic over the body, dread over telling my family that our worst-case scenario has come true . . .

I shift my car back into gear, then pull a tight U-turn and head back the way I came.

I called Eliana on my drive to tell her about the hiker who found Guy's body, the impending helicopter ride his corpse will take later this morning, and the very narrow window of time we have to get to the sleeping bag before it's too late. So, by the time I park at Campsite #34, Eliana and Maeve are waiting for me at our barren picnic bench.

In the ten minutes since I left, they've taken down the sunshade, returned the rest of the chairs to Salli. My parents watch as I get out of my car and wave, but they don't approach. Good. The last thing we need is them panicking while the rest of our family is within earshot.

Eliana told me she'd tell our parents we'd handle it.

I hope she's right.

I unlatch Buffy from her seat and set her outside. She's ecstatic to be back in the campground, stretching her leash to the maximum extension as she follows her nose into a nearby bush.

"Long time no see," Eliana says as I walk over to them, plunk myself down onto the bench.

"I knew it was too good to be true, no one finding him," I say with a sigh. "But I'm trying not to panic. Leo said ten minutes, so he should be here soon. Look for a ranger's truck."

"Are we going to talk about Leo seriously white knighting it, or no?" Maeve asks, tapping her flawlessly manicured fingers on the table. "Because this man is risking his job for you and, TBH, probably doing something illegal. This is so romantic."

I drag my palms over my cheeks, which are flushed. "We're not talking about it," I say, because oh god, Leo could lose his job over this. He loves this job. A queasy voice inside my head says that I shouldn't let him do this. But then I look at my sisters, my parents at the campsite beside us.

I don't really have a choice.

"Did you really say 'TBH' instead of 'to be honest'?" Eliana says with a frown, and Maeve waves this off with a flick of her wrist.

A forest-green truck pulls up alongside Campsite #34, and we hurry over to it, waving goodbye to our parents. I climb into the front seat with Buffy, and my sisters slide into the back. We've barely said our hellos and gotten our seat belts on before Leo speeds up the road. We lurch as the truck dips off the paved road and onto a dirt one.

"Not sure how much Remi told you," Leo says, not taking his eyes off the road, "but they found him on the Historic Fallen Lake Loop. Best I can do is drop you off by the base of the trail and keep the ranger who's guarding the entrance busy. Y'all can sneak past, then hike up. It's steep and muddy, so be careful."

"Leo," Maeve says dreamily, "do you have any brothers? Or sisters? I'm not picky."

"What?" Leo's brows scrunch together as he glances at my sister in the rearview. "No, I'm an only child. Wait, why?"

"No reason," Maeve says with a pout and crosses her arms.

I lean around into the back and say, "Really, Maeve?"

"What? I'm not flirting with *him*," she says, and I guess she's got me there.

I settle back in my seat and hug Buffy to my chest. The unpaved road we're on is narrow, an access road for rangers. Branches scrape the sides of the truck, the rolled-up windows, and the tires dip in and out of more potholes. Between the bumpiness and my anxiety, I'm nauseated.

But I can't puke. I hate puking, and I don't think I could live with myself if I puked in front of Leo. He's way too hot of a person to see me throw up; I'd never live it down. Not like I'll see Leo after this, but it would haunt me for the rest of my life. Just that memory, playing over and over again in my head, when I try to fall asleep six months from now. I try to not think about vomit or dead bodies as Leo slows around the curves; then eventually, he parks between the trees.

"Okay, this is as far as I can take you." Leo turns toward me. "I'll drop you off here; then you need to walk north for about five minutes, okay? I'm going to drive toward the cordoned area and join the ranger on duty. I'll try to keep her in conversation. If you stick to the trees and are quiet, you should be able to slip past, then follow the Historic Loop trail markers. When the trail splits, keep to the right."

"Thank you, Leo," Eliana says, and I'm shocked by the rare sincerity in my ice queen of a sister's voice. "You're saving our asses. And our parents'. We owe you."

Leo's cheeks flush slightly. "Just trying to do the right thing. And also, I never saw you three, okay? None of this ever happened."

"Understood," I say, and while I want a moment alone with Leo, to kiss him one last time, I thank him and clumsily climb out of the truck before my sisters can give us privacy. I've never been very good at goodbyes, and I shake off the regretful feeling in my stomach as we begin our hike north, through the trees.

# CHAPTER TWENTY

*July 6 / Late Morning*

The cordoned-off area is marked by an unrolled length of caution tape draped around the trees like a PTA mom's last-minute Halloween decoration in the cafeteria. Only one ranger stands guard at the Historic Loop trailhead—an older woman with gray curls in a topknot—and as promised, Leo has her chatting away. From where we're tucked between the trees, I can't hear the conversation, but the older woman is listening intently, nodding along to whatever Leo says. Despite the distraction, fear paralyzes me, first my feet, then my legs, and as my sisters creep beneath the saggy caution tape, I can't move.

"Remi," Eliana hisses beneath her breath. "C'mon!"

I force myself forward. If the ranger were to look to her left, she'd see us. Leo has her facing the other direction as they chat, but still, it causes a cold, sticky sweat to break out on the back of my neck. This isn't like the one time I broke into my math teacher's office to prank him senior year; this could have actual, serious consequences.

Gently, I tug Buffy after me, and the dog—oblivious to her situation—trots happily forward. Then she yips in excitement as a fluffy ground squirrel darts in front of her, lunging forward until her leash goes taunt.

I run to Buffy and scoop her up, now successfully on the other side of the caution tape, and glance over my shoulder. Leo and the woman are still chatting, but he has his hand on her shoulder, almost as if he's stopped her from turning around, from seeing me. The relief makes me loose limbed and clumsy, and I stumble up the trail behind my sisters with Buffy in my arms.

Only when we're up the trail and around the bend do I let her down. Puppy-paw mud prints smear my white T-shirt.

"You had to bring the dog," Eliana says beneath her breath.

Okay, it wasn't the smartest thing ever to bring Buffy, but sue me. I haven't exactly been the most logical version of myself the past twenty-four hours. No one would be, and it's irksome that Eliana can still climb onto that high horse of hers whenever the mood strikes.

"Whatever, we made it," I say, not wanting to get into a fight. Not when we've made it this far, metaphorically and physically. But I've never done well under pressure, and the magnitude of what's at stake weighs on me as we carefully hike our way up the mud-slicked trail.

Maeve, who's wearing sandals, complains every thirty seconds—yes, I'm counting—about how disgusting it is. Eliana mostly ignores her except for the occasional promise that we're almost there. And I, in all my unathletic glory, can barely keep pace with them. My calves hurt, and I regret not breaking in these boots before the trip. A blister on my heel pulses in rhythm with my heartbeat.

The Historic Fallen Lake Loop would be a steep, high-grade, and difficult climb even if it hadn't rained last night. Only Buffy seems to be enjoying herself on this hike. She's enamored with all the squirrels and birds, the bevy of smells that she—a bona fide city dog who thinks "nature" is the YouTube videos I leave on for her when I leave the house—has never smelled before.

After twenty minutes of hiking, the trail splits into two directions— one leads back down to the entrance, and the other leads higher up, to another trailhead. "Leo said to the right." I motion toward the right with my hand, wondering why the hell I didn't bring water. Or an inhaler. This is a serious wake-up call about how out of shape I am.

"They think the rain caused him to slide down?" Eliana asks as she pulls a sip from her water bottle's straw. Noticing my parched mouth-breathing, she sighs and passes it to me. Maeve picks at the sunburn on her shoulders, then taps some mud off her sandals.

I nod, sipping the water and feeling slightly better with some hydration. "That's what he said."

"Whoever dumped him, then," Eliana says as she takes back her bottle, "probably went up even higher on the trail. They had to have been in good shape."

I wipe my forehead on my shoulder. It's nearing eleven in the morning, and even if I weren't on my first-ever hike to find a dead body—thanks, I hate it—I'd be sweating. "Probably, yeah."

We keep right at the trail split, and the mudslide Leo mentioned earlier quickly becomes apparent. The trail is waterlogged and slippery. One side is a mud-slicked wall, and the other is a steep drop-off that disappears into a ravine. I've always hated heights, and my vision blurs, a bendy parallax as I peer over the edge, regretting it immediately.

"Be careful and stick to the wall," I tell both of my sisters and lift Buffy into my arms. The trail here is mostly flat but curves around the mountain up ahead. Guy must be around the bend.

Even though I want to panic-sprint to the body and rip the sleeping bag off him, I move slowly, leading our little group. My hiking boots are soaked, mud squishing between my toes as it permeates my socks, and if I don't find at least one tick somewhere on my body when this is all over, I'll be shocked.

As I curve around the bend, all the tension I didn't know I was holding in my muscles expels like an exhale—because there he is. Guy's body lies in the middle of the pathway. The mud isn't as thick here; I'm not sure if the hiker who found him moved him out of the sludgy mud, or if he just . . . slid this direction, but I lower Buffy to the ground and hurry over.

The second I step down I know that I've stepped wrong. My hiking boot slides over something smooth, like a rock, and my ankle twists to the side. My entire leg buckles, tossing me forward into the mud. "*Fuck*," I whimper, and Buffy yips little worried barks at me as I try to push myself upright. A burning, aching pain radiates from my ankle.

"I'm fine, I'm fine," I say to my sisters as they carefully rush over. Because who cares about my ankle. I landed in front of Guy's body. The bane of my existence, the ghost that's haunted me this entire trip, is finally within my grasp. We need to remove the sleeping bag and get out of here. I probably sprained my ankle but, in the grand scheme of things, whatever. It'll be worth it. It has to be worth it.

Eyes watering, I readjust onto my butt and stick my injured leg out, tucking the good one beneath me as I peer over at the lump of sleeping bag material. The fancy, expensive sleeping bag I researched online—so many hours of my life wasted, and for what?—is stained with mud and blood and damp from the rain. The pleasant lilac color is a mottled gray-brown, and it's zipped all the way around. Like whoever moved him didn't want to see his face.

Eliana walks around to the head of the sleeping bag, and Maeve crouches to my other side, wrinkling her pert nose. "This is so much grosser than I imagined," Maeve whispers, and nudges the toe of her sandal at the sleeping bag.

"Warning that it's about to get much, much grosser," Eliana says, and unbuckles her purse. She hands us each a pair of latex gloves.

I take them skeptically. "Why do you have these?"

"Kids, Remi," Eliana says, snapping hers on. "Kids are sticky. Now put these on. We're here to remove DNA, not leave any behind."

I wipe my muddy hands off on my jeans as much as possible, then put on the gloves. The sobering thought of *I can't do this* overwhelms me as I stare down at the outline of Guy Moran.

Eliana draws in a slow, deep breath and looks from me to Maeve. "Are we ready?"

Maeve's hands shake as she readjusts her gloves, an errant curl loose behind her ear and falling over her eye. "All this buildup is stressing me out. Let's get it over with."

Eliana lifts her gaze from the sleeping bag to meet mine on the opposite side. "You can do this," she says to me, and I'm unnerved how well my sister understands me in this moment. "We can *all* do this, okay?"

"Do it," I tell her, my stomach queasy.

Eliana unzips the top of the sleeping bag without fanfare, then peels back the sodden fabric from the body, and as she does, a thick, heavy smell—like rotting fish—seeps out into the fresh, mountain air. When we saw Guy on the forest floor two nights ago, he could've been sleeping or concussed. But this? *This* is a dead body. I don't know what those kids in *Stand by Me* were going on about, because there's nothing cool or exciting about this! My entire stomach heaves, and I hang my head back, squeeze my eyes shut, willing myself not to throw up.

"You okay?" Maeve asks, and I crack open one eye to look at her.

"Peachy." I breathe in through my mouth and, when I'm 90 percent positive I won't upchuck my breakfast and coffee, I look down at the body. Because that's what it is, and I'm not sure if reminding myself that this *isn't* a person is helping or hurting. Never has the yoga term *corpse pose* ever been so literal, because Guy's body is posed in a perfect Savasana, palms up at his sides. His eyes are open, vacant pools of brown, and the skin of his face is shiny under the intermittent sunlight that reaches us through the trees. But the skin around his mouth and jaw is loose, like putty.

The khakis are stained with dirt and who knows what else. The nice camel hair jacket is bunched up around his chest, his stomach bloated. His hair is matted to the skull with blood. And if I had any doubt that Guy hadn't been murdered, it fades as I stare at the wound. That didn't come from hitting his head on the firepit—not a chance. It's a divot of splintered wood.

Maeve leans forward and pulls at the collar of the jacket.

"What're you doing?" I ask.

"Checking the label." Maeve peers closer. "This jacket is *amazing*."

I snort, half delusional laughter, half disbelief. Even Eliana tries to cover up her laugh with a cough. "If I didn't know you better," I say to Maeve, "I'd wonder if you were a sociopath."

Maeve scoots back from the body. "What? I've been looking for a nice winter coat."

I literally have no response to that and refocus on the situation. "Okay, what's the plan? We slide the bag out from beneath him?"

Eliana shrugs, using her shoulder to push her hair off her face. "Yeah, but . . ."

"But what?" I force myself to look across the body, at my sister.

"Did Leo say if they identified him yet?"

I shake my head. "No, not officially. Wait. Why?"

"It's just, Guy's right here," Eliana says with an almost manic laugh. "What if we take him with us? Dispose of him properly? Then we'll for sure be in the clear. No one will ever find him!"

"You have got to be kidding me," I say flatly. "*No.* Not a chance! Everyone knows there's a body. They'll be looking for him."

"We don't know what other DNA might be on him," Eliana says, and that's when I realize my sister is desperate. She's genuinely worried that Guy's murder will somehow lead to her losing her kids, and it makes me want to scream. Because, as always, Eliana's needs eclipse ours, ever since we were young.

"That wasn't the plan," I say, almost hopelessly.

"Let's take the coat too," Maeve suggests. "Not sure about you, Rem, but that's what I grabbed when I moved him the other night."

I glance at my sister. "Is this some weird attempt to get that coat? Because it has blood on it, you know."

"Oh my god, Remi," Maeve says with an annoyed sigh. "It's not even my size. But Eli has a point! DNA evidence is, like, huge. And if we take him . . ."

"No," I repeat, a little firmer now. Because I'm thinking of Leo seated beside me in my car, putting his job on the line, me promising we'd only take the sleeping bag, leave everything else untouched. If we take the body, this won't bode well for the Fallen Lake rangers, and maybe it's sappy and pathetic of me, but I *care*. I can't do that to Leo.

Eliana's mouth twitches. "Your little ranger boyfriend will be fine."

"This isn't because of Leo," I say, almost pathetically, because nothing about my tone is convincing. But there's more to it than Leo. "Eliana, we can't do this. We didn't kill him. If we just remove the sleeping bag, there's a chance this will look like an accident, and that'll be that. Detective Diaz will get her man. They'll all move on. If we take him . . . they won't know he's dead. They will keep looking for him, and I don't know about you two, but I don't think I can live with myself if I have to move a dead body. The other night was one thing. This is bad, Eli."

"Stop being so selfish, Remi," Eliana says, and she begins to zip the sleeping bag back up. I reach out, grab her wrist, and stop her. "Seriously? You know that this is the smarter call."

I gape at my sister, the dead body of my would-be rapist off-gassing like a cheap rug between us. And I, officially, snap. "Then what, Eliana? If we take him with us, *what*? How do we get rid of him? Make sure no one finds him? What, do you want to remove his fingertips too? Get some pliers and rip out his molars while we're at it?"

Eliana's face hardens. "No, of course not. We'll figure out how to get rid of him later. We'll be smart about it. Thorough."

"Maeve," I say with a choked laugh and turn toward my other sister. "Come on. You have to agree with me here!"

"I don't know," she says, and shrugs her slender shoulders. "Eliana's right—what if there's something else on his body that leads to us? But I also don't know what we'd do with him either . . ."

I clench my molars. God forbid Maeve actually take a side for once in her life, rather than play the apathetic middleman. I let go of Eliana's hand and, instead, grab the end of the sleeping bag. Pushing to my feet makes me dizzy, almost wanting to scream due to the pain in my ankle, but I pull as hard as I can, trying to wiggle Guy Moran's body free.

Sure, I don't want to go to prison, but there are *lines*. This entire trip I've managed to hold myself together because I told myself I hadn't done anything wrong. Like Leo said earlier, we were trying to protect each other. If we take this body, if we get rid of it, we *can't* come back from that. Not when we have another solution—a good solution—right in front of us. I don't think I'll be able to live with myself if I help cut off someone's fingers or play dental student with a dead body.

"Remi, stop it." Eliana lunges to her feet and grabs the other end of the sleeping bag. And just like that, we're playing tug-of-war with a dead body in a sleeping bag. Maeve yelps and jumps out of the way, shrieking at us to calm down.

"I am calm," I snap at Maeve, and grip the end of the sleeping bag with my fists. My ankle wails in pain, but I ignore it. "Can you listen to me for once in our lives, Eli? I'm not okay with this! And sure, leaving him is a gamble, but the body is out in the elements, in the mud. The likelihood of DNA, with the sleeping bag gone, is so slim. Please, let go!"

"I can't lose my kids." Eliana's mouth quivers and she shakes her head. "And I really, really don't want to go to prison and leave them to be raised by Chad and my judgmental bitch of a mother-in-law!"

For a moment, the trees around us are silent, and I almost drop the sleeping bag in shock.

Then Maeve says, "*Whoa.*"

Eliana swipes back her hair from her cheeks with her shoulder. "What? Allison is a judgmental bitch, and I will die—literally, my soul will perish—if she or Chad are the ones who raise my kids. Or whatever second wife Chad scoops up at the gym or Tinder or wherever sad divorcé men pick up women. Whatever. We're way past worrying about the morality of this. Look at us! We're fighting over a dead body! The least we can do is make sure we all get away with this and live our lives."

"You never listen to me, Eli." Maybe it's because now that I'm putting weight on my ankle, I'm almost positive it's broken, but my eyes burn with tears. Or maybe it's because I am constantly railroaded by the women in my life, the ones who're meant to support me, lift me up. "You treat me like a kid, like someone who doesn't have two brain cells to rub together. And sure, my life is miserable and pathetic, but I'm still an adult. I still have autonomy and get to make decisions that impact the rest of my life. If we do this, the anxiety—"

"Oh my god, shut up." Eliana yanks harder on the bag, and my feet slip, sink into the mud. Tears sting my cheeks and my vision blurs, like I might pass out from the pain. "News flash, Rem: everyone has anxiety! We all deal with it, but you act like a victim, and I'm so sick of it. Like, ninety percent of your problems are *your* fault. You need to grow up."

The pain radiates up my ankle, to my knee, but I'm not sure what's worse: my probably broken ankle or my oldest sister telling me I'm a victim, that I need to grow up. All this time, I was worried that's what Eliana thought of me, and I guess it's nice to know the truth of how she feels. I will never be good enough for my sister. Never be her equal.

"Eliana, come on," Maeve says, but it's weak, a half-assed protest. As if she knows it's impossible to diffuse Eliana when she believes she has the moral high ground. "Let's take the sleeping bag and get out of here?"

I yank once more on the sleeping bag, and my ankle gives, my body careening to the side. Eliana yelps and lets go as she falls to her knees in the mud. The combination of the sudden weight and my weak ankle causes me to lose my grip, and Guy Moran's body—still inside the sleeping bag—tumbles off the trail and into the ravine.

# CHAPTER TWENTY-ONE

*July 6 / Late Morning*

The lilac human-shaped bundle tumbles down the side of the ravine, catching on branches, slamming into rocks, until it lands with finality at the bottom, in a muddy stream of water, and disappears from view. If I had to guess, the body is eighty or ninety feet below us. The walls of the ravine are slippery with mud, no handholds, nothing. Guy's body is gone, and the sleeping bag is gone with him.

My breath comes out as a strangled sob, and the pain in my ankle pulses, too hot and itchy to ignore. I hobble back from the ravine, my vision blurring with panic and pain, and lean against the muddy wall of dirt and rock. Buffy, who's watched all this with benign curiosity, whimpers at my feet. If I had the mental fortitude to put aside my pain and comfort my dog, I would, but if I bend over, I'm not entirely sure I'll be able to get back up. "I'm okay," I tell her, not believing the lie.

Eliana's muttering "No" under her breath over and over, both gloved hands woven through her blonde hair, streaking it with mud. "We have to—"

"We have to what?" I swipe my forearm across my face. "Eliana, he's gone. The sleeping bag is gone. We're done."

"This is . . . this is all your fault," she says with a crack in her voice. "All of it."

"Why? If I'd listened to you, then we'd be okay?" I ask sarcastically because, no matter the dread slowly filling my body, I'm relieved that Guy's body is in a ravine. That Eliana can't fish him back out and cart him to the nearest incinerator.

"Yeah, but we're in this entire mess in the first place because of you," Eliana says. "Why'd you have a beer with Guy? Why didn't you tell him to leave? If you had, we wouldn't be here!" Her voice is almost a whine, pathetic and cruel.

"*Eliana*," Maeve says, her voice a harsh snap. "Uncool. None of this is Remi's fault—you know that."

Eliana's mouth is tight, frozen in a snarl of disgust. Either toward herself or me, I'm not sure. I think of Grandma Helen, nearly twenty years ago, telling me Guy had a crush on me, even when I could still taste chlorine in the back of my throat. I don't know what it is with some women and their inability to admit that sometimes men make victims out of us. And it's *not our fault*.

It's not my fault.

The tears are freely flowing now, and Eliana's frozen expression melts into one of disdain. She's always hated it when I cry. Like whenever I show too much emotion, it reminds her of her own limited emotional capabilities.

"Yeah, all my fault," I say with a broken laugh, and if it weren't for my ankle, I'd walk over, get into my sister's face. "Everything I did, since we realized Guy was dead, was for *you*. Because you married a douchebag named Chad and were surprised when you finally realized what we've all known for years—that he sucked! Just because you blew up your marriage doesn't mean you get to blow up my life."

Eliana's nostrils flare, and for one hot flash of a moment, I wonder if my sister might tackle me to the ground. But she stays put, her hands fisting at her sides. "I only married Chad because I was pregnant, you asshole," she spits, and this is news to me. News to Maeve, too, by the look on her face. Not like I've ever bothered to do the math, but Eliana and Chad had kids quick. I didn't realize it was *that* quick. "I wanted an abortion, but he talked me out of it and proposed. So yeah, fuck me for trying to make the best out of an unideal situation. For trying, because I had a kid! You don't know anything about my life, Remi, so shut up!"

Silence settles around the three of us. Eliana's cheeks are flushed pink, strands of her hair sticking to her face with sweat and mud, and her eyes are glassy with tears. Maeve takes a half step toward Eliana but pauses as if she's approaching a wounded tiger and determining the statistical likelihood of getting her head bitten off.

For years, I've judged my sister for her marriage to Chad. Not only is Chad a low-key misogynist who hates that my sister works a full-time job, but I'm almost positive I saw him checking out Maeve's cleavage one Christmas. He's the type of man who is so unremarkable, so *ordinary*, that he's forced my brilliant, strong sister to dim beside him in comparison. Like his fragile ego can't take being outshone. But I'm starting to realize that my sister hates him a little bit, too, but feels like she doesn't have any options.

"Um." Maeve tilts her head up. "I'm pretty sure that's the helicopter. We need to go. Now." Then I hear it, the thwap-thwap-thwap of the propeller blades, the rustling of branches overhead.

I attempt to step forward, but I wobble on unsteady legs, the pain radiating.

"C'mon, Remi," Maeve says, and wraps her arm around my waist, letting me lean on her like a crutch. "Eliana!"

Eliana's standing at the edge of the ravine, her hands still balled up at her sides. An actual tear tracks down her muddy face. After a long, stress-inducing moment where I worry that she might stay behind, try to reach Guy, she swears beneath her breath and runs over.

Maeve supports me as I hobble on my good leg, and we continue down the trail. It's all downhill, slick with mud, but if I'm remembering this particular trail from the map correctly, it will connect with the main road near the Buckeye campgrounds. So, I grind my teeth together and bear the pain.

"I shouldn't . . ." Eliana's voice warbles, fades out, from behind me. "I shouldn't have said that, Remi."

I'm too tired and too hurt—in too many ways—to process what my sister is saying. My entire nervous system is drenched in pain and adrenaline.

"Whatever, Eli." I wince as I step down the built-in wooden steps in the mountainy trail. Because that wasn't an apology, or at least, the apology I deserve to hear. Sure, emotions were high, and we both said some not-so-nice things, but Eliana's always known how to cut to the core with me.

We escape down the trail before the helicopter spots us, but we're not out of the woods yet. *Literally.* Guy's body slid into a ravine and took the DNA-covered sleeping bag with him. But the police will be able to fish out Guy's body. A dead dude in a sleeping bag isn't going to look like an accident. They'll investigate. They'll trace my DNA or use the brand of my sleeping bag to link it to my REI order from two weeks ago. Who knows.

*I should really find a lawyer,* I think woozily.

"Can we slow down? I need some water," I say, trying to tether together all my scattered thoughts, which only drift further apart with every step I take on my messed-up ankle.

Maeve lowers me onto a nearby rock, and Eliana wordlessly hands over her water bottle. I take a moment to sip the water and breathe. Look around. The trees are thinning out. Hopefully we're nearly at the end of the trail. The paved road will be easier to weather with my ankle, but numbly I wonder if I'll be able to leave camp, due to the whole lockdown. Because I'm pretty sure my ankle is broken. I need to go to the hospital.

I've always had a high threshold for pain—almost as a defensive mechanism, after too many adults in my life telling me I was overreacting to each and every bump, every tiny discomfort—but now that my adrenaline is fading, the pain feels like a tidal swell trying to drown me.

"What're we going to do?" I fiddle with the cap on Eliana's water bottle.

Eliana—who has stayed silent since her attempted apology—says, "Can you talk to Leo? See if he's heard anything?"

If I had more energy, I'd lift my brows sassily at my sister. But all I say is, "Not a chance. I'm leaving Leo out of this. You were perfectly fine doing something that could've lost him his job earlier, so it's kind of hypocritical that you want Leo's help now."

Eliana sighs, kicks an errant pine cone with the toe of her once-white Ked sneaker, which will surely never be white again. "You want to do this now? I'm *sorry*, okay? I crossed a line!"

"You crossed, like, six lines," I say and, partially out of spite but also thirst, drink the last bit of water in her bottle, then hold the empty bottle out to her. I keep hearing what she said, over and over again like a cruel echo. My ankle throbs and there it is: *victim*. Another throb: *grow up*. Another: *your fault*.

"You don't think I've wanted to blame myself for what happened with Guy? All I do, Eli, is blame myself. I should've said no, okay? Told him to get lost. But I didn't and it's not my fault, and I fucking hate you for saying it was."

Eliana looks down at the trail, curtains of muddy hair hanging against her cheeks. "Yeah, well, I hate myself, too, for saying it. It was wrong, and for what it's worth, I'm sorry. I don't . . . actually believe that."

My sister's tone is sincere and, strangely, I believe her. I know, better than anyone else, how easy it is to say the wrong thing at the absolutely worst time. But if I'm being honest with myself, I don't forgive her. Not yet at least. It still hurts, a little too much, to let go. "Okay, well, I'm sorry, too, for saying you blew up your life. I don't know anything about your life or your marriage."

Eliana lifts one shoulder in a shrug. "I did blow it up," she admits quietly. "I wanted to damage my marriage beyond repair, so we'd have no choice but to divorce. I wanted a clear out, the chance to start over . . . Do you both really hate Chad that much?"

"*Yes*," I say honestly, and Maeve nods.

Eliana bobs her head. "Huh. In the future, if you think the man I'm going to marry is an asshole, please tell me."

Maeve snorts, then holds up her hands defensively. "Sorry, but I'm pretty sure you would've tried to bodily harm one of us if we said we didn't like Chad."

"Probably," Eliana says with a humorless laugh. "I'll try to be more open to feedback in the future."

"Any ideas on what we're supposed to do next?" I ask my sisters, and stretch out my injured leg, wincing as my heel presses into the dirt. I don't say what I'm thinking, what I'm afraid of: that there's nothing else we *can* do.

Eliana crosses her arms over her chest. Lifts her gaze the way we came, up the trail. "No. They probably have him out of the ravine by now."

Anxiety can do a lot of funny things to your body. Pump it up with adrenaline, turn your gaze hypervigilant, your hearing fine tuned—a naturally occurring danger radar. But sometimes, it drains you, leaves you empty. And as I slump on that rock and consider my lack of options, my body feels more deflated than a Mylar balloon after a kid's birthday party.

Maeve scrubs her palms over her cheeks. "I don't know, but all I do know is we need to not turn on each other. You do realize one of y'all could've fallen down that ravine? Or the helicopter could've spotted us because you two dummies were too busy fighting?"

A prickle of shame heats my face. "If I'd fallen down there, at least I would've been able to get the sleeping bag," I joke, and Maeve groans. "Sorry, I was joking. Obviously, I'd be dead."

"Maeve's right, Remi," Eliana says, and it's my turn to groan at the burgeoning high-horse tone in her voice. "We almost messed up."

"Given our lack of sleeping bag, I'd say we really did mess up," I point out. "But did either of you hear me disagreeing? For once, I wasn't the problem. Eliana was."

Eliana sniffs loudly. But she also doesn't argue. After a moment, she says, "You were also right, Remi. Taking the body was a completely unhinged idea, but you can't say any of us are thinking straight lately."

If these were different circumstances, I'd relish the fact that my sister said I was right. I genuinely cannot name another time when she's admitted this. As the oldest, Eliana's hierarchy-fueled ego has made her impervious to ever admitting someone younger than and related to her could be right. About *anything*.

I remember the desperation in Eliana's eyes, and I sigh heavily. "Chad's not going to take your kids away from you. I know you're scared, but you're a great mom, Eli. No judge would agree to giving Chad full custody, not even if you end up in some legal trouble. It's not like you murdered someone."

Eliana hiccups a laugh, smiles slightly. "That's . . . very nice of you to say, Remi. I'm not sure if I deserved that. But thank you."

"Yeah, yeah, don't get used to it," I say, emotionally discomforted by a vulnerable Eliana. "Anyway, there's not a chance this doesn't trace back to us, to our family. What if we tell Detective Diaz the whole truth before she connects the dots? It might make us look better if we tell her what we know."

"What about Mom and Dad?" Maeve lowers herself into a squat to pet Buffy.

"We leave them out of it," I say. "That's the only lie we'll tell, okay? That we have no idea what happened to the body in the morning. And . . . if you'd be willing, I don't want to tell them Leo's involved. We'll say we overheard where the body was and went off on our own. Is everyone in?"

"Yeah," Maeve says immediately.

Eliana takes a longer moment to think, then she nods. "I'm in."

# CHAPTER
# TWENTY-TWO

*July 6 / Afternoon*

Mom and Dad are waiting for us at their picnic table by the time we limp around the bend in the road, and even though I'm not responsible for my parents—their emotions, how they handle this entire situation, which *is*, technically, kind of their fault—I feel so incredibly guilty that we've come back empty handed. Because, if Eliana and I hadn't fought like children, we'd have the sleeping bag.

Guilt and shame. What a toxic combination.

Mom hurries over to meet us at the edge of camp. "What happened? Remi, baby, are you okay?"

I'm still slouched against Maeve and glance down at myself. My mud-covered clothes, my mud-covered dog, my rapidly swelling ankle. "Long story, but we didn't get the sleeping bag," I say with an undignified sniff. "And I'm pretty sure my ankle is broken."

My entire life, I've hated being the center of attention. And I'm embarrassed as my mom frets over me, my sisters helping her situate me in a chair near a rock so I can prop up my foot. I'm relieved to hear that everyone else went on a walk and that we don't have an audience. News of the lockdown spread fast, and my extended family is apparently roaming the nearby sites for gossip and information.

As my parents fret, we vaguely describe what happened. No one brings up the fight, the tug-of-war. We say Guy's body fell into the ravine when we tried to get him out of the sleeping bag. I guess we all agreed, without speaking, that it was too embarrassing to admit the truth out loud.

Dad brings me a half-melted bag of ice from the cooler, and my mom unties my hiking boot, peels back my sock.

"Oh, that's nasty." Maeve pulls a face, then backs away from the semicircle of loved ones huddled around me. But I force myself to look. My ankle has swollen to almost twice its normal thickness, the skin bruised. Ugly and unfamiliar.

"My bone isn't poking out of my skin, so that's good?"

"Definitely," Mom says with a strained, worried smile, and after she wipes the mud off my foot, Dad plops the melting bag of ice on my ankle. "We'll need to take you to the ER."

My hippie parents admitting that I need actual medical attention is astonishing. I'm surprised Mom didn't whip out a salve and wrap and try to fix it for me. Oh god. Am I dying?

"What about the lockdown?" I ask, and as if I summoned it, we hear a familiar thwap-thwap-thwap overhead. We all look to the sky in time to watch the helicopter glide above us, disappearing toward the south. I can only hope that's the last time I ever see Guy Moran, but, knowing my luck, he'll rise from the grave like a zombie or come back as a ghost and haunt my ass.

"Doubt camp will be locked down for much longer," Dad says, and his thick mustache furrows. "Well . . . What's the plan, girls?"

"We'll take care of Detective Diaz," Eliana says, and her flustered, emotional state has seemingly calmed now. Or maybe she doesn't let our parents see that side of her. "You two never saw Guy. Got it?"

Mom and Dad exchange nervous glances.

"Oh my *god*," Eliana says, "not take care of her like that! We're coming clean."

"I think it's our only option," I say. "There's no way they're going to think Guy's death was an accident, and it'll only be a matter of time until Detective Diaz realizes we're the ones who invited him here."

Mom's face falters—and I am once again reminded at how bad my parents are at crime, considering they apparently never even thought of this.

Dad tugs on the corner of his mustache. "Girls, I—"

"Dad, we'll be *fine*," I tell him earnestly, even though I don't believe it. At all. My parents clearly feel guilty enough for moving Guy's body, and I don't want them feeling any worse. But who knows if I'm thinking straight. I've barely slept since the night Guy attacked me. I'm running on coffee and adrenaline. I accepted a job offer and slept with a stranger and I like my family way more than I did seventy-two hours ago. I'm not sure if this is character growth or the first step toward a mental breakdown.

"This isn't up for negotiation," Eliana adds, almost menacingly.

My parents exchange yet another look, one that's harder to decipher.

Then Mom nods, clutching the dirty towels she used to clean my ankle to her chest. "Okay," she says simply, quietly. "Okay."

"I'm going to call the rangers' kiosk, see if we can get an ETA on when we're allowed to leave," Eliana says, then she glances at me. "Are you holding up okay?"

"I wouldn't say no to some Tylenol or ibuprofen," I say.

Mom mutters something about poison and scuttles off into Atlas. She returns a moment later with a CBD salve that smells like rotten moss that she lathers onto my skin. So now my appendage is slimy, covered in bruises, and smells. Great.

"I have Midol in my bag," Maeve says quietly and winks, then dashes to our partially torn-down campsite.

Mom and Dad ask me if I'm okay several times before I convince them I'm not dying, and they leave to use the showers. I should probably do the same, but the thought of standing makes me want to throw up. So, I stay in my chair, with Buffy in the dirt by my good, non-propped-up foot, and try to breathe. To calm myself down.

The last time I broke a bone, it was at the New Age summer camp that was supposed to heal my anxiety or whatever. Not sure what it says about my family that both times I've broken a bone can directly be correlated to my parents' poor decision-making. The ice is helping, though, and the pain is easier to ignore compared to everything else that's broken in my life. That fight with Eliana was so . . . pointless. I shouldn't have said what I said about Chad—although my sister really does have atrocious taste in men—or been such a bitch. But she also needs to realize that my opinion matters. I might be eight years younger than her, but I still *matter*.

Depending on how the next few days go, it's possible I could be arrested for Guy Moran's murder, which is the most broken thing of them all. Just when I felt like everything was aligning—Tasha's job offer, hooking up with Leo, my sisters, Seattle—my life blows up. Naturally, I'm the kind of mess who would get arrested right when I've finally gotten my life on track.

My life, the Shakespearean tragedy.

I shove my hand beneath my butt and find my phone in my back pocket. A small amount of mud is caked into the corners of my case, but the phone is unscathed. I exhale slowly and open my messages. I have several from Leo. The one he sent hours ago, warning me that they found Guy—vaguely worded, of course—and a few from the last half hour.

LEO: How'd it go? Are y'all back at camp? They're preparing to helicopter him out now.

LEO: Okay, I'm not sure if I should be worried about you, or if this is you letting me down gently

LEO: If this *is* you letting me down gently, don't reply and I'll stop bothering you. Otherwise, pls let me know if you're okay

A small smile cracks my face.

ME: We're okay. Well, okay-ish. I think I broke my ankle?

And because I'm weird, don't know how to talk to men, and delirious from the pain, I snap a photo of my ankle and text it to him. *Sexy.*

LEO: Yikes

LEO: Lockdown is lifting soon, do you want a ride to the hospital? Because you definitely need to go to the ER. There's one nearby

ME: I'll let you know. Thanks, for today

LEO: Did you get what you needed?

ME: Nope 😶

I watch as Leo types a reply, then stops—the ellipses that show he's writing a response pause, then dance back to life.

LEO: What now?

ME: I wish I knew. Nothing good probably. Maybe whatever jail or prison I end up at will have conjugal visits if you're into that kind of thing

ME: Hahaha sorry, I think the ankle pain is getting to me. Please ignore me

I groan and lock my phone.

"Hurts that bad, huh?" Maeve returns and dispenses two Midol into my hand, then passes me a canned iced coffee.

I crack the top and toss the pills back. "Yes, but that groan was because I don't know how to talk to Leo. I'm making conjugal visit jokes, Maeve! Take my phone away from me." I shove it at her, but she doesn't take it. The phone flops awkwardly back onto my lap.

"Remi, be yourself," she says with an annoyed sigh. "You have a weird sense of humor, so own it. If Leo doesn't find that funny, then it's on him."

My phone buzzes and I peek at the reply.

LEO: How'd you know? Caged Heat is my favorite movie

I snort, and Maeve smiles smugly, sitting on the rock beside my busted ankle.

"See?" My sister raises both of her brows and crosses her leg over her knee.

I roll my eyes at her and reply.

ME: How convenient for us

LEO: Are you still leaving today?

"There's no way for me to drive myself home," I realize with a groan. "Which is an optimistic worry, considering we probably won't get to leave Fallen Lake because we're going to be arrested."

"How about this," Maeve says. "*If* we're let go, I'll drive you back to San Jose, then fly from there to LA."

"Really? You'd do that?"

"Remi, it's only a five-hour drive." She has her phone out now, no doubt canceling tonight's flight out of Reno. Either way, she won't be on it. "Your ankle is broken."

"Thanks," I tell her. Then I text Leo back.

ME: Probably not. Whenever we can leave—if we can leave—Maeve is driving me back home. Don't think I'll be behind the wheel for awhile

LEO: Is it too much to ask you to keep me posted?

ME: Oh I'm sure you'll hear about it in the news

LEO: You're funny

ME: I'll let you know how our talk with Diaz goes. And don't worry, we never saw you today

Leo Tapbacks my response with a heart, and I lock my phone before setting it on my lap.

"So, are we calling Detective Diaz or what?" I ask Maeve as Eliana returns to my area of convalescence, phone in hand. "You still have that flyer, right, Eliana?"

Eliana chews on her bottom lip. "Yeah, we probably should. According to the front, the lockdown will lift within the hour. Think you can hang in there until then?"

"My ankle is broken, I'm not bleeding out," I say, still uncomfortable with this much attention on me. Seriously, it's the worst. I don't understand people who like this much attention. Like Maeve. She'd *bask* in the injury spotlight if our roles were reversed.

Eliana plops down into a nearby camp chair, then unzips her purse. She removes a folded square of paper and takes her time unfolding it, smoothing out the flyer on her thigh. She stares at it for a moment, then lifts her gaze to us.

"We're sure about this?" she asks.

"Yeah." I focus on the pain in my ankle now, to distract me from the panic of this decision. Because I'm not sure. I also don't have any other ideas, any other plan of action. I'm wrung dry, emotionally and physically. We *lost*. But now it's up to us to decide how much we're going to lose.

"Do it," Maeve says, propping her chin in her hand.

Eliana sucks her teeth, then nods, almost to herself, and she dials the number on the bottom of the flyer.

The line only rings twice.

"Detective Diaz," the woman's voice says, authoritative yet warm—such a hard line to walk.

Eliana clears her throat, then says, "Yes, Detective Diaz, this is Eliana Finch-Campbell? You spoke to us at Fallen Lake State Park. We were hoping to talk to you about Guy Moran. Can we come in?"

"No need," Detective Diaz says. "I'm doing the rounds in the campground right now, talking to those still in the area before the lockdown lifts. I'll be over at your campsite shortly if you don't mind waiting for me."

Eliana says that we will, then hangs up.

The three of us look at one another.

Me, with my busted ankle, sprawled out in a camping chair.

Eliana has mud in her hair, eyes bloodshot from her once-a-year cry.

Maeve's normally unaffected exterior cracking as she jiggles her foot, twists one of her rings around her fingers.

Throughout this trip, we've come together and torn ourselves apart, more than once, and I'm not sure where this puts us, how we'll move forward. Or if we'll even have the chance to try again.

# CHAPTER TWENTY-THREE

*July 6 / Afternoon*

"Do you think this is how old-timey criminals felt while awaiting their executioner?" I ask, wondering if I've missed the slim window of time where I might pass out from my ankle pain. Wouldn't hate being unconscious right about now. Because, as resolved as I am that coming clean is the right choice, that doesn't mean I'm not dreading our confession.

Eliana laughs at this, but it's forced. Like she knows she should laugh but would rather gouge out one of her own eyes than enjoy herself in this moment.

Only three minutes have passed since we called Diaz, but I hope we won't need to wait much longer. Our extended family is still on their hike, and I'd rather not have an audience for what's about to happen. But it doesn't matter. Everyone is bound to find out what happened to Guy Moran sooner rather than later. Will Detective Diaz handcuff us? Arrest us? Take us downtown—or whatever the Podunk equivalent of "downtown" is for a town like Fallen Lake?

Five minutes pass, and we don't talk.

I further destroy my nails and cuticles, swatting Maeve away when she tries to stop me.

A burst of laughter reaches our dramatic huddle, and I glance over my shoulder, then groan. Grandma Helen, Bill, Salli, and Aunt Lindy have returned. Aunt Lindy walks toward the showers, passing our parents on their way back, and Salli disappears into her tent. Grandma Helen and Bill don't seem surprised to see me here—guess they realized the lockdown, well, locked everything down before I could leave—but as they pepper me with questions about my injury, I try to explain my "hiking accident" before Detective Diaz shows up. But the sleek Sacramento police cruiser pulls around the horseshoe bend and parks alongside the front of our parents' campsite before I can get rid of Grandma Helen and Bill.

Grandma Helen—who doesn't share my parents' disdain for law enforcement—checks her reflection in her silver compact before fluffing her gray curls, as if trying to appear as put together as possible. Bill eases himself down onto the picnic bench, the lower half of his back strapped into a padded brace.

Mom and Dad huddle beside Atlas, their arms crossed as they watch Diaz climb out of her cruiser. She looks identical to yesterday— same hairstyle, same neat uniform, same gun on her belt that could totally kill me. The only difference I can clock is the exhaustion on her face, the mud on her boots. The same mud I have on my own boots, my clothing; the same mud that's in Eliana's hair. If Diaz has any doubt about the story we plan to tell her, we're literally covered in evidence and didn't bother cleaning it up.

"Afternoon," Detective Diaz calls cheerfully as she walks over to us, sliding her sunglasses from her face. Her gaze narrows as she notices my propped-up foot, which I can proudly claim has *officially* swollen to twice its original size. She opens her mouth for a moment, then closes it, and turns her attention toward Eliana. "You're the one who called?"

Eliana sits up straighter, dusting mud that's dried into dirt off her pants. "I am, yeah. We were hoping to talk with you about Guy Moran."

Grandma Helen lifts her thin brows imperceptibly at this, and I can't imagine how lost my extended family is. Last Grandma Helen and

Bill heard about Guy was our first night, when everyone merrily shit all over him and celebrated his absence.

Detective Diaz stops in front of us, hooks her thumbs through her belt. "That's actually why I've been doing my rounds," she says. "We've had a development, and I wanted to follow up with the guests I spoke with yesterday, to provide answers and ease any concerns. On behalf of the Sacramento Police Department, I apologize for any inconvenience this unfortunate situation has caused and any disruption to your vacation."

Eliana blinks, a quick fluttering of eyelashes. "Not a problem at all," she says smoothly, and I want to shriek that there is a huge, *huge* problem. And I'm dying inside the longer my sister procrastinates. "What's the development?"

"I'm sorry, Detective," I say because I have no interest in the details, in drawing this out any longer than necessary. If Detective Diaz is my executioner, then drop the axe already. "We have something we need to tell you. That's why we called. Um. You see, we haven't been—"

"I'm sorry, miss," Detective Diaz interrupts, "but I have several more stops to make. I wanted to inform you that Guy Moran has been found. The lockdown will lift shortly."

"That's it?" Maeve blurts out, and Eliana swiftly, covertly, kicks her in the shin. And while the rock where I've propped my foot blocks the attack from Detective Diaz's sight, she's glancing between us now. Looking closer at us. The mud. My obviously broken ankle. Our shady energy, as Leo identified last night.

Detective Diaz readjusts the walkie-talkie on her belt, smiles politely. "As I was saying, we found the fugitive's body on a trail in the northern end of the campground. From what we can surmise, he fell while hiking, no doubt trying to escape on foot after dumping his car."

I can say, with utmost certainty, that the Finch family has never been stunned into silence before. But here we are, not a word between the seven of us. The ever-throbbing pain in my ankle fades into the static of my mind as I repeat what Diaz said. They think Guy *fell*. Did the sleeping bag rip off his body on the way down the ravine? Even if it did, the initial reports were that he was found on the trail. Not in a ravine. Is Detective Diaz a truly awful cop, or is something else going on here?

"He fell?" I'm the first to speak, and I ignore the bug-eyed look of warning from Eliana.

Detective Diaz nods, her eyes locked onto mine. "Yes," she says with a tight, professional smile. "He fell."

"But—" My words die on my lips because Diaz interrupts me.

"Ms. Finch, trust me when I say that he fell. The rangers reported that the trail was most likely fragile due to the rain. Erosion and whatnot," Detective Diaz says; then she shifts a half step closer to us and adds, "A fall like that, it did some nasty damage, but I can't say I'm sorry. Guy Moran wasn't a good man. The hit-and-run? He left a teenager dead on the side of the road. Like she was *trash*. Don't quote me on this, but he deserved worse than he got. An accident like that is far too fast for someone like him."

"Oh dear." Mom presses her fingertips to her lips.

Detective Diaz nods, then checks her watch. "I wish we could've caught him, put him behind bars, and given the family more closure," she says, mouth ticking in a frown. "But it's better than Moran escaping, I suppose. Do you folks have any questions for me?"

My confession hangs on the tip of my tongue, the anxiety of a kept secret pressurizing my chest. As a kid, I could never keep a secret or lie for very long. Maybe it was due to anxiety, I don't know, but I'd always blurt out the truth sooner rather than later. Like the act of being deceitful to another person undoes me from the inside out. In hindsight, this is probably why my sisters never told me anything.

Right now, this is my chance. My chance to do the right thing and come clean. Because what happens if I don't? Will I always be haunted by what happened to Guy? Or will I be able to move on, convinced that he got what he deserved? My palms are slick with sweat and my stomach roils, part Guy Moran guilt and part nausea over my ankle. But then my gaze darts over to Eliana's face, which is slack with relief. Maeve's no longer spinning her ring around her finger—a red mark mars her skin from the repetition. Even my parents, who never let their guard down while in the vicinity of law enforcement, seem looser, calmer.

I swallow, my throat dry and full of knives. "Nope."

"Again, apologies for the inconvenience," Detective Diaz says, "and thank you all, so much, for your cooperation." And with that, she returns to her car and drives away.

Eliana and Maeve both look at me, and I widen my eyes. "What just happened?"

Eliana picks at the mud in her hair. "I think . . ." She twists her lips to one side. "Do we think Diaz is looking the other way? There's no chance that looked like an accident."

"Who cares," Maeve says and shimmies her shoulders, as if flicking off the anxiety like a dog after a walk in the rain. "It's over. It doesn't matter. It doesn't matter who moved Guy. Or who even killed him. It's *over*."

A smacking noise draws my attention from my sisters to my parents' picnic table. Grandma Helen is smacking Bill in the arm with her fanny pack, and I hear the end of her fervent, whispered sentence: ". . . him farther away from camp! What were you thinking?"

"Um." I try to sit upright, having forgotten about my busted ankle, then hiss in pain as I swing my foot onto the ground. "Grandma?"

Grandma Helen turns around, smiles sweetly. "Yes, chickadee?"

"What did you just say to Bill?"

Bill looks at his hands, picking at his nails. He's still slouched at the picnic table, the strap of his back brace unsticking from its Velcro, and something clicks into place inside my mind.

"Bill didn't throw his back out having sex," I say, my mouth dropping open. Bill told the truth yesterday. They didn't go to bed until one in the morning. But not for the reasons we thought.

Eliana turns to look at our grandmother, her eyes slitted into an assessing gaze. "You actually never said that's what happened. Maeve assumed. Grandma, what did you do?"

Grandma Helen reattaches her fanny pack around her waist. "Nothing."

"Ma," Dad says, the word a question as he stares at his mother, "don't lie to my girls. What happened? What did you just say to Bill?"

"Oh, fine," she says with a flustered raspberrying of her lips, and Bill meekly voices his protest, but she waves her hand at him. "I couldn't let this family go to jail because of Guy Moran! Sue me."

"Hold on," Eliana says. "Start over from the beginning. *You* killed Guy?"

Grandma Helen's face pales. "Goodness no! Although I can't say I blame whoever did. That boy was a menace. We properly hid the body after your parents dumped it in the middle of a goddamn hiking trail." She turns to glance at Bill. "Or, at least, I thought we properly hid the body."

Bill holds his hands up in innocence now. "I drove to the farthest trail that had car access," he says by way of explanation, and I recall what Leo said. That the Historic Loop trail was only inaccessible due to the rains, the mud. The person who disposed of Guy had barely carried him anywhere. They put him in a car, drove him into the hills, and dumped him. "Like I told you, Helen, I concealed the . . . er, body. I did a great job," he adds defensively.

"The rain," I say to no one in particular, my mind slow like I'm five steps behind everyone else. "The rain caused a mudslide. He must've, um, come loose during that."

"See? That hiding spot should've been flawless," Bill says.

"It should have been *waterproof*," Grandma Helen says with enough sarcastic wit that I finally believe that we may be related after all. "Besides, it doesn't matter! Can someone fully explain to me what happened? Because until this moment, I thought you two killed Guy." She gestures at her son and daughter-in-law.

"I need a flowchart to follow this," Maeve says, massaging her temples. "Grandma, Guy attacked Remi, and we got into a fight. He fell, but he was fine and ran off. When we found him, though, he was dead. Mom and Dad moved the body from the tent because they thought *we* killed him. But Grandma, you and Bill moved the body from the trail our parents dumped him on, because you thought *they* killed him?"

I snort. "It's like a true crime version of telephone."

"I'm not proud of what we did," Grandma Helen says, her cheeks flush, "but family sticks together! And I've always hated the Morans, Ernest. I've told you for years . . . that's beside the point! I thought you were in danger, and I did what any good mother would do: I took care of it."

"Technically," Bill says, "I took care of it."

"Did you?" Grandma Helen sasses, lifting a brow.

"Ma, did you really ask Bill to move the body?" Dad asks, his arms hanging limp at his sides.

Grandma Helen sniffs. "What? I did what I had to do."

"No offense, Dad," Maeve says, "but you're in no position to be upset at Grandma for what she did, considering you did the exact same thing to us."

Dad deflates a little, his shoulders rolling forward. "You're right."

"Maybe," I say, "Guy really did fall. That stick with the blood on it . . . he could've just bled onto it. We assumed that it was a weapon . . ." My words trail off as I frown. Does that mean we were partially responsible for Guy's death?

Does it matter, at all, beyond the anxious and bruised remains of my conscience?

"We all have assumed a lot of things." Eliana stands up, massaging the space between her brows. "But I think we can agree that all the cards are on the table now, yes? Something tells me Detective Diaz saw the discrepancies but looked the other way. Either due to her dislike of him, or maybe she wanted to wrap up her case."

"The American judicial system is deeply flawed," Mom says with a mournful shake of her head.

Eliana ignores this. "That, or something happened after the body fell down the ravine. The sleeping bag could've ripped off his body; maybe the water carried it away. We don't know. We probably will never know, but this is a free pass that, frankly, none of us deserve. You all seriously messed up on this trip."

"Careful on that high horse," I murmur to my sister.

"Myself included," Eliana adds with an annoyed wave of her hand. "But somehow, it's all . . . okay."

While that's a rather optimistic way of looking at the situation, I kind of agree with Eliana. This shouldn't have worked out. I mean, I was ready to spill it all, primed to confess when Diaz arrived, but she didn't want to hear it. And maybe, deep down, I didn't want to say a thing, too worried that the end of Guy's life might lead to the end of my own. To the consequences I don't believe I deserve to suffer.

I'm relieved and guilty and exhausted and the pain in my ankle is, somehow, getting worse, despite the Midol. Given that Maeve was my supplier, there's a solid fifty-fifty chance it expired four years ago and has been riding around in the bottom of her purse with a ball of lint ever since, so I shouldn't be too surprised.

Grandma Helen readjusts her tidy outfit, a hiking getup of a zippered fleece and leggings. "While I apologize for thinking you'd be capable of murder," she says to my parents, "I'm not sorry for intervening. The two of you dumped him out in the open." Then she turns to us, sighs. "And girls, I'm sorry for not speaking up about the Morans sooner. I've never liked their family, but your grandfather . . . well, he never listened. He insisted they were good people, but I should've listened to my gut."

My paternal grandfather passed away when I was ten. Despite spending the summers in Humboldt County, I rarely knew him. He was distant, often outside doing various yard work projects, avoiding us kids when we descended on the house like a summertime hurricane.

But from the stories my father told—infrequent as they were—I got the vibe that he wasn't a very nice man. A rare flare of sympathy for my grandmother heats my chest. I've spent nearly two decades upset over how she responded after Guy's little drowning joke, but sometimes you tell a lie to convince not only others but yourself.

"This isn't your fault, Grandma." I shift in my chair as I carefully lower my leg from the rock. As the blood rushes back into my limb, the painful pounding intensifies. "As great as this family-bonding moment is, I think I need to go to the hospital now?"

# CHAPTER TWENTY-FOUR

*July 6 / Afternoon*

When Eliana drove out of Fallen Lake State Park, I half expected Detective Diaz to jump out from behind a tree and say the entire thing was a joke, then read us our Miranda rights. But we were let out of the park without incident, the barricades unceremoniously dragged to the side of the road. A few official-looking vehicles were still in the parking lot, but the mood was subdued, the energy calmer. I didn't see Leo anywhere, and I pretended not to be disappointed.

The adrenaline that has kept me upright the past few hours has all but dwindled, and I watch numbly from an uncomfortable waiting room chair as Eliana berates a poor nurse, asking when I'll be seen. We've only been here for ten minutes, and I just finished filling out my paperwork. That poor woman.

Maeve's seated beside me, flicking through a three-year-old copy of *People* magazine.

Both of my sisters cleaned up before taking me to the hospital, and our parents promised to pack up anything Eliana left behind at our campground. Then they're meeting up with us later for a proper goodbye and to bring me Buffy, since dogs are apparently not allowed in human ERs.

We already said goodbye to Salli, Grandma Helen, and Bill before leaving for the hospital. And while I'm still not that fond of my judgmental, vaguely misogynistic grandmother, my heart has softened toward her. Maeve kept her promise and will drive me home to San Jose, but along with Eliana, we're staying the night at a local hotel. Who knows when I'll actually get out of the ER, and we're all exhausted.

"The nurse said you're next," Eliana announces as she returns, lowering herself into a chair on the other side of me. "They'll take you in for an x-ray, then you'll see a doctor. I looked up the Yelp reviews for this place, and it's surprisingly good, given the location."

Maeve tosses the magazine onto the coffee table and yawns, stretching her arms overhead. A pervy-looking dude across the waiting room with a bleeding hand wrapped in a T-shirt stares at my sister's breasts. ER waiting rooms have to be a special kind of hell.

"Are we going to talk about it?" I ask, mostly because I don't want to focus on the pain in my ankle or the pervy dude leering at us. "I can't believe Grandma Helen and Bill . . ."

Eliana crosses one leg over the other. "Me either, but it makes sense, I guess. They were acting so suspicious yesterday when Maeve questioned them. But someone moving the body—*again*—never made any sense. Unless they cared about whoever dumped it originally. Otherwise, why bother?"

Even though it's been over a half hour since Grandma Helen outed herself and Bill, it doesn't feel *real*. But Eliana has a point. Whoever moved that body didn't want it found, which meant they cared deeply about who'd dumped it. We should've thought of that, as it narrowed the pool of suspects considerably. "Do you think I was right? That he fell or he was more injured than we thought?"

"I don't know," Eliana says, lips thinning as she presses them together. "I don't want to think about it. It doesn't matter anymore."

"I'm with Eli on this one," Maeve says, her voice low to match our whispers. "What's that saying? 'Don't look a gift horse in the mouth'? Don't do it, Remi. This was a freebie."

I grunt and lean back in my chair, shut my eyes. I wish I could let it go that easily, but I never have liked unfinished business, loose ends. They're the fuel and fire for anxious thoughts. Why should I care if I accidentally contributed to Guy Moran's death? It's not like he gave that teenager anywhere near the same amount of empathy or guilt when he drove his car from the scene of the crime. Still, it'd be nice to have a clear-cut answer, but I need to embrace the unknown, something my therapist has been encouraging me to do for years.

Guess I might as well start now.

"Since everything is calming down," Eliana says, her tone softer, more deferential, and I open my eyes, glancing over at her, "I really want to apologize for what I said earlier."

Eliana has gone from barely ever apologizing to me in our entire lives to apologizing multiple times for what she said back on the trail, and I'm not sure how to handle her sincerity.

"I appreciate the apologies," I tell her, "but you can stop, Eli. It's okay. Emotions were running high, and I'm not holding it against you. Besides, I'm sorry too. I have no idea what's going on in your life—because I've never asked. Not like it's an excuse for what I said, but sometimes I get so fed up with you treating me like the kid who accidentally killed your Tamagotchi."

"You killed three of my Tamagotchis," Eliana says automatically, and even though it's been over twenty years, I shouldn't be surprised that she's held on to this piece of information.

Ignoring her revisionist history—I only killed *two* Tamagotchis—I say, "You weren't completely wrong, though. I have allowed my anxiety to hold me back, and it's something I'm going to work on. But if you ask me, we're even. No more apologies, okay?"

Eliana nods, brushes some invisible dust off her clean pair of jeans. "Thank you. Earlier wasn't my finest moment."

"This entire weekend wasn't our finest moment," Maeve mutters and picks up the old *People* magazine again, sniffing a dried-out perfume sample.

"Remi Finch?" The same exhausted nurse from the front desk pushes a wheelchair over toward us, avoiding Eliana's existence beside me.

I raise my hand like a kid in the fourth grade, then allow the nurse to help me into the chair. "Thanks," I tell the nurse and add beneath my breath, "Sorry about my sister. Please don't do the nurse equivalent of a waiter spitting in my food?"

The nurse laughs lightly, and she smiles, some of the exhaustion fading. "Oh, I've dealt with far worse," she says as she wheels me down the hall for my first-ever x-ray, and I wave goodbye to my sisters. "C'mon, honey, let's get that ankle looked at."

Not only did I break my ankle, but I dislocated it too.

Earlier, the ER doctor—who was, to my fifteen-plus years of *Grey's Anatomy*–watching disappointment, not super hot—assured me it was a simple dislocation and fracture and that I shouldn't succumb to compartment syndrome. Now I'm alone, staring at the white ER privacy curtains while my cast dries, my phone limp in my hand. My sisters left for the cafeteria in search of snacks and to call our parents.

After suffering through an x-ray *and* a CT scan—not to mention the not-hot doctor poking and prodding my ankle, which felt like being stabbed with a knife—I'm even more exhausted than I was earlier today. My brain is numb, trying to rationalize this entire trip. Put it into tiny, organized boxes inside my head that, above all else, will make sense. But there are too many unknowns for this trip to make any kind of logical sense, and I should be happy that I'll be leaving Fallen Lake tomorrow with only a messed-up ankle. It could've been so much worse.

I unlock my phone and pull open my email. I was serious when I told Leo that I had my resignation letter drafted inside my head. And maybe it's because of the painkillers and the haze that's getting progressively harder to ward off, but I decide now's as good a time as any. Probably because I'm scared that once I leave and return home, the comfort of my humdrum existence will lure me back into the safer choices. That I'll chicken out, which I *can't* let myself do. Not after surviving a weekend like this one.

Should I resign from my job while high on painkillers? Probably not. But it's happening. I tap away at my phone, and I make the resignation short but sweet. For the most part, I do like my coworkers, and if I had to guess, they'll be happy that I'm moving on to somewhere where I'll be able to do more of what I love. Or, at the bare minimum, not suffer on a daily basis.

I reread the message once for typos—or drug-fueled streams of consciousness, of which there are two—then hit send. The email whooshes off, then silence fills my room. Well, the curtained-cubicle area of the ER. It's a Monday afternoon in a tiny tourist town, and the ER is quiet. A machine beeps in the cubicle next to me. Someone pages a doctor over the PA system. Two nurses laugh in delight over something that sounds gossipy and delicious but is meaningless without context.

Even though I've accepted Tasha's job, quitting is a big deal. I've never quit my job before. I don't think I've ever quit anything before. I'm a "suffer in silence until it's over" kind of person. At least, I used to be. I don't want to be like that anymore.

Life is far too short to be spent miserable.

I stare at my phone, chew on my chapped bottom lip. I haven't told Leo what happened with Diaz yet. Honestly, filling him in slipped my mind after the whole Grandma Helen reveal. Then I was carted to a hospital and prodded at for two hours. But I don't have any more excuses now—because that's what they are, excuses for a coward like me—and I open up our message thread, considering what to say.

After enough years of therapy, I know the importance of patterns. That's what therapy is often about, anyway. Identifying our patterns and trying to break them. In a lot of ways, I've broken some patterns with my family during this vacation. And I quit my soul-sucking job. The amount of personal growth correlated with the accidental death of Guy

Moran this weekend *is* a little disturbing, but hey, I can't change my circumstances. And as loath as I am to admit it, I have a pattern with men.

Not a good pattern. Obviously.

I'm almost thirty. If I don't figure this out now, then when?

Leo has been wildly outside my normal, well, *everything*. And even though I'll be moving even farther away in a matter of weeks—I cringe mentally at the logistics of moving states with a broken ankle, which has to belong to a new, more stressful life-stressor category, and the last thing I should want is to maintain some kind of long-distance . . . communication with Leo—I feel panicky and sad at the thought of never speaking to him again.

My old pattern would be to delete Leo's number and pretend he never existed, then continue to shut myself off from meaningful connection until I die alone. Because I actually *like* Leo, and I don't let myself like people very often. Actually, the more I think about it, the more ridiculous it seems that my first attempt at having a one-night stand ended up like this. Not only with my feelings for Leo but with Leo getting himself involved in the chaos of the Finch family and a dead body. I wanted something physical and distracting and surface level, and now Leo knows my deepest, darkest secrets.

Sounds about right, honestly.

ME: Sorry to crush your Caged Heat dreams but things have taken an unexpected turn

ME: Also sorry if I'm a little loopy, I'm on painkillers for my ankle

A reply buzzes not long after I lock my phone.

LEO: Diaz just left after debriefing all of us. Sounds like a freak accident

ME: Mmhmm. Very freaky. Very accidenty.

LEO: Any chance I can see you before you leave?

ME: I'm staying at the Antler Inn tonight if you wanna come by

ME: I am NOT propositioning you. I'm sharing a hotel room with my sisters. That'd be weird

ME: Also I have a cast now. It's not very sexy

I send him a photo of my cast. Because, even drugged, I don't know what I'm doing when I talk to Leo. You'd think texting would add a layer of filter, of thinking before I speak, but it's like the opposite. The drugs aren't helping.

LEO: Get your mind out of the gutter

LEO: I want to say goodbye since you ran off earlier

ME: Oh okay

ME: I wouldn't hate that

LEO: See you tonight then

# CHAPTER TWENTY-FIVE

*July 6 / Early Evening*

After a long weekend in Fallen Lake State Park, the Antler Inn might as well be a Four Seasons resort.

Two queen-size beds flank a bedside table that looks like a kid's enlarged Lincoln Log creation, topped with a lamp that has antlers inexplicably sprouting out from either side of the shade. The art on the walls is exclusively paintings of deer nibbling grass or fish with multicolored scales. Not my aesthetic, but even I have to appreciate the commitment to their brand.

Eliana and Maeve deposit me on the bed closest to the door, and I toss my backpack onto the ground before flopping back, staring at the wood-beamed ceiling.

"Even the little soaps are antlers," Maeve calls from inside the bathroom.

Eliana sets her suitcase on the luggage rack by the window and peers out at the lake. "Mom and Dad should be here soon to say goodbye."

"Where'd they say they were headed next?" As transient seniors, my parents never stay in one place long. Given the events that happened here this weekend, it's smart that they're fleeing to parts unknown.

"Arizona, I think." Eliana sits down on the other queen bed and removes her phone from her back pocket. She taps aggressively at the screen. "Sorry, one sec. Chad's throwing a fit that he has to watch the kids another night."

"Isn't that what he wanted?" I turn my head on the comforter to look at my sister.

Eliana's mouth twitches into an evil grin. "Yeah, I'm pretty sure he's gonna back off the whole custody situation once I get home." She finishes her text message, then tosses her phone onto the bed. "Guess this weekend wasn't all bad."

"It had more upsides than I anticipated." I drum my fingers on my stomach, then add, "Leo's going to come by later, to say goodbye."

Maeve flicks off the light in the bathroom and walks into the main room. "Ooh, should Eliana and I make ourselves scarce?"

"What," I say flatly, and gesture to my collapsed body, the cast-covered foot awkwardly sticking off the edge of the bed, "about this image makes you think I want to have sex tonight?"

Maeve sniffs. "I'm trying to be considerate."

"Gee, thanks."

Maeve walks around my bed, then pauses to grab something off the floor. "Is it just me, or did we *all* completely forget about Guy's phone?" She holds up the fancy iPhone, which must've fallen out of my bag.

"Not just you," I say, then push myself upright. Finding Guy's phone feels like a discovery from weeks ago—not yesterday. "We should probably get rid of it."

Eliana tucks one leg beneath her on the bed. "Definitely."

"We can dump it on the road tomorrow?" Maeve sets it—along with my bag—on the dresser beside the TV. "Like at a gas station or rest stop?"

"Sure," I say, because I don't have any other bright ideas on how to dump a phone, but the conversation is cut short by a quick burst of knocks on our door.

Maeve lets our parents inside, and I use my crutches to push myself upright and onto two feet. Well, on one and a half feet, I guess. "I'm fine, I'm fine," I insist as they fret over my cast, my crutches, the hospital bracelet I forgot to cut off earlier. My parents, the overreactors. Buffy barrels into the room after them and proceeds to sniff each and every foreign surface.

Mom cups her hands over my shoulders, looks me in the eye. "I love you, Remi, and I'm so sorry about this weekend. We only tried to help, but we made it so much worse."

"We could blame each other until the end of time," I tell my mom, "but none of this would've happened if it weren't for Guy. He's to blame, not you and Dad. Or any of us, for that matter."

Mom's mouth softens in the corners as she smiles. "Thank you, sweetheart. But I think your father and I have learned our lesson."

"Not to interfere with our lives?"

"Not to do drugs in state parks," Mom says, patting my shoulder before releasing me from her grasp.

Dad wraps me in a bear hug, asks me to keep in touch over the next month as I make my move. I promise to do just that, and while I won't miss this trip, I might miss my parents. They shuffle back into the hallway, and we collapse onto the beds.

Buffy, having investigated the entire room and my cast, hops up onto an armchair by the window. The hotel is pet friendly, with a deposit, and I'm pretty sure the concierge said no pets on the furniture, but I'm too tired to care.

"Room service?" Maeve holds up a slender menu that had been tucked in the drawer of the bedside table.

All I've eaten in the last few hours is a vending machine candy bar because the prescription bottle of painkillers the hospital gave me said to take them with food, and my stomach rumbles.

"I could eat," Eliana says, and leans over Maeve's shoulder to peruse the menu. "Good god, there's a lot of venison on this menu."

"Where'd you think they got all the antlers?" I ask darkly, and Maeve throws a pillow at my head.

Once our orders are placed, I scratch the itch that's been bothering me ever since Detective Diaz gave us that wanted flyer. I google the hit-and-run, and several articles from the *Sacramento Bee* pop up. Eliana and Maeve sit on my bed, and together we read what exactly Guy Moran did. Morbid curiosity, or an attempt to make ourselves feel the tiniest bit better? Who knows. But I don't feel any worse about Guy's death as I read what happened on the night of July 3rd.

A white Ford F-450 hit an unnamed teenager near Rick's Dessert Diner. The victim was crossing the street to get into her mother's car, who was picking her up, and the truck blew through a red light, hit the girl. The driver didn't stop. Not the smartest thing, because the red-light camera caught the driver in the act. The newest article names Guy Moran as the driver of the Ford, the journalist recounting what we already knew: that Guy fled on July 4th after a warrant was put out for his arrest, and he was later found deceased at a state park north of Sacramento.

"According to this," Eliana says, "his death was officially ruled an accident."

"Good," Maeve says as she relocates back onto her bed. "If this isn't proof that karma is real, then I don't know what is."

While I don't buy into Maeve's ideology, I have to admit that there's a certain amount of poetic justice about what happened to Guy. The article also named Diaz as the detective on the case, and I think back to earlier this afternoon. She knew it wasn't an accident. Maybe she didn't know how we were involved, but she had to have known. Detective Diaz writing her own ending to Guy's story wasn't ethical or moral or *good*, but I don't blame her. Even if I hadn't been involved, I wouldn't blame her.

Men like Guy Moran usually get the last laugh. They *win*. What happened this trip . . . I'm not proud. But I feel a sense of wonder—or maybe it's closer to horror—knowing how far you'll go to save yourself and the people you love.

Leo texts me from the lobby of the Antler Inn later in the evening. And after I shoo off my sisters, insisting I'm able bodied enough to crutch myself to the elevator, they watch Buffy while I meet Leo downstairs. Similar to our hotel room, the lobby of the Antler Inn has more sets of animal horns than I've ever seen in one room; it's a little unnerving and briefly makes me wonder if my parents are really that off the wall when it comes to veganism, because I'm pretty sure they're all real. I shudder as I pass a particularly beautiful set of antlers mounted near the elevator.

I hobble past the check-in desk and into the sitting area, where a small fire crackles in the pit. Two plaid couches are arranged in an L shape with a coffee table nestled between them, the shadowy lick of flames dancing across the fabric. Leo's seated at the couch facing the fireplace—his back toward me—but he hears my ungraceful approach before I reach him, turning around with a smile.

"Need any help?"

"Nah, I'm a crutches pro," I tell him, and when I finally reach the couch, I collapse onto the cushion beside him. My arms are Jell-O, and I'm a liar, because crutches suck. But maybe I'll finally have some kind of upper body strength once my cast is finally taken off.

"Wow. And after only a few hours," Leo says, and I struggle with the crutches as I try to lean them against the coffee table, but they end up clattering onto the ground. He leans over and picks them up for me, gently resting them beside the couch.

The heat of the fireplace is definitely not helping my nervous sweats. At least I showered earlier, after we ate our room service. Eliana wrapped my cast in a spare trash bag we found in the cupboard beneath the bathroom sink, and since she had the foresight to book a handicapped room, I used the shower bench and handrail as I rinsed the mud and hospital smell off my body.

Leo peers down at my cast, then lifts his gaze to mine. "How're you feeling? Still drugged?"

"Nah, they've mostly worn off by now," I admit, "but I'm doing okay. The cast helps with the pain, since I kept moving or accidentally using my foot."

"You're never going to go on a hike again, are you?"

I shake my head mournfully. "Nope. I knew they were bad for me, and now I have proof."

Leo's grin widens, and it's like all my bones and muscles soften. His hand slips over mine on the couch, and he says, "Have I said how glad I am that you weren't seriously hurt?"

"I'm glad too," I say with a breathless laugh, hyperfocused on the heat of his hand on mine. "I'm well aware that almost everything this weekend could've gone way, way worse."

"Speaking of," Leo says, his voice dipping into a whisper that shouldn't be seductive, given the subject matter, "Diaz really thinks Guy fell?"

I shrug, then adjust my body toward Leo's on the couch. "We were going to confess, and she . . . cut me off. It was the weirdest thing. She kept insisting it was an accident. Hey, do you know if they found the sleeping bag with the body?"

"No idea. I figured I was starting to look a little suspicious, asking a ton of questions," he says, cheeks flushing, "so I backed off. None of the other rangers were remotely as interested."

"Well, they're clearly boring."

"Clearly." His gaze lowers to my mouth and, even though I feel like a disgusting blob of a person wrapped in plaster, I want him to kiss me. One last kiss for the road. "But I also have a . . . vested interest."

"Am I the vested interest?" I joke, and he answers me by pressing his mouth to mine.

I've never liked PDA, and I haven't changed my viewpoint on it now, but besides the concierge—a teenage girl who was playing a game on her phone when I hobbled by—the lobby is empty. *Basically* private. Private enough. Leo's palm cups my cheek, and the kiss is very, very sweet. Surprisingly tender. And I'm extremely flustered when he pulls back, tucks some of my wet hair behind my ear.

"You're leaving in the morning?" Leo asks, his hand settling now on my thigh.

"As soon as Maeve's ready, yeah," I say, then add, "but she rarely wakes up before ten in the morning of her own volition. So sometime tomorrow."

Leo's smile is sad. "I hate goodbyes."

"Me too. They suck. The worst. Zero out of ten stars."

"I know things are gonna be busy when you get home," he says, "with the new job and everything. But if you're ever up in the Seattle area, let me know. This weekend was . . . honestly kind of wild, but it was also the most fun I've had in months. Is that messed up to admit?"

"Seattle?" I repeat with a scrunched brow. "Don't you work here?"

"For the season, yeah," Leo explains, and he seems confused by my confusion. "With AmeriCorps, we rotate around. I swear I explained this earlier . . . I was in Fallen Lake for the past year, but my rotation wraps up in September. My next is up north, working at a few parks in the Seattle area, mainly Discovery Park."

"Oh." I swallow, my throat oddly tight. Because Maeve's kismet, rom-com bullshit isn't real, but Leo and I do keep getting flung together. And I'm not . . . okay, I'm not *mad* about it. Sure, the dude is too hot for me—on the Richter scale of hotness, he'd cause tsunamis—but Leo is nice. Easy to be around. He finds me funny, which is a turn-on I didn't know existed. Oh, and he not only knows the worst thing I've ever done and didn't turn me in to the police but also helped me cover it up.

Real boyfriend material.

And yet, I hesitate for a half second, considering not telling him about my move north. Because—just like Leo never mentioned his next rotation was in Seattle, I never once mentioned that Tasha's company was also in the same rainy city. Leo has, until this moment, been a concept. Not *real*. A one-night stand gone sideways. Always, always temporary.

Some of that temporariness made my feelings for him . . . safe. Now, they're the opposite of safe, and my thoughts are too loud for my brain.

"Remi?" Leo's brow creases in the middle as he stares at me, unaware of the complete spiral happening mere inches from him. "Are you okay? Is it your ankle?"

I force myself back into my body. "No, no, my ankle is fine. Well, it's not fine—it hurts like a bitch. But I had no idea you were moving to Seattle."

Leo squints, as if trying to figure out what the hell is wrong with me. "I swear I mentioned it earlier, but maybe not the details. No offense," he adds with a laugh, "but you're being extremely weird. What's going on? Did you once shoot a man in Seattle just to watch him die or something? Sorry, bad joke."

"My new job," I say, and force the words out because the new version of me doesn't self-sabotage like it's her favorite hobby, "is in Seattle."

Leo's expression freezes, and it's entirely possible he's having his own freak-out spiral. "Really?"

"Really, and I'm not a stalker who is making this up," I say, and grab my phone from my bag, pulling up Soft Cat's website before shoving the device at Leo's chest.

He laughs, the freeze thawing. "Yeah, that actually didn't cross my mind," he says, and barely glances at the screen—my not-a-stalker proof—before handing it back to me. "You're moving to Seattle too?"

"Yeah, I quit my job earlier, so there's no going back." A smile tugs at the corner of my mouth, a smile that I can't possibly contain. Because Leo's unattainability was comforting, yes, but I think it was holding me back a little. I like him. A lot. Too much, given the circumstances. And maybe whatever *this* is will have the chance to grow and expand, and sure, Leo might have absolutely no interest in me beyond sex, or even if he does, we could be an absolute disaster together, but I won't lie: I really want to find out.

"Any chance you'd want to go out on a date that doesn't take place at a dive bar or a Dairy Queen?" Leo asks, and this time, it's my turn to kiss him.

# CHAPTER TWENTY-SIX

*July 6 / Evening*

After Leo and I say goodbye—for now, not forever—I hobble my way into the elevator and ride to the second floor of the Antler Inn. I catch a glimpse of my reflection in the mirrored walls of the box around me. Despite my damp hair and no makeup and exhaustion, I look . . . happy. An emotion that's always been difficult for me to admit ownership over, to embrace. But whatever. I'm owning it now. I'm happy.

The crutches dig into my armpits as I slowly make my way down the hallway to our room. But I'm not alone in the hall, and I smile when I spot a familiar figure dressed in a caftan standing in front of our door. My crutches are loud, heralding my approach as they clack against the hardwood, and my aunt glances toward me before I can say hello.

"Oh, Remi," Aunt Lindy says as I reach her a moment later, hands fretting around me nervously. The sleeves of her caftan flutter like a magician's scarf. "You poor thing! Your parents told me you'd gone to the hospital but were vague. What happened?"

I dig my key card from my back pocket and unlock the door, Aunt Lindy holding it open for me. "I fell hiking," I tell her, because Aunt Lindy, along with Salli, missed our talk with Detective Diaz and Grandma Helen's confession in the campsite earlier. This is the lie—the cover story—I'm going to have to tell every single person who asks what happened to my ankle. Stephanie. My old coworkers when I come in for my last paycheck. The movers. Tasha, when I'm in Seattle. But it's close enough to the truth that the lie isn't too uncomfortable. "Look who I found outside," I say as I enter the room, and my sisters look up from the armchairs by the window.

Buffy hops off Maeve's lap and trots over to Lindy, wagging her tail. I set my crutches on the bed, then lower myself onto the mattress.

"Hey, Aunt Lindy," Eliana says, and sets her phone on the bedside table before standing up to hug our aunt. "What're you doing here?"

"You thought I'd leave without saying goodbye? Who knows when I'll see you three next, especially all in one place!" She laughs huskily at this, then adds, "This entire day has been such a cluster you-know-what, and I'm glad I didn't miss you."

Rather than force me to stand again, Aunt Lindy leans down and wraps her spindly arms around my shoulders. The scent of her is over-whelming, rose perfume and nicotine and the haze of campfire smoke, and as she releases me, she says, "Before I forget, congratulations on the new job. And the date last night. Va-va-voom."

I bite back a groan. Me slipping away from the party last night was never going to go unnoticed, but Maeve or my mom must've filled Aunt Lindy in on the details. "Thanks, Aunt Lindy."

My aunt still leans forward, exposing way too much cleavage, and cups my cheeks in her palms, stares at me. "Good for you," she says with a serious nod of her chin. "You deserve the world, doll."

Rarely does Aunt Lindy act normal, but not even I can dissect her behavior right now. Then she smothers Maeve in a hug before withdrawing her Tesla keys from the pocket of her caftan. But rather than step for the door, she moves toward the dresser beneath the wall-mounted TV, picks something up.

"Where did you find my phone?" Aunt Lindy holds Guy Moran's phone aloft in her hand.

My sisters and I exchange glances.

"Wait," I say. "*That's* your phone? The background photo is a close-up of someone's tits."

"Yes, mine," Aunt Lindy says, her eyes widened with confusion. "From when I was younger. It's always nice, to remember how good you once looked! Before, you know, gravity."

"Aw, I think you still look great, Aunt Lindy," Maeve says.

"Thank you, doll." Aunt Lindy frowns at the dried smear of blood on the phone case, rubs it off on the sleeve of her caftan. The whole scene is so absurd that I'm actually speechless.

"Hold on," Eliana says with an awkward laugh. "Lindy, you're saying that's your phone? We found it near Guy Moran's body."

Aunt Lindy's face whitens. "His body? Oh dear," she murmurs beneath her breath. She doesn't speak for a moment, only grows paler and paler. "Oh *dear*. I really hoped I'd imagined . . ."

"Imagined what?" I ask, but I'm pretty sure I know the answer.

Aunt Lindy covers her mouth with her hand. "I . . . think I killed Guy?"

We force Aunt Lindy to sit on the other bed after she says she feels faint.

"I was outside my campsite having a smoke," she says mournfully. "And girls, I know how disappointed you are, but I never quit smoking. I lied, okay! I *lied*." She manages to drag out this last word dramatically, like an actress on the stage.

"Really, Aunt Lindy?" I laugh, the sound truly unhinged. "We've known for years that you didn't quit! Who cares! What does this have to do with Guy?"

"I'm trying to get to that point!" Aunt Lindy's hands flutter manically. "I was a little buzzed, you know, and craving a smoke, so I snuck out into the woods. I was enjoying my cigarette when this man came running at me," she says, and presses her eyes shut tight. "He was bloody, and I was so scared! He was coming right at me, so I grabbed a stick off the ground and whacked him! Then I ran off to my campsite. The next morning, I went back . . . I thought I imagined the whole thing when there was no one there, no sign of anything. So, I told myself I imagined it."

Eliana lowers her head into her hands and groans loudly. "You didn't think that it was real when the campground locked down?"

"No one told me *why* the camp locked down," Aunt Lindy says helplessly. "Remi, when you came by my campground to talk about the fugitive in the park, I won't lie, it made me *wonder*. But . . . no offense, doll, but you've always had a weird sense of humor."

Eliana grunts in agreement.

Then Aunt Lindy moans. "Oh my god, I'm a murderer! A *murderess*!" She hangs her head between her knees, hyperventilating now.

I look to Eliana, who tosses her hands into the air. Maeve spins a ring around her finger.

*What are we supposed to do?* I mouth at them, but they shrug.

"Aunt Lindy," I say unsurely, and I can't exactly kneel down to my aunt's level with my gigantic cast, so I nudge her in the leg with my crutch until she peers at me. "Guy wasn't a good person. He was the fugitive the cops were looking for, because of a hit-and-run," I say, and hesitate over how much to tell my aunt about that night. I'm tired, so tired, of retelling that story, of reliving that moment. "Guy was bleeding because we got into a fight with him before he ran into you. His wound must've been worse than we thought if it just took one more blow to . . ."

"Kill him?" Maeve supplements helpfully, and I shrug. Because there's no nice way of saying that, is there?

"Yeah. Kill him." I swallow the watery bile in my throat. "We tried to help Guy, when we saw that he was hurt, but he took off. Didn't want us to call the cops, which makes even more sense now that we know about the warrant. I can't imagine how scared you must've been when you saw him running at you."

"I just . . . reacted," whispers Aunt Lindy, and she swipes back a wave of graying strawberry blonde hair from her forehead.

"So did we," Eliana adds, her tone soft now, almost mothering. "What you did wasn't wrong, Aunt Lindy."

"It wasn't right, though," our aunt says.

"No one thing is right *or* wrong," I say. "After this weekend, I can say with confidence that our lives have a lot more nuance than good or bad, right or wrong. I doubt even Guy was all bad."

"That boy," Aunt Lindy says beneath her breath. "That *man*. I always disliked the Morans, both as a kid and when we got older. I met Rico through Jim, you know, and they were always around. But Jim . . . Jim was a lot like his son. Didn't like women very much. Can't say I'm surprised Guy turned out the way he did."

I remember that holiday party all those years ago, Guy breaking into Rico's gun vault, Jim Moran begging Rico not to call the cops. I always wondered why Rico didn't, but if they were friends, it doesn't surprise me. Society encourages women not to trust one another, but men? Men will always cover for each other.

"You okay, Aunt Lindy?" Maeve asks, and gently rubs our aunt's shoulder.

"Don't worry about me." She sits up straighter, sucks her teeth. "I'm just so sorry, girls, that you went through all this . . . nastiness. Do you know if they found the body?"

I hesitate, unsure of how much to tell Aunt Lindy. This isn't just our secret. Telling Lindy about my parents' and Grandma Helen's involvement would open up the conversation, and all I want—seriously, the only thing in the world right now—is to stop talking about Guy Moran.

"Yeah," I tell my aunt, "and his death was ruled a hiking accident. From what I've read, there won't be an investigation."

Aunt Lindy audibly exhales, the loose strands of hair puffing off her cheeks. "Good, good. I mean, it was self-defense. We didn't have anything to worry about."

"Right," Eliana says with an efficient nod. "Self-defense."

"But I'm glad we won't have to deal with that," Aunt Lindy says, and she squeezes Maeve's hand before standing again, much steadier on her feet. "You three have been through enough. Especially Remi."

"Yeah," I say with an exhausted laugh—then hesitate. "Wait, why especially me?"

Aunt Lindy blinks. "Because of what Guy did."

"I didn't . . . I didn't tell you that," I say, and glance to my sisters. Did our mom or dad tell Aunt Lindy? They swore they weren't going to tell anyone what happened, and Aunt Lindy might be our family's leakiest faucet. There's no chance they told her he'd tried to assault me, let alone the mess they'd made afterward.

"You sure did," Aunt Lindy says, and kisses the side of my head before walking to the door. She pats her pockets, checking for her phone, and removes her keys.

"Lindy, Remi didn't tell you about Guy attacking her," Eliana says, and her voice is odd. It's a tightrope. "All she said was that we got into a fight with him."

Aunt Lindy rubs her thumb along the teeth of her house key, back and forth. She's standing close to the door, just a few steps and she'd be gone. But as my aunt looks from me to Eliana to Maeve, she sighs heavily. "Oh, girls, I was hoping it wouldn't come to this."

# CHAPTER
# TWENTY-SEVEN

*July 6 / Late Evening*

Aunt Lindy slips her keys back into her pocket and walks into the center of the room. "I saw what happened, Remi," she says, her hazel eyes meeting mine, and there's no guilt in her expression. Just sorrow. "I lied. I *was* out having a smoke when I heard a commotion, and I followed the noise, saw Guy . . ." Her nose wrinkles and she trails off. "I've never been good in the moment, girls. I freeze up. Memories have a way of holding you hostage, and when I saw Guy forcing himself on you, Remi, I froze. But your sisters showed up and did what I couldn't do in that moment. I couldn't let that man hurt you again, though."

Maeve lets out an inappropriate laugh, then clasps both hands over her mouth. "Aunt Lindy, it wasn't an accident, was it?" she asks between her fingers, eyes widened. She's equal parts fascinated and horrified.

Aunt Lindy smooths her hands down her linen pants, glances away from us. "No, it wasn't. Guy ran past me in the woods, muttering . . . oh, girls, he was muttering all kinds of awful things about you three. And I knew he was going to come back, wasn't going to let this go. So, I grabbed a log, snuck up behind him, and whacked him in the head."

My entire body goes numb as my aunt retells the truth of what happened that night. Because it's the truth; I can tell. There aren't any theatrics, like earlier, no crying or despair. My kooky aunt has never sounded more serious, and I don't know what to think, what to do, in a moment like this.

"This family," Eliana mutters from beside the armchairs, her fingers massaging her brow, "I swear to god—"

"I'm not sorry," Aunt Lindy interrupts, her cheeks flushed. "Girls, I'm not proud of what I did, but I had to protect you three. I never had kids of my own. You three girls are like daughters to me, and if you let Guy go . . . men like that don't change. If he assaulted you, Remi, he was going to do it to another woman. And another. If you'd called the cops, he'd get a slap on the wrist."

I stare blankly at the wall behind my aunt, the wooden paneling, the dusty TV with fingerprint smudges. That was my fear, wasn't it? That the police wouldn't take me seriously because Guy hadn't finished what he'd set out to do. What would the Fallen Lake police really have done? I force my gaze to my aunt's, and she smiles sadly at me.

"I wish the world was different, but it's not," Aunt Lindy says softly, almost apologetically. "And we should've done something about the Morans years ago; the whole lot of them were rotten."

Maeve laughs, her tone disbelieving. "You're an amazing actress. You had me fooled earlier."

"Maeve, seriously?" Eliana shoots our sister an exasperated look, then turns to our aunt. "What are we supposed to say, Aunt Lindy? You . . . killed someone."

"You don't say anything." Aunt Lindy crosses her arms over her chest. "We don't talk of this ever again, you hear?"

"Okay," I say, surprising myself. "We won't say anything or tell anyone."

"Remi," Eliana begins to say, then sighs. Pushes her bangs off her forehead and says, "Okay, okay. Fine. We won't tell the police."

"Thank you," Aunt Lindy says, and the pinched look on her face softens. "That's all I ask. No police. Not with a past like mine."

"What does *that* mean?" Eliana asks.

Aunt Lindy tuts. "We all have skeletons in our closets, girls; now come give your aunt a hug goodbye."

Numbly, I push to my feet with the help of a crutch, and when I hug Aunt Lindy goodbye, I hug her as tight as possible. I don't know if I should thank her or blame her. Was Guy running off toward his parked car, prepared to flee a second time? Or would he have come back, later in the night? Assaulted me again—or worse? I have no doubt that he could have killed me. I don't know what would've happened, and the only reason I don't know is because of my aunt.

But for once, this is the kind of unknown I can learn to live with.

# CHAPTER TWENTY-EIGHT

*July 7 / Morning*

Eliana shuts the passenger door of her minivan, then lowers her sunglasses onto her nose. "Forget anything?"

"My dignity? Ooh! My conscience," I say, and even though her face is obscured by her sunglasses, I feel the heat of her disapproving scowl. "I definitely left that behind somewhere. Calm down, I'm joking. I'm . . . okay, given everything that happened this weekend."

After Aunt Lindy left, I wasn't sure if I should laugh or cry. Neither of my sisters were faring much better, but as we stress-ate a bunch of vending machine candy, we decided to keep our promise to our aunt. We wouldn't call the cops on her and expose what she'd done. But I haven't quite figured out how I feel, knowing my aunt killed someone for me, to protect me.

"Same," Maeve says, both her hands wrapped around her steaming to-go coffee, her poodle jacket zipped up, hood on, "but fuck Guy Moran."

Eliana picks up her to-go coffee from the roof of the minivan and lifts it in a silent cheers. I tap my to-go coffee against theirs, and shiver in my sweater. It's early, but we wanted to beat traffic. Eliana's still stopping in Eugene on her way to Seattle, but Maeve and I should be back in San Jose by the afternoon. Her flight back to LA is booked for tonight.

"Drive safe, okay?" Eliana wraps her free arm around Maeve in a quick, efficient hug. Then it's my turn, my oldest sister squeezing me slightly too tight. "See you soon, Remi."

I maneuver my crutches until I can hug Eliana back, pleasantly surprised that the thought of not only seeing my sister again but moving to the same city as her doesn't fill me with deep, existential dread. "Thanks, Eli."

Eliana pulls away, sniffs. "Yeah, yeah. Don't mention it. Seriously. Ever again." Then she gets into her minivan and backs up, zipping out of the Antler Inn parking lot.

"Let's roll," Maeve says with more enthusiasm than I knew she could muster before eight o'clock in the morning, and we climb into my sedan. Well, Maeve climbs. I hobble ungracefully, struggling with my crutches, but eventually fold myself into the passenger seat.

Buffy lets out an excited yip from the back seat, already squared away in her safety harness. I toss my crutches into the space beside her and buckle my seat belt. Maeve blasts the heat as she programs her Google Maps, and then we're on the road.

Too much time around my optimistic family has rubbed off on me because this weekend wasn't all bad. Chad overdosed on childcare and will most likely drop his witch hunt to prove Eliana's a bad mom. Maeve and her life circumstances are the exact same as they were four days ago, but given that she's the happiest and most well-adjusted Finch sister, I'm not worried about her. If anything, this weekend has changed my view of Maeve for the better. And broken ankle or not, I'm starting over in Seattle, close enough to my oldest sister to have weekly dinners and spend time with my niece and nephew.

We hit a nasty pothole, and I narrowly avoid spilling my coffee, Maeve picking up speed a moment later as she merges onto the I-80. I flip off the THANKS FOR VISITING FALLEN LAKE! COME AGAIN SOON! road sign, and my sister snorts.

My mind drifts back to that summer, nearly twenty years ago. Guy Moran's fingers woven in my hair as he pressed my head below the surface. My legs kicking out and my toenails scraping the stucco tiles. That first panicked gulp of water into my lungs before the pressure released and I kicked to the surface. Coughing, choking, and realizing that, for the first time ever, some men only view you as a plaything. Guy wouldn't be the only man to treat me this way, but he was the first. And if I have my way, he will be the last.

That afternoon at the Arcata Community Center, I was obsessed with the thought that I would die before anything real ever happened to me. I've been waiting—since that moment—for my life to begin. I'm done waiting, though. I'll always be an anxious mess, to varying messy degrees, and when it comes to my family, I'll always be the youngest Finch sister. That's not a bad thing, though.

Some families will do anything to protect one another, and for so long, I never thought I belonged to a family like that. Or, if I did, then I was the odd one out. The one they'd accept losing, if push came to shove. Dark as it might be, I'm happy to belong to a family that will help me bury a body. Figuratively speaking, of course. How far Eliana might go with the proper motivation and a shovel is a mystery I'll die happy never solving. But I'm glad I have my misguided yet well-intentioned parents. My judgmental grandmother, who's doing the best she can, given her circumstances, the era in which she grew up. My kooky yet complicated aunt, whose comments about Rico and skeletons in her closet have echoed in my mind ever since last night. And my sisters. In ten, twenty, thirty years, I'll need someone to talk to about this weekend.

I'll have Eliana and Maeve. The two people I've never asked for— and who would be harder to get rid of than a dead body.

# ACKNOWLEDGMENTS

*Drop Dead Sisters* may be my adult debut, but it's my fifth published book, and this process never gets any easier. Publishing is one of the greatest joys in my life—and my most talked about topic in therapy. Go figure. But I'm incredibly lucky to have had such an amazing team backing this book from the earliest inklings of a pitch in 2022. From start to finish, working on this book has been incredibly fun and rewarding, and I have so many people to thank. So let's dive into it!

Thank you to Melanie Figueroa, my agent. Without you, this book simply would not exist. This industry can be soul crushing, exhausting, and defeating, and I can never thank you enough for picking me up after each of the publishing industry's KOs. Thank you for encouraging me to find the joy, even though it meant writing this weird camping murder book. And thank you to Root Literary for being the absolute best agency; I'm so lucky to have y'all on my team.

Thank you to Megha Parekh, my editor. You're the fiercest champion, and this has been such a wild ride! Thank you so much for seeing the potential in Remi and her sisters, as well as the encouragement to go full unhinged with my revision. And a massive thank-you to my developmental editor, Selina McLemore, for so many things, including (but not limited to) sending me emails in the middle of a literal snowstorm to brainstorm this book's absurd twists and turns. I appreciate not only your time and energy but also the enthusiasm and care you have shown toward this book. I can't wait to kill off another character with you.

Additional thanks to Thomas & Mercer and Mindy's Book Studio, with a special thank-you to Mindy Kaling, a name I truly never thought would end up in the acknowledgments of one of my books. I've been a fan of Mindy's for over fifteen years, and I'm beyond honored/humbled/still-in-disbelief that she felt this book was worth supporting. Thank you to my production editor, Emma Reh, as well as copy editors Anthony Dosen and Bill Siever, for ensuring that my sentences make sense. Thank you to my art director, Tree Abraham, and my designer, Jarrod Taylor, for so wonderfully capturing the essence of this book with such an amazing cover. And many more thank-yous to everyone behind the scenes whose talent, hard work, and time went into making this book possible. This has been such a lovely experience.

A very special thank-you to Sabrina Lotfi, who called me in the middle of a revision self-confidence crisis and talked me out of a horrific anxiety spiral while she was grocery shopping on the other end. You are such a supportive, lovely friend, and I cherish all of our meandering phone calls and our texts about publishing, reality TV, and what Steve made me for dinner. Additional thanks to Emily Miner, Page Powars, Elizabeth Urso, and Britney Brouwer, and to Natalie Sue and Lauren Thoman for the kind blurbs and reading on such a quick deadline!

Thank you to my nonpublishing friends, Cooper, Becca, and Phil. Y'all are my absolute favorite nerds, and supporting me—your weird writer friend who talks too much about publishing—has always meant the world to me. Thank you to my therapist, Laura, who helps me wrangle my OCD on a weekly basis. And all the thank-yous to Prozac; I almost dedicated this book to you. For over a decade, I was worried that I wouldn't be a good, productive, or funny (because my suffering is the basis of my humor, I guess . . . ?) writer if I was on anxiety medication. It's been such a pleasant surprise to discover that I was, in fact, dead wrong.

Thank you to my parents, not only for their unwavering support but also for taking me camping every single summer of my childhood and giving me the perfect setting for this book. Hearing about this book's sale on the annual Coombs family camping trip and celebrating with you was such a joy. Thank you to my two big sisters, in particular, for internalizing the disclaimer in the front of the book. You know, the one that says this entire book is a work of fiction and any similarities are purely coincidence? Seriously. They're all coincidences. Not everything is about you. Jeez.

Thank you to Steve, my unfailingly supportive spouse, best friend, and all-around favorite human being. Thank you for keeping me fed while on deadline (and let's be real, even when I'm off deadline) and ensuring that I don't fall too deeply into the rabbit hole of my anxiety. I love laughing, gaming, and wandering the rain-wet sidewalks of Seattle with you. And it wouldn't be one of my book acknowledgments without mentioning Sofiya, my sweet old lady cat, who has kept me company for nearly fifteen years while I type away on my computer, no doubt wondering why I'm not hand-feeding her chicken treats instead.

# ABOUT THE AUTHOR

*Photo © 2023 Jessica Whitaker Photography*

Amelia Diane Coombs is the author of four young adult novels. Her most recent title, *All Alone with You*, was named a JLG Gold Standard Selection by the Junior Library Guild. A Northern California transplant, Coombs lives in Seattle, Washington, with her spouse and their Siberian cat.